by Laura Chester:

Tiny Talk (1972)
The All Night Salt Lick (1972)
Nightlatch (1974)
Primagravida (1975)
Chunk Off & Float (1978)
Watermark (1978)
Proud & Ashamed (1978)
My Pleasure (1980)
Lupus Novice (1987)
Free Rein (1988)
In the Zone: New and Selected Writing (1988)

Editor:

Rising Tides, 20th Century American Women Poets (1973)
Deep Down, The New Sensual Writing by Women (1988)
Cradle and All, Women Writers on Pregnancy and Birth
    (1989)

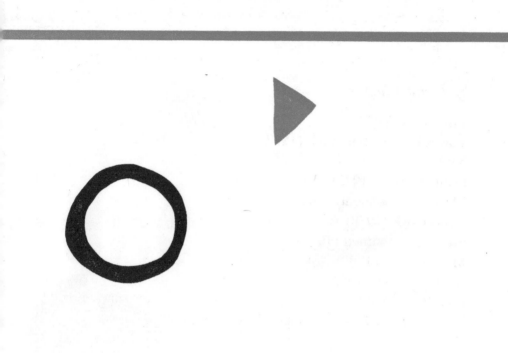

LAURA CHESTER

THE
STONE
BABY

BLACK SPARROW PRESS

SANTA ROSA   1989

ACKNOWLEDGMENTS

Sections of this novel were first published in the magazine *Notus,* and the anthology, *Cradle and All, Women Writers on Pregnancy and Birth,* Faber and Faber, 1989.

With special thanks to Betsy Uhrig and John Martin.

This project is funded in part by the California Arts Council, a state agency. Any findings, opinions, or conclusions contained therein are not necessarily those of the California Arts Council.

Black Sparrow Press books are printed on acid-free paper.

LIBRARY OF CONGRESS CATALOGING-IN-PUBLICATION DATA

Chester, Laura, 1949
   The stone baby / Laura Chester.
      p.   cm.
   ISBN 0-87685-777-2 (autographed). — ISBN 0-87685-776-4 (hard). — ISBN 0-87685-775-6 (pbk.)
   I. Title.
PS3553.H43S7   1989
813.'54—dc20
                                     89-39003
                                         CIP

for Summer Brenner

The Stone Baby

PART ONE

It appeared as if Julia were at the center of this throbbing hive—just the bustle and bombardment of getting three boys off to school—Thomas, Ross and Alexander, with their vying demands for different kinds of eggs, her insisting on scrambled, getting their lunches composed and tucked into three wooden boxes, as Juba wanted out, and the freezing cold morning wanted in. Then the lacing of Sorel boots, the location of mittens, catching each boy as he bundled by— only Thomas didn't allow for a real kiss—she had to steal one each night from his available sleep.

They were on their way now, and the house would calm down for a couple of hours before Alex came home from nursery school. Mark, her husband, would collect him later that morning. At the moment Mark was preparing a lecture, locked into his study at the far side of the house. Room onto room onto room onto room, as distant as the engine from caboose, she thought. She was tired of pulling the load.

Last night she had tried to sound casual, knowing how he always resisted a plan if it weren't his. "I've got two tickets for the O'Keeffe show," she said. "Do you want to make a weekend of it?"

"What's this?" He was preoccupied, reading the Week In Review.

"Georgia O'Keeffe, a big retrospective at the Met. Kate gave me tickets as a birthday present. Partly nostalgia, because of New Mexico."

"Oh," he looked nonplused. "The erotic flower lady. Haven't you had enough of that?"

"Well, there should be some smaller works, drawings and watercolors I've never seen, and I thought we could spend the night, do some early Christmas shopping."

Mark got up and headed for the kitchen. "I don't exactly have a ton of extra money at the moment to be throwing around New York."

"We could pack a lunch," she trailed after him, "and just make a day trip out of it."

"When is this?" He sounded irritated now, hedged

in. No cookies in the can, not even store bought.

She studied the tickets, "December 3rd, 10 a.m. It's not for a couple of weeks, but I'd have to get a sitter ahead of time."

"Why don't you go, and I'll stay here." He was looking in the fridge now for God knows what. No milk either.

But she was standing there, still waiting. "I'd really like you to come."

"What's the big deal? You make everything into an issue!" He slammed the fridge shut, and she winced, because the boys were sleeping right upstairs. "I just don't happen to know what my plans are, o.k.? My life isn't as simple as yours."

She didn't bother to answer that, but glancing back, she could see that he was pleased with himself.

Maybe she would take Philip.

The house was clean and dark and quiet. No one was sick. Their chow dog slept. She headed for the stairs, then remembered, "Could you pick up Alex tomorrow morning? I can get the big boys at three."

"Whatever you say," he responded. She knew he would sleep downstairs again.

It appeared, it all appeared, that they were actively engaged in this job of busyness together, but now that her children had departed for the morning, she could drop into the true state, which was alone. She held onto this feeling, kept it under her tongue, with all that went unspoken, a kind of sweetness that never seemed to melt.

Slinging the mouton coat over her shoulders, she trudged the snow-packed pathway to her studio in the barn, past the hexagonal sandbox, entombed with snow, the stone walls looking like extended lumps. Even the woodpile, with its black plastic flying, seemed like some hindered vamp. She would turn the heat on high, sit huddled on the paint encrusted stool and wait until the chill had diminished. She felt alone because Philip was away. Business and pleasure, a little bit of both.

"A *lot* a bit of both," she had corrected. He had asked her to go with him, Italy then France, but her answer had been obvious and immediate, "I could never do that. I couldn't possibly." But that didn't keep her from imagining.

She pictured a village near the Arno, at some kinder time of year. She wanted him to come into her presence as if into some protected room, with its own dark entrance up. She would open the window onto the smell of a warm and generous harvest, the strumming of big machines in the distance, and even the sound of the children would remain down the road, and nothing too real would approach them. This would be a place where they both could be unburdened, right down to their unencumbered skins. It was a big load, that world of his, the regular risk of different versions, spun and spewed out there like overlapping webs.

She wanted to be the clear canal down which his long boat could glide, peacefully, smooth-minded. She wanted his lovely dark head in her hands, the close cropped hair upon the hard skull, feeling the contours, as she rubbed the knot at the top of his neck. His mind was constantly juggling. She wanted to take those three busy balls right out of the air, and place them, at rest, upon the bedside table.

There was something very nice about settling herself down upon his buttocks, so that she could work her fingers down along his back, moving from the rounded shoulders, for his arms were bent up like wings, making his muscles appear thicker, then thumb inch by inch, down the strong smooth back, down to the lower portion of that plane, where a small plantation of hair grew, low and flat, and she gave just enough pressure to make him groan a little, and he murmured, "Great, don't stop."

She thought of the wheat field out there being cut, swath by swath, and knew that he'd feel better when this was over, just as the earth liked to feel itself shorn, and she would keep it up for as long as she was able, until her hands felt worn and hot. Then making small circles lightly over all of him, with the entire flat of her palm, she let him sense that it was almost over. And then he rolled over, and had to smile at her, such a sweet smile at last without resistance.

There was no reason to perform here, no need for fabrication, but still it almost felt too good, just to lie down next to him, and she did, slightly on top, with one leg between his, and he looked a little funny as he tried to lift his head, craning his neck to get a glimpse of her. She wondered if he found this ease anywhere else, the warmth of the cloth she drew over them, the quiet of their happy breath, listening for the other's gentle rise and fall, the curtain filling out like a well-draped breast, the light and the wind both swaying together, and the slightly spicey smell of the lemon oil.

The bed was small for a double, with big square pillows, the comforter slipping, the clothes from both their bodies scattered together, and it made her smile to think she could just reach down and pull on his underwear, his shirt, his khaki colored pants, so that he'd have to grab her and topple her, face forward — strip her all over again.

He could do whatever he wanted with her, though she'd never had to tell him that. For the moment, the slow, subdued caress of his hand was assurance enough, reassurance. Even if this were nothing but some form of illusion, even if her need to give, to love, was only in part because of him — still, these were the arms she'd chosen to succumb to, the smell which she found so appealing, and the brow she kissed lightly on impulse.

But suddenly, looking at him lying there, she felt the pain of this possession, and the ultimate loss. Perhaps it was just her perfect happiness, that at last they were together, alone like this, yet something so private and good must have an inner lining, and her heart could feel both sides at once.

You live in a fantasy," her older brother, Winthrop, had said, as if to condemn her. Why had that bothered her so much at the time?

She had been excited about Winthrop's visit, planning

14

dinners, a tour of the Berkshires, a horseback ride.

"What a place you've found!" he said in his overly loud voice. "This is fabulous!" It was a charming old Colonial on twenty acres, a modulated landscape, usually covered by snow in January, but they'd been enjoying a warm spell. "Look at you Alexander," he lifted the three year old up to the ceiling, "how big and tall you are."

"And don't forget my strength," Alex answered. Win had brought a brand new mitt for each boy, but only one ball. This presented a problem.

"I thought you boys knew how to share," he laughed.

"We do," Ross answered, "but it's difficult," extracting the ball from Alexander's grip. When he succeeded, Alex crumpled to the floor and Mark began his retreat to the far end of the house.

"You coming to the retirement bash?" Win called after him. Julia's father would soon be sixty-five.

"I might have to be somewhere else," Mark reappeared briefly in the doorway.

"Oh?" she said. This was the first she had heard of it.

"I might go to Florida," he continued. "By myself. I need a little peace and quiet."

"Don't we all." Julia looked at her brother, while the boys yelped, "We want to go. Can we go?" But Mark had turned and made his escape and Win looked ready for a drink.

Normally Julia didn't allow the boys to throw balls in the house, but she overlooked it now. Juba also got into the action, bouncing back and forth, lowering her dark red mane to bark.

"Are you sure this dog's safe?" Winthrop wanted to know. His spaniel had just bitten a neighbor's child, and the dog had been banished from all the comforts in the world to exile in Wisconsin.

"How's Ethelred adjusting to the farm?" Julia asked.

"Just goes to show what can happen to you if you make one wrong move in this life," he answered. "I'll teach you boys to play pickle in a minute. But first — I've got a question for *you*," he grabbed Rossie by the leg. "Who's your favorite uncle?"

"Uncle William," Rossie yelled, wriggling out of his grip.

"What!" He snatched up his Harris tweed coat, pretending to leave, just as Thomas arrived, dragging in his hockey equipment.

Winthrop always looked perfectly dressed in materials suggesting some other country or generation. He'd taken the train from Philadelphia, and that too seemed old-fashioned and suited him.

Winthrop was divorced, no children. William, their younger brother, was also still a bachelor. He was going to join them, driving down from New Hampshire. Julia always got along well with William. He was light of mood and physically affectionate, a slightly milder version of their dark, handsome brother.

William took the backseat, while Winthrop commented on her excess speed, flying in the direction of old Frank's place. Frank was seventy-nine years old, but he still rode every day, keeping a few people's horses to help pay for his own, but the place was truly an eyesore, yard sale stuff left piled and rusting, heaps of boards for some future use. There was a shelter, corral and watering hole, but Frank lived in the shell of an ambulance, backed up into a small, dilapidated barn.

Philip was bridling Sensation, and his dark green Jag, parked between Frank's two heaps, signalled the high contrast they were involved in. Philip came right over and went directly to Winthrop, shook his hand, "I've heard a lot about you." Julia knew her older brother would legitimize her in a whole new way, while Frank waved and stumbled around the junky yard. "Great day for a ride," he called out to her, and she had to go and reassure him that he *was* included, that they wanted him to come.

She asked Philip if Win could ride Senny, since Winthrop

was the biggest of them all. He graciously complied and took Frank's Morgan, while William got a gelding named "Bad Weather," which suited his sense of humor. Julia rode Western on Bunko, and Frank took Candy, but first he had to put in his teeth, and pull on the cowboy hat she'd given him for Christmas.

Swinging up into their saddles, they followed her. She turned to talk, wanting to put them all at ease. "You know Philip went to Yale too," she told Winthrop. William had been the only male member of the family in five generations not to get in—"This jelly broke the mold!"

"What year?" Winthrop asked, and she could see Philip wince, when her brother added, "Oh you were way ahead of me," even though Winthrop seemed older than forty, and Philip younger than forty-eight.

When Philip first told her that he'd gone to Yale, she'd been surprised. He didn't seem the type. But he had put himself through school doing yard work for people. "Nothing was ever given to me, flat out," he had said, and she admired his determination, that he had the obvious smarts, but that he also loved gardening, and had a talent for color and for things which grew.

"All the men in my family went to Yale," she had told him. It didn't matter where the women went. She remembered how her father and uncles used to hang their class years going up the front stairs, and how she had loved reunions as a child because of the crazy excitement and the tents, the foaming beer. She had felt like she was part of something. Now she knew she hadn't been part of anything at all.

She liked talking to Philip on horseback. It made their conversations easy because the words came and went, and the gaps or interruptions were filled with the sensual movements of the horses' shining legs. She liked to watch his body as he rode, and told him that he had good posture, and she knew that he was watching her when she stripped off a sweater, tied it around her waist, or turned around to talk, twisting around in the saddle, her blue jeans nice and tight.

Today she rode ahead and let the guys talk together. Frank trotted up next to her, "I'm not going to charge you for this today."

"Don't be crazy. We're all going to pay you. The money's for the horses, not you."

"Not today, sweetheart," he took her hand and squeezed it hard. Ever since they'd started riding with Philip, Frank had become oddly affectionate, and it was probably her fault, because in her enthusiasm she showered more attention all around, gave Frank a hug goodbye, because she had this energy. But lately she was afraid he was getting senile, confused.

The horses had warmed up now, so they cantered up to the mound, with its big rolls of hay placed at intervals along the field. They seemed to lend a certain hospitality to this already generous landscape, the available view of the valley. She pointed out Kate's house in the distance.

"How's Kate doing?" William asked.

"Better," Julia said. "But grief's a slow process."

He didn't want to talk about that. The horses were eager. They hadn't been ridden for a while. She rather liked being the only girl. It reminded her of her childhood, all of her brothers' friends about, how they showed their affection through teasing and commands, how eager she'd been to please.

They walked the horses downhill, across Barston Road, her blond horse, Bunko, leading them all. He always seemed to know the way, and when they got to the field where they often ran along the edge, his little ears curved more tightly inward. They seemed to stiffen with alertness, and he started dancing sideways, until she gave him the go ahead with a tiny click and urge. He made a small leap to start off with, though she had him under control, the reins held tight, until Frank pushed up behind her, a bad habit of his, which sent Bunko hurtling even faster, and she yelled at Frank, "Please, don't."

Now all the horses were pounding, and Julia led the way along the side of the field, where the tractor path had been created, but she decided to turn her horse to the right, to bring him in — they were headed straight for Miss Litchcroft's. Julia saw her out in her yard, white hair rising, hands on hips, observing this thundering spectacle. She didn't like horses on her land. Julia turned Bunko hard, and he gave in to the turn, cutting over the edge of the field off the path, and the others followed, fanning out behind. Luckily, no one hit the lawn. In any case, Miss Litchcroft was apparently heading for them anyway. "Mister Mercato," she landed abruptly on Philip. "Is this how you improve your terrible reputation?"

"What do you mean?" he asked, disturbed by this outbreak in front of Julia's brothers.

"What do you want, a litany?" she replied. "You don't ride over fields! You walk, along the edge."

But this was mid-winter, the field wasn't planted, and Julia didn't feel they'd done anything wrong.

"I'm really sorry," Philip said. "It was entirely my fault," which it wasn't. "We were going too fast."

"Well you certainly were!"

"And this is Julia Chapin," he introduced her.

"And *you* should know better too," she glared at Julia, who remained silent, thinking — she means, riding with him and his reputation. "I think you had better go on out to the road, and ride around my place today," she said as her final reprimand, and it was indeed a blow to have to skirt her three hundred acres and be banished to the pavement.

"Let's get out of here," Julia said, turning her horse down

the drive. The others followed silently, and the woman was left there with her hands on her hips. Julia felt justifiably insolent.

But as soon as they were out of range, Winthrop lit into her. "You can't talk that way to a woman like that. She owns that property, and *you* want to ride over it. You can't just get in a huff and react."

"I'll write a letter, an apology," Philip put in, "*Mea Culpa.*"

"Make it sincere," Winthrop suggested, "and send it over with a bottle of champagne."

"Oh no," Philip shook his head. "She'd find that much too New York, too *nouveau riche.*"

"Send her a case then," William said, and they all laughed.

Further on there was another dirt road that led to other fields, and they found a gigantic log which Winthrop jumped, over and over again, as they all cheered and clapped. She could tell that Philip loved it. Senny was sensational, big easy strides.

"This is a wonderful horse," Winthrop patted him, riding up to the rest of them with that hefty exuberance in his voice which comes from the elation and control it takes to make a horse jump properly.

Then cantering down an incline, the three boys leading, Frank and Julia walking behind, having a chat about winter shoes for the horses, whether borium was necessary, she saw how they took the corner at the bottom sharp, very fast, and Philip went soaring from his saddle, sideways, gracefully landing right in a huge pile of cow shit, a load of manure some farmer had dumped there and hadn't yet spread.

He wasn't hurt, slightly stunned, but laughing now, as he wiped some crud off his pants, took off his sweater and knocked his hard hat on his boot. It was getting very warm, and they all followed suit, stripped down to their jerseys — a clear blue, glorious day — a big swipe of stain across the back of Philip's white shirt.

20

After unsaddling, they brushed the horses down. Julia wrote out a check for Frank. He always took the money if she thrust it on him. She heard Winthrop telling Philip, "You know cleaning the outside of a horse certainly makes the inside of a man feel better."

Philip was working on the hindquarters of the Morgan. They seemed to agree on everything.

Philip suggested that they all come have a drink. He wanted her brothers to see the magnificent view from his deck. Gigantic stones composed the fireplace which ran up the outside wall.

"We haven't eaten out here since early November," he said, rearranging the chairs.

Winthrop admired the expanse from this lookout. "So this is your retreat from Wall Street."

"From the world," Philip laughed, pouring everybody wine.

It was a striking, modern place, built right into the hillside. Paula, his housekeeper, an older woman in her sixties, brought out a plate of crackers and some chèvre, another bottle of wine from his vineyard in Tuscany, and then a platter of chilled duck with sliced oranges.

William had to use the bathroom, so Julia took him inside, past a rather tacky painting of a nude. William stopped and waved at her. They were getting giggly. "Do you think he's a little light?" William whispered, peering around the next corner.

"Not from what I've seen around here," she responded.

William sashayed to the bathroom door, then swivelled, "I just want you to see my *view*."

Outside, Winthrop and Philip were engaged in the more serious discussion of the event that had occurred with Miss Litchcroft, and how you simply could not alienate these people. As Julia reappeared, Winthrop said to her, "You must live in a fantasy world," and she wondered why she never measured up.

"Oh Bill, come and join us," Philip leaned back in his

chair as a very tall, elegant man walked out onto the deck. "Bill Brenner, this is Winthrop and William Chapin. You know Julia."

He clucked and said, "My favorite equestrienne," tapping a cigarette and lighting up. The smoke seemed appealing outside there. "But may I ask where such a lovely lady keeps her husband all the time, while she's galavanting over these fields?"

"He's allergic to horses," Philip answered for her.

"Can I have a smoke?" she asked. She hadn't had one for months.

"That's a good looking sweater," Philip admired Winthrop's pullover, which he'd draped over the balcony of the deck. Philip hadn't changed his shirt. Now there's a real man, Julia thought. He wasn't even bothered, but gave a big laugh while telling Bill about the incident with the *merde*.

Renata came out to join them. Renata was his main squeeze. That's what Julia called her, even though it seemed he rarely paid her much attention. She spoke Italian, which helped with his foreign guests, and she was easy to have around. He brought a variety of girlfriends up to the country, and they usually bordered somewhere between glamorous and cheap, but Renata did have an elegance, and she came when it was a special weekend, when his daughter was along, or if there was a big party, because they looked well together. She was smart.

Renata's dark brown hair was pulled back with a clip, exposing her fan-shaped earrings. She said, "Darling," often enough to Philip, so that he, too, became slightly affected. She had the prearranged desire to go out and be amused at some auction. He gave her his checkbook and said that he trusted her taste, but she wanted *him* to go with her. Her big brown eyes gave a moist little plea, but he said, "Why don't you pull up a chair and join us? The duck's even better than last night."

As she went inside for another plate and glass, William,

the brat, snapped up the last bit of duck, so that when she returned she looked hungry and chagrined.

"My brother took it!" William squealed, hands up, what an infant, but Julia and he giggled, as they were both getting pretty drunk, and Julia had another of Bill's cigarettes while Winthrop admonished her about her health.

She knew what she wanted to paint, but it was still swimming in that vague amniotic intuition. Just as a mother might sense the look of her child before it's born, so too, her paintings were never exactly what she imagined. They brought their own life and energy with them, though she had given them everything that was hers.

The studio was warm now, and the huge canvas was waiting on the floor, stretched out with its plain raw cotton duck. The cans of liquid color were mixed, the brushes clean and upright.

Her last series had focused on interiors, not that one saw them literally that way, though a corner might appear out of some carmine red, a tilted chair or a ledge of prussian blue, the intimation of a vase or the umbilical twist of telephone, linking two angles while the objects would float — giving these "interiors" breathing room, making the space less constricted.

But now she wanted to look outward, toward landscape — aerial fields of color, patches with sky and mound in them, bales that appeared as presences, placed. Energy, light, in the air, contained. The pressure of a storm approaching. She wanted to compose these landscapes, control them, just as she had wanted to liberate restricted space.

She wanted something new to arise, but was it the truth she wanted? What kind of truth was she asking for, from him, or even from herself? Wasn't she avoiding the possibility of an honest marriage? Or intuiting Mark's own game of deceit, wasn't she just getting honestly even? Didn't she really prefer illusion anyway, her little fantasy world, and her art, the overlapping veils of color, where the images arose and subsided at the same time, where nothing was seen too clearly, never the wholehearted, hard-edged truth to contend with, for that kind of truth might upset her. It had.

Bill Brenner had tried to warn her, in that discreet and overly eloquent way of his, "Listen my dear, I can see that you're getting involved here. But you must realize that he'll have no more concern for you and your family than for the next woman he passes on the street." Julia didn't want to believe this, though she knew Philip didn't want any woman in his way. He had to have his own way there. It suited him to play the field, and not get too attached to anyone.

How do you manage it?" she asked, wondering what all these women thought of one another.

"I'm very upfront," he answered. "But what's curious, the competition seems to excite them. I'm sort of a challenge."

"Yeah," she flashed back, "like trying to seduce a gay man." Bunko leapt the rivulet of water that ran through the ditch they were crossing, hating to get his feet wet, and the surprise of the leap delighted her. She knew he admired the easy way she rode. She had a great seat, quick reactions, and she liked making those instant decisions which felt like impulse geared into nerve.

The phone rang. Mark had given her a flat, white phone for her thirty-fifth birthday, which sounded like a cross between a throttled chirp and a stuck squeal. Mark answered inside the house before she had a chance to get it. It was Kate. "I've got it," she told him. "Mark? It's for me." She never felt private enough, waiting until she heard him hang up.

"Are you working?" Kate asked. She sounded apologetic, slightly desperate.

"Just pondering the inevitable, thinking about you know who."

"Not that same subject."

"You got a better one?"

"Actually, I have," Kate huffed, jokingly, "Me!"

"One of my favorites."

"I just wanted to tell you about my session with that psychic," she said then, and her voice seemed shaky. "Do you really have a minute?"

"Of course!"

"You won't believe what he told me. First, I explained what I've been going through, how anxious I've been lately, unable to eat or sleep properly, basically asking for a little reassurance, but then he had the audacity, I am *still* so furious! I had to lie there for about ten minutes, while he concentrated, and then he had me sit up on this table and then just point blank he put the gun to my head and said — You've got a brain embolism."

"A what?"

"A time bomb, in my head, which I can do absolutely nothing about. He said he wasn't even going to charge me, because I should save up all my money for a CAT scan, which also isn't true."

"What a jerk."

"So I called Dr. Kale, the neurologist, and he said the whole thing sounded ridiculous, that any tests were out of the question. But now I have to live with this."

"He must be a phony."

"But what if it's true? What if he was picking up on something? I knew there was something wrong, but there's nothing I can do about this, even if it *is* there. I just wish I had never gone."

It had been late October when Frank and Philip and she took Kate riding. Kate wasn't too sure of herself in the saddle, but Frank didn't mind going slow, happy to have a new ear to bend.

Philip and Julia had ridden quite a ways ahead, so far that they decided to wait beside the corn field. Philip seemed to want to know more about her past. "How did your family make its fortune?" he asked. She felt his hesitation, choosing that last word, but it was accurate enough.

"Pencils," she said, "yellow pencils. Then investments. My grandfather was a brilliant investor. He bought Carnation when it was only a dollar a share," and now because Carnation was merging, the family was selling out at sixty-nine times the original cost. "Actually, they tried very hard not to spoil us," Julia said. "I never had many clothes, and my grandmother insisted that we share everything. She'd give all of us a horse for Christmas, or a boat." Frank and Kate were still out of sight. "Every summer, I wore my brother's old hand-me-downs." She looked down at the faded overalls she was wearing now, the big man's shirt she'd picked up in a thrift store. "I've always been sort of a tomboy."

"You're very feminine, actually," Philip said, riding up closer, and then she did feel feminine, felt it radiating out from her center as she turned to look into the look he was offering, and they let that look linger and then he leaned way over and barely kissed her on the lips, and though she had wanted to allow for it, her return had been more of a playful peck. She wanted to be soft with him. But she was nervous now, glancing back in the direction they had come, as if the corn stalks themselves had witnessed, some hunter hidden in the corn stalks, with the golden kind of clatter they set up, as the wind blew through them, and something new was stirring in her also.

26

The mind is not what makes the decision in some matters. And it wasn't just her heart, either exactly, but her whole being. The change seemed to begin with a quivering in her gut, as if some jellied bone had come alive in her, awakened to another life and begun to grow, and now it was as if some other woman lived inside her, who wanted to have this new life, her own way, and as Julia became weaker this woman inside her grew. She had given away her power. She had fed her feelings on luscious, wet living color, and she'd woken up laughing with his kiss on her lips.

"You know what I think I hear you saying," Martine had called from California that evening, and it was such a relief to unload all this, "is that, what appears to be happening out there, in the world, is actually a process going on inside yourself."

Martine had been too long in therapy, Julia thought. "I don't know, Martine. Perhaps. It does help to think of it that way," she paused, "for about three seconds."

She felt herself swinging back and forth, like a pendulum on a big brass country clock, and it always kept swinging his way, listing, and she was waiting for him to catch it, to calm it, control it, to let it rest in his hands, center stroke, not ticking so wildly, but it only seemed to swing faster, more frantic inside her, as if time could be sped up.

Philip said there were three kinds of people. There were those who had no instincts. There were people with instincts who denied them, and there were those who followed them. She thought about that. She told him that she had retreated back toward the safety of the middle, for her instinctual life was so strong it could be appalling, and she found she had to keep herself in check.

But he was clearly a man who followed his instincts, and that made him seem almost cold-blooded. His instincts came from gut level, but weren't softened by the heart nor tempered by the wisdom of the mind. It was more a matter of palette, craving or drive. He knew what he liked, what stocks to invest in, what company to get behind. He recognized the kind of person that impressed him, the kind of woman he liked, and he acted upon that. Brilliant, but not wise.

"I guess it's clear by now that I'm very attracted to you," he told Julia. That hadn't been clear. She didn't say anything. She was almost frightened, because nothing seemed to stand in his way. Nothing was sacred.

She laughed out loud when she realized she wanted to paint horses. Big, dumb ones that filled the canvas. Horses that flew over flat rounds of color—just intimations of speed and the freedom of it all, as if music itself could be captured. She wanted to get the astral energy of the animal—a liquid blue force, saffron colored friction, the quality of night stars riding down a river. Strokes that disappeared into the infinite, hooves.

She hadn't been influenced by the current trend, the blood and guts school she saw on her occasional visits to Soho. Painting itself was now back in, but she thought it even more risky to make the colors clash and yet remain appealing, to make a painting which was grand, which reviewers had called, "Strangely beautiful." The look was hers. It was readable, recognizable, no matter which direction she chose. Extremes of color—chartreuse, cerise, lavender grey, burnt sienna— she used them all, while the middle ground of the canvas was often inspired by touches of metallic, bronze leaf, that she'd scribble like embellishments at the end. Only there, through the painting, could she give herself free rein, and know that she could trust her instincts.

You know it was on that second ride we took together," he told her, "that I realized how much I wanted you."

She laughed, ready to up-him-one. "Well, it was the very first time I saw you. When you came out of your house in those tennis togs." Why was she always just a step ahead? He wasn't the kind of man who wanted anyone leading him. He enjoyed it when women adored him — he thrived under the gentle spray of their affections, but he had to remain in control.

Yes, it had been the first time, when she'd driven Frank up to his house on the mountain. Philip had been in contact with Frank about boarding Sensation, and Frank's description had made her curious — "This rich feller, with a tennis court, and a roundy-bout swimmin' pool, just about everything you could ask for."

Julia had offered to drive Frank up in her weather-worn Volvo, bleached red, and Philip had come out of the house with his metal racquet, all in white, very sun-tanned, and he'd peered down into the window. He had thick dark hair, cut short, and she kept trying to catch the fastener on the top of her peasant blouse, realizing, even then, that she was distracted by those intense blue eyes of his, his whole being bearing down, pouring in through that open window. It was August. Rossie was in the backseat of the car, looking like a little blond twig, busily engaged in studying the library books he couldn't quite read yet.

"So you teach riding?" Philip asked her.

"No, I only ride for fun," she responded. "But Frank wouldn't mind instructing your daughter."

Philip spun away from the window, and she wondered why he felt so protective. But if his daughter looked anything like Dear Ole Dad, she was probably spectacular and needed a little protection.

"So I'll have them trailer the horse over to your place tomorrow," he said to Frank. "Why don't we all ride. Nine-thirty?" He looked at her, and she shrugged, why not. Frank and he had agreed on a monthly boarding fee which was lower than anyone else's.

That next morning, she had ridden in a most unbecoming

outfit, an old turquoise turtleneck that had holes along the shoulder seams, torn, loose blue jeans, and the big heavy boots, which Frank had given her the previous winter when she'd complained about her feet being cold. Frank had splurged because she was all he had. He had no wife, no family, only the horses, and Julia. She took him jars of food weekly, and he was dependent on her small kindnesses. He loved it when she sang as they rode, because then he knew she was as happy as he was, even though he couldn't sing a note. "Just don't ever desert me," he'd say, and she'd pooh-pooh that. She would never let him down. He was important to her too, for it was only while riding that she could be at one with the kind of freedom she craved, where she was totally released from the churning.

Frank and she liked to race their horses over the open farm land, and they were sometimes reprimanded for their speed. People involved with horses were often a fussy, persnickety lot. They liked to have the last word. And it wasn't just an upper-crusty group of snobs, because one heard the same kind of one-up-manship coming from the Western roughneck crowd—how to do this, what the rider was doing wrong, how and when and where to go—as if having imposed their strength of will so consistently over the power of the horse, they'd overdeveloped this capacity, and needed to extend it onto people as well.

But Julia didn't want to tell anyone how to ride. She told Philip that he was doing fine. She liked his gumption. She knew he should keep his knees pressed in, heels down, hands at a steady tightness—he let his elbows fly—but she didn't like giving instructions.

Philip seemed confident enough. He wore a hard hat for protection, blue jeans and black boots, a striped cotton sweater that looked brand new. He was dazzling. "We should do this every week," he suggested.

"We're going to lose our cowgirl," Frank said.

"Oh?" Philip looked disappointed.

"I'm just flying back home, to Wisconsin, for a couple of weeks."

"Where do you fly from, Albany?" he asked.

"From here," she said, meaning the small local airport. Her father would pick them up in the two-prop Aztec he flew on weekends. Mark was going to stay at home this time, while she took all three boys.

They had crossed the highway and were headed over a field toward the Marvell Woods, when Julia spotted a white horse racing toward them, a torn rope hanging from its neck. Julia was riding Candy that day, and the mare had a full udder, and it was only when Candy spooked that she realized this horse was a stud. He came on like some intense pack of protein, raging, all teeth and hoof, and Candy began bucking like a rodeo bronc, but then stood there, on alert, as the stallion raced over to Sensation, kicked at his face, then over to Frank's Morgan, who was swerving frantic off into the edge of the corn field, and then back straight out for Julia, who was screaming, "No! NO!" as if that could prevent the urges of a stallion. Candy perceived his intensity and took off in a bolt, no way to control her. She was headed for the highway, and Julia had to make a decision. She could stay on, and risk the road, cement, oncoming cars, or she could bail out. She chose the hard-packed field, throwing herself to the left, landing hard. Her head jerked forward, smacking the ground. But then she jumped up to make sure the stallion didn't trample her. He was hot on the mare's tail, running right down the middle of the highway, luckily no cars. Julia felt stunned, haywire, jerked alive by the jolt, adrenalin cruising with its many little bumper cars all over her body. She had lost her hat. Philip went and found it, then handed it to her. "I hope you'll still ride with me," he said, as if this accident had anything to do with him. "Are you o.k.?"

"Why not," she answered, distracted by her physical state. "I'll try to hitch a ride back to the car," she told Frank. "I'll make sure that Candy gets home."

"How long will you be gone, in Wisconsin?" Philip asked.
"Three weeks, I guess."

"I'll be counting them," he said, and she gave a little laugh that contained its own beware.

She got a ride almost immediately from a woman who had seen the horses run. Julia was in a state of mild shock, but Julia assured the woman that she'd be o.k. Then it started to drizzle, but she got in her car and found Candy on a dirt road halfway up the hill. She'd been caught by a man in a red truck. He was walking her, calming her down. The owners of the stud already had him in tow, but they didn't apologize. They thought it was all a big joke.

The man who held Candy said that he had lost a horse once that got loose on the road, hit broadside, and how the car hadn't even stopped. He suggested that she milk the mare's udder. "That milk'll sour in her baby now." So Julia squeezed the udder from each side, and watched the milk squirt onto the dark dirt road.

The corn field by their house seemed to be condensing daily, as Farmer Watten cut in on its square, closer and closer, on each edge, making the field appear shorn. She got Thomas to hang up the laundry, and the bright string of clothes on the line seemed alive. She liked seeing the sequence of colors, the faded blues and big white sheets. Nothing like the smell of air dried sheets. A liveness packed the air. Birds were travelling toward some warmer climate. The boys shook the tree for "apple thunder," and the thudding of apples landed ripe on the ground. Frank was going to help them press cider.

That weekend the boys made a fort out of a pile of old fence posts, built great weightless buildings out of leaves. They roamed as freely as the wind which took the leaves from the giant maple—took them, tore them, set them free. It was the season of vigorous preparations, stocking up cords of wood for fuel, and then one morning the meadow out front turned

32

grey with frost, first sign of winter, and the travelling thrill-cry of geese flew over, leading her eyes to their chevron.

At sunset the colors fused. The palette of the sky was a shifting rose against the bruised blue hills. The trees exposed their framework, their brooms against the sky. Color to her was like some pure emotion, she could enter completely and become part of it. She felt peaceful now with Mark gone, teaching in Boston. He spent a good part of the week there, and she liked having the boys alone. Walking with the three of them out onto the cut field that evening, she suddenly stopped, and they all stood still as the full moon began to rise before them, huge and singular over the rounded earth. It looked so close, enormous. Keenly, she felt herself, right there. Earth as planet. Moon as moon. But how quickly she came, how pregnant.

As a child, she had found her greatest times of togetherness riding with her father, just off through the open fields of Wisconsin, off into the dairy wind, wildly galloping over the grassy airplane strip, linked in spirit on horseback. But sometimes they just rode quietly together, lost in their own calm world that had the sweet dry smell of oats ready for harvest. They rode wherever they wanted, ignoring *No Trespassing* signs. She was privy to secret trails, certain spots where accidents had happened, where Gramma had broken her neck on Shareef, and it all became a kind of legend in her childish mind, and she was part of the story, rescued from mother, and that interior world of bridge club and kitchen knives.

Now as a woman, when she thought back about her father, she realized that this element of escape had been an important feature for her. She was his only girl, his darling. She pictured herself in his grey Mercedes. The seats were soft, a very fine velvet, and the windows rolled slowly up and down. She laid her head in her father's lap, and they were all alone, driving out to the country. He had one hand on the steering wheel, the other on her hair, smoothing out the silkiness. She was half asleep, so warm and comfortable, glad to be off like this, cruising just with him, with the sunlight filling the soft dove-grey interior, making it warm as some sleeping hive, only his hum as they drove.

She felt that she was like him—fair, green-eyed, phlegmatic on the surface, apparently good-natured, easy to be around, yet driven underneath, full of a self-possessed will. He loved to laugh, to have a good time, and his circle of friends embraced him. But when Julia saw him leaving the house those evenings, she felt a twinge. He'd be all dressed up in sleekness, black and white, and they were "going out," leaving her in the breakfast room with Winny and Willy, eating creamed tuna out of potato baskets, and the swinging doors that led to either kitchen or dining room opened, then closed, as their parents moved through to wish them good-night. Her mother smelled like the evening in her slippery-looking sable. All of her sparkled—her shiny nails, the jewelry, even her dark brown hair, her freshly made-up mouth, leaving an imprint on Willy's cheek, even the sound of her stockings—all of her seemed to be slippery, something Julia didn't want to hold onto. While Daddy was soft in his camel hair coat. His gloves were immense and lined with cashmere, and his ring was a garnet signet ring. The emblem of that impressed her. She even liked the roughness of his cheek when he came home from work, the smell of newspaper on his hands, and the laden briefcase with his initials above the lock. How utterly spent he seemed, but still ready to get down on the dark red carpet on all fours and let her ride him, bouncing before the fire, giving her a good buck.

When she told Philip how her father used to take her out to have Chinese food once a year, how it was their big date, Philip was only appalled. "Once a year! Why not once a month?" He took his daughter out every week, but then she was an only child, and he didn't live with her, being divorced. Still, it struck Julia that maybe she hadn't gotten enough at that early age. "Enough is never enough for you," was her mother's summation and refrain.

When she asked Kate about it, Kate only said, "Well my father *never* took *me* out."

Andrea, Philip's fourteen year old daughter, was very possessive of him. She was even blunt enough to announce, "I don't want my father having any more children. I want to be the only one."

Julia was amused by this, and liked the fact that Andrea could express herself, but Julia also remembered how important it had been for her to hear, "Your mother's the most important person in my life." At the time, she didn't want to believe it, but it freed her from the bonds of that first love.

Philip told Julia that she was a wonderful girl, marvellous, quite a rider, and Frank filled in the picture, saying that she made these great big paintings, and that she was a very good cook.

"Frank always thinks it's 'something different' when he eats at my house," she laughed.

"You are something different. You're fantastic," Philip said.

"Don't flatter me!" But to tell the truth, she liked his compliments. If everyone got a good dose of that every day, wouldn't they feel a whole lot better? Just two or three compliments, like sweets from the sky. She blossomed under the warmth of his rays. She almost didn't realize that she was becoming dependent on his presence. She couldn't help it.

When he missed a weekend, she craved. She languished, suffered even. Only much later would she declare, "I *won't* become addicted to you."

One day they rode to Kate and Conrad's house. Even though the garden had begun to fade from its midsummer splendor, it was still impressive. Philip surprised her by knowing the names of certain unusual perennials. Then Kate had accompanied them down to the bottom of the drive, chatting with him, while her daughter, Atea, rode double with Julia, thrilled and silently alert to the strange high movements of the horse, but reaching for her mother at the mailbox.

"Nice seeing you Phil," Kate said, beaming, and he flashed a look back in her direction."

"Great seeing *you too*."

Later Kate said, "You should have seen the look he tossed my way as you were leaving, Julia. We were talking about a mover! Will you please just be careful, and don't DO anything." Kate believed that he could easily wreck Julia's high-strung heart, and for what purpose.

"I'm not going to do anything," Julia smiled. "We just ride, and I like him, that's all."

"Well, keep it that way. You know how violent Mark can be, and you just *can't*. I KNOW YOU, don't forget."

"I know," she acquiesced.

"But damn," Kate threw in, "you *do* have good taste."

One week Julia thought it was cooling off, that she was getting cold feet. She refused to flirt with him. She saw through it all, his tactics. But by the next week she was back dancing on hot coals, and by the next week the trees were aflame, and every turn of the countryside was enlivening.

That week they rode alone together. Frank had to go to a funeral. It was the first time they had to handle the trails all by themselves, and they wanted to go somewhere remote. Conversation came easily to them now. They chatted about his ex-wife, his daughter, her sons, while she gestured toward the intense autumnal blue of the lake against the forest of birch leaf gold.

They let the horses wander through the woods on an old logging trail, until it was clear they were far away from everything. Finally the trail itself seemed to disappear, and she wondered if he would want to stop, get off, sit down beside that big boulder, or crush back into that layer of leaves, but he wasn't making a move. The tensions that led up to the act seemed more interesting to him, but it made her frustrated. Did he just like to talk? He held her horse while she dismounted, walking back into the woods to "make use of nature." Coming back out, she looked up at him, offered to tighten his horse's girth, just so that she could get closer.

Nothing happened, though she longed for it. Getting back up on Bunko, she rode past him, and popped him once on his hard hat— he reached out and took her hand. This one little gesture made her feel unglued, but then Bunko moved forward and she lost him.

When they got back to Frank's place and put the horses away, he asked her to drive on up to his house, have some lunch, and she agreed, though it was getting late and she could tell he was in a hurry now.

His daughter Andrea was there on the deck. Julia came in on the scene. "You know you were supposed to be back by 12:30!" It was now after one and Renata was there, maintaining her reserve and calm. Philip had become a different man. He brusquely asked Paula, the housekeeper, to put a plate of cold cuts and a glass of wine out for Julia. She could have lunch on the deck. The rest of them had an appointment. Julia wasn't hungry, though she did drink all of her wine while he took pictures of Renata standing in front of the table, and Julia asked, "Should I move out of the way?"

"What?" he sounded almost angry. But she didn't repeat

it, and he didn't sit down or take a picture of her. He had to patch things up, and it was working. His daughter came back outside and hugged him fiercely.

"I feel so bad when I get angry," she said. "Forgive me?" And he hugged her, bending down over her small fourteen year old form, while looking up at Julia, his little daughter with her swank, dark hair, and slender body, decked out with bangles and teenage rings, securely in his grip, and the way he collected her in his arms seemed almost too physical, too close, but nice in a way, so firm. Julia felt too distant for food or comfort, not in this group shot today, not interested in what stared up at her from the cold white plate, not even keen on the view.

He waved goodbye then, mentioned something about next weekend, his arm sliding around the shoulder of Renata, reassuring her, while Julia wondered why she was there.

It was only much later that he changed her memory of that day when he said, "I could have raped you up there in those woods."

She wondered what it was that she needed to indulge, to escape. What was it that she craved? Her fixation on him seemed distasteful. But by the next Saturday she was ready to ride again, as ready to forgive him his rudeness as the little daughter had been eager to be collected in those strong fatherly arms.

Philip, like Julia's father, had this aura of the unattainable, and that was thrilling, his aloofness, and directness, striking at a particular moment. He was someone to look up to, to revere, if you wanted to worship money, which she did not, but still she had a certain amount of awe for his place of power in the structured world.

Philip had his emotional limits, but knew how to control both the rod and undulating line, knew how to throw temptation out into that waiting pool, to set up a dilation of ripples drawing the hook back slowly, throwing the fly back in, with a certain skillful snap and tease. This went on for a month or so. Julia had a fantasy.

She imagined that Philip had a special saddle made for her. It was an English saddle with a big leather cock rising out of the seat, and he also gave her these black leather pants with a slit in the crotch, and she'd wear these with nothing underneath them. They were hot and close against her skin. He'd tell her to open her blouse, and her breasts would be exposed, fleshy and warm, and he'd feel them before he helped her mount, holding her ass in his hands, and then she'd settle herself down onto this firm, prick-like form, and the horse would begin to move, around this pasture that was far away from everything, and then he'd want her to trot the horse, and he'd stand there, pleased, leaning back against the fence, as she rose and sat down, rose and sat down, on this leather cock-saddle he'd given her, and then she'd have to canter, slowly, but she'd get into it. It would start affecting her, deeply, making her want to clutch, as it pressed up and down inside of her, and now she was just hanging on, with her eyes closed, for she couldn't get enough of it, and then the horse would glide up before Philip, and she'd lift forward, dislodging herself from the member of the saddle, and he'd pull her down and take her there in the field, reaching around to squeeze her breasts, and she'd be blindfolded at this point, and he'd take her from behind, then make use of her mouth, and she'd still have on these black leather slit pants, as she rocked on all fours, and then he'd get underneath her, and she'd sink onto him and ride as she'd ridden the saddle, and he'd move all over and handle her, pushing and rubbing on her as she rode, and she'd come and he'd cry out, "Fantastic," and the horse's head would be down in the semi-darkness, eating the tall, drenched grass.

She wondered about her lewdness, why she fabricated, why she needed these little scenes to get off. Why riding with him excited her. She would bring that excitement home, and Mark certainly reaped the benefits, though sometimes he'd ask, "What's with you two?"

And she'd answer, "Nothing. We're just friends."

"You like him, don't you. A new crush object."

She'd keep her grin turned in another direction, as she pulled off her scarf or unbuttoned her vest, and she would admit that yes, she liked him, why not, but that he was a terrible materialist.

"Well if you try anything," Mark took hold of the base of her ponytail, "it'll be the end of you."

She made a point of reading religious books, which Kate had lent her. It was Kate's interest, not hers. Julia only felt grounded in this new earthiness. She felt connected to the leaf, root, flower and stem — dependent on the sun, which was his presence, and the rain, which was his absence, but also on the elements of earth, the minerals of his darkness.

Now the leaves of that season had a vibrating quality of lightness about them, barely hanging on, fluttering between heaven and earth, and torn, they sailed in a swirl across the field, and how she too wanted to be collected, taken, thrown — into some unknown element. She didn't want it to end, this season of rides, though she could feel it coming, and when she mentioned it to him, he could only reassure her, pointing out a place that would make a kind of love nest in the snow, and she'd shake her head, "Incorrigible."

It had been such a warm fall, and on one of those Indian summer afternoons after a long ride, Philip invited Julia to come back to his place for a swim, but she didn't have a bathing suit with her.

"That's o.k.," he responded, "you don't need one at my place."

She didn't answer, looking down at her pommel, but she could tell that Frank, who overheard this, didn't like it one bit — who did this rich man think he was, embarrassing his girl. He could have punched that young feller right in the mouth!

"Or you could borrow one of my girlfriend's suits. Come on."

She didn't think so. She didn't believe the suit would fit. She didn't even know who it was he had with him that weekend. Some woman from Belgium. He didn't understand her reticence. "I thought you'd be the type who'd just throw off her clothes and dive in," he grimaced, getting off, unsaddling.

"I guess I'm more modest than I look," she said. He didn't know that she'd never even had a lover, that her husband had been her first man. She had fallen in love once before, and something might have happened, but Mark got wind of it and broke the thing wide open.

"Well bring your suit next time," he instructed, and she said she would, but when she did, keeping it rolled up in a towel in the back of her Volvo, he didn't even ask her. Later it became a kind of metaphor, "Got to get you into that water."

For a while it seemed that he had a different woman every weekend, and that didn't seem natural, but he thought it kept life interesting—This one was so smooth, such fun, and that one was brilliant in business, another was Julia's age, he made a point of mentioning, "at the peak of her womanhood," and these things both titillated and disturbed. It was hard to know what he wanted, what he was preparing her for. She began to feel special, because these other women came and went, transient lovers, while Julia had a kind of permanence.

The first time he said, "My daughter's the most important woman in my life," Julia had responded, "I hope you didn't tell her that." He had. But it didn't appear that he brought Andrea up to the country very often. She probably had her own teenage concerns in the city. He'd been divorced for seven years.

"Are you still bitter?" she asked him. Why else would he use and discard so many women.

"I was never bitter," he said.

Perhaps he just couldn't feel very deeply for any one woman anymore, so he kept a lot of lovers in flux, to protect himself from the pain of failure. If one woman left him, the others could fill in, and he'd never have to face the problem.

Nothing seemed permanent in his world, nothing truly solid. His wealth was acquired, on the level of risk, though he cultivated older money — the Piersons, the Welch family, the Metfords, attaining a certain grace through imitation. The old Yankee families in the area considered him a rash wheeler dealer, and yet they were still intrigued by the lifestyle they could never pull off. Julia thought they were envious. She liked his style, his flair.

He had a custom-made navy wool suit and when she saw him in it that day, she thought she'd die to get her hands on it. She had been taking Rachel up his long driveway. Rachel, Julia's best friend from California, and her new boyfriend Richard, were visiting for a couple of days. Rachel had heard the whole story, what there was to tell. It was Monday morning, and Julia figured that he'd be back in the city by now. They were driving up to his place to pick up a broken bridle. She had agreed to come get it out of the garage during the week, but mainly she wanted to show Rachel his place, and as they went speeding up the drive, taking the curves at high speed, she hit the brakes and he slammed also, lurched his car off to the side of the driveway, as she screech-turned to a stop. He had been flying down just as fast as she'd been ascending, and they had just missed collision. Her heart was pounding, bashing inside of her, not only because of the close call, but because he was now pulling back, and driving his car up beside hers. Was he angry? No, not even shaken. Luckily, she had an excuse, the bridle. His girlfriend of that weekend looked flashy, probably a model. Julia leaned back to introduce Rachel, who seemed restrained, taking this man in.

When he drove away she commented, "He looks like he owns the world."

"God, he disturbs me." Julia felt that same old adrenalin after-rush she'd experienced with the stud in the corn field, but Rachel was a little concerned, happy, excited for her friend, yet concerned.

"Do you think he's trustworthy?" she asked.

"No way."

Her Richard, at least, was trustworthy. For the first time Rachel considered it a good quality. "I saw how he looked at you, Julia. I can tell, you're about to explode. If I were you, I'd sleep with him. It would help disperse some of that tension. I'm not recommending you do that. That's just what I'd do."

She loved Rachel for being so easy and accepting. Sometimes she wished she had Rachel's confidence. She looked beautiful that morning, with her grey wool hat pulled over her shoulder-length black hair. Usually she wore her hair longer, and this new cut made her look more kempt, probably more acceptable for Richard's lecture tour. He had a brilliant reputation. He didn't exactly seem Rachel's type, not splashy and glamorous enough in a wasp way, what she usually went for, but Jewish, like herself, very tall and dark, nice, but apparently difficult. Julia wondered if it would last, or if being a doctor's wife was what Rachel really wanted. It certainly was what her mother, Renay, had always told her to want, "You know what I'd do at *your* age."

Rachel wrote Julia: *Hi darlin — Was wonderful seeing you surrounded by orchards and mown fields. How are "things" with your dangerous man? Don't do anything I wouldn't do! Took the kids to Sacramento last weekend, and we loved it so much. I kept thinking of you — our Rodeo Queen. We spent an hour at the animal exhibit (there's a pregnant animal section and we saw a calf only seconds old) then the Rodeo itself was all glitter and golden. Being IN AMERICA*

I truly realized why the population isn't pounding the pavement to read my poetry. Berkeley represents such a small % of the cultured and privileged that one's perspective gets extremely warped.

You should see Lianna right now, her hair is shorn to pixie length and she looks like a luscious strawberry that I have to take a bite of every night. Vergil, on the other hand, has a spikey haircut and is into sports and the pursuit of fun. His charming dad condescends to spend an occasional evening with him. I just wish he were a man who understood what it meant to be responsible to something other than a suntan.

Meanwhile, Richard's work continues to possess him, but is he happy with it? Not much. We've been close, closer even, but sometimes this step we're about to take towards cohabitation worries me. I'm tired of fretting about personal relations with men, and want to worry over my writing instead. We're going to the mountains soon, and I hope we can have some fun. You know I always do, but he has such a hard time relaxing and taking pleasure in the unexpected.

I actually delight in the fact that I don't know where I will be in ten years or with whom. I just want to be surprised!

There was no possible way Philip could have guessed about the wacky workings of her head. How she literally did everything for him. When she made the bed first thing in the morning, she imagined that he might like the feel of the flannel covers, under the careful lay of the quilt. When she dressed for tennis, she went with him in mind, imagined that he'd be batting balls on the next court. Even when she made a fire in the fireplace, or chose a dress, or had her hair lightened, all of it was for him.

Of course the paintings were for him, and he began to understand that, but this other more mundane process he could never comprehend, how every time she made a special dish, she believed that he was going to taste it. She even wanted her boys to look nice on the weekend, in case they should meet him on the street in town. When she took out a book, had he read it? What kind of wine would he choose? Where would he go, if he were going out to dinner, as Mark and she both were. She thought of him watching the movie with her, and if he'd seen it already, had he liked it, and what would he say? What would he remember? And when she gave that party, how she really overdid it, with a sumptuous heap of food, red roses and champagne, her fanciest pink satin and her grandmother's crystal, all set out like some sort of display, for him, who never even made it as it turned out. So how could he know? How could he even begin to understand what her husband understood too well?

"Mark can read me like a book," she said to Philip, her arms around his waist, because they were riding double, and she loved it, hanging on behind, on the rear of his horse, while he sat in the saddle. "He knows I've got a crush on you."

"I don't want to complicate your life," was his response. But it damn well was a complication. The arrangements, the babysitters, the timing, the calls, the hair just right, the question of clothes, the confirmations, the sudden change of whim, the endless anticipation, the vacant stretch of waiting, the storm that cancelled out, the basic do without, the managing of time, the shuffling of emotions, the confusion of her feelings. Life could have been more simple. Much less complicated.

But she didn't want to think about any of that now, riding that short distance there behind him with her arms around his waist. He felt thicker than she'd imagined, and the wool of his yellow sweater felt nice. She put her fingers through the loops of his blue jeans, got the horse to trot a little, so that she really had to hang on. He mentioned that he'd heard riding bareback could be exciting for a woman, and she confirmed that there and then. It was not just because of the horse's high backbone, but because she was finally, in this limited way, in possession of him. She let her hands rest on his thighs, his waist—she went so far as to hug him.

"You know I'm very attracted to you," he said. "I want you to come to Italy with me. I'm going next month on business."

"I couldn't do that," she interrupted. "I couldn't possibly." And she meant it. She was the mother of three boys. But she was also flattered. No one had ever been so daring with her before.

Once she began the new series of paintings it was almost easy. Nothing else mattered as much. It was a kind of substitution to fill up his absence. Mark, at least, understood these flare-ups of hers, her chronic need to escape, to be in her own world, inside those colors. She loved this first phase best, when she was ready to move for the clean, bare canvas, trusting herself as she poured the colors on, brushing the liquid stains up next to each other, where they merged, forming another color all their own. The brilliance of the paint was so much more intense at first, fluid, in a living state, and she sometimes felt, in her concentration, that she was looking through a kind of magnifying glass, observing an organism that couldn't be seen in real life, but which was even more alive.

Only later, after the stains became subdued, did that first phase pass, and then she got down to the second level of work, painting with colors straight from the tube—more layers of stain would come later—layer upon layer, like a courtesan slowly getting dressed. She wanted her paintings to seduce him, yes, like the right perfume could intoxicate a man. She wanted her paintings to be that luscious—voluptuaries of color and form. When Philip finally saw them, on his return, he'd be taken by their newness, dazzled by those spurs of metallic, that burst of cobalt blue. He would have to have one for his big wall, and she would offer it to him, though he would insist on paying. He'd been generous in many other ways. Think of all those compliments she'd reaped and stacked like sheafs in the field of memory.

He was a man who fed on compliments himself, and maybe that's why he doled them out. Once, while riding, she told him that he did have very good posture, and then the very next week, he had wanted her to repeat that, asking, "How's my posture?" And she had said, "Terrible!" He needed a little teasing, she figured, though he didn't quite know how to take it. He knew how to get back at her. He had a little story of his own.

There had been this attractive young woman in the city, who was serving on the same committee as he was, and he noticed after the first few meetings that she kept looking at him rather oddly, and finally after one of these sessions she came up to him and asked if they could meet sometime, after work, so he suggested that they get together for a drink. After they sat down, she wasted no time in telling him that she had decided it was time for her to have an affair with an older man, and she had selected him. "She was almost militant about it," he went on, "but I wasn't interested. She was so pushy. I told her I couldn't help her out, but that I could introduce her to a few of my friends."

Julia knew that the girl had handled it wrong, but she sympathized with her somehow. "What do you think she wanted, the generic older man?" Julia pushed her horse into a gallop. She wanted to get away from him, but his horse started up and followed her. The girl had been attracted to *him,* not to just any older man. Didn't he understand that? Didn't he realize how he affected women? Didn't he know what was happening to her? Or was he just trying to tell her to cool it.

Exalted and frantic, she didn't know how long she could keep it up, and wondered if it wouldn't be best to just bail out, before any real damage was done. She knew she'd be sore for a while, aching from whiplash of the heart, but at least this craziness might stop, this wildness, and she thought of the thunder of that maniac stud. But just as she began to imagine writing him — *You've become too much for me, too important in my life, and I can't live like this, divided,* for she was living in two worlds, two minds, one body, monogamous, torn, and luckless in love, just as she was about to announce that she couldn't see him for a while, not until the fields had thawed and they could ride again, not until those dark turned fields and her changed emotions registered the same deep coolness, just when she was ready to fish up her will and turn her head, he'd call and ask her over, and she'd be as willing as water.

The invitation to the Solstice Ball came on heavy, cream-colored paper stock that folded out into the shape of a star, embossed, black tie — both Julia and Mark were invited.

Philip's place looked transformed, silver balloons pushed up against the cathedral ceiling, long curling ribbons attached, which brushed the heads of the taller guests, including Mark, whose first impulse was to reach up and gather a bunch. She turned to their host who welcomed her with a kiss on the cheek. "Darkest night of the year," he murmured, and the way he said it made her spin inside. Silver tinsel hung over the windows, making the big, cleared living room look like a winter palace. He could create an ambiance most men could not bring off without the help of an inspired wife, but he liked to be in charge of the details, the canapés, the music, the silver pitchers filled with white roses and starburst mums, what label of champagne.

There were so many people, most of them from New York, weekend people, that Julia felt she could meander without having to talk to anyone in particular, dipping in and out of conversations like a taster of hors d'oeuvres, listening in on what others had to say, gossip amplified rather than whispered. "And now Margery wants the summer house too, even though he gave her the co-op. Just handed it over."

"Now there's a case of outright guilt."

"Veronica! When did you get back?"

"I didn't know you came up here in the winter!"

Julia felt under-dressed somehow, not enough glitter. She wore a floor-length dark red velvet dress, classic, but not in style. For the first time she missed not having the flash and glamour of jewelry which these other women displayed. Big gobs of it seemed to hang from their necks, their wrists, their hands, a cascade of brilliance, of roped gold, a feminine kind of clustering, drawing the eye to its scintillation as if to make up for some basic fact.

The band was set up on a little platform in the corner, and she was in the mood, but Mark didn't know how to dance. Their bodies fought against each other, and it made her feel awkward. Maybe it was her fault. Maybe she didn't know how to follow. Mark stopped, mid-beat, tried to think, and then began again. When they missed, he groaned and said, "Let's forget it. I'm going to get a stiff one from the bar." She stood there alone, and watched him, detached, as his tall, gangly form wove in and out, away from her.

"You'd think the locals could be more grateful."

"Why should they be? Take a look at the cost of real estate," a retired full-time resident answered. People were often surprised that Julia lived here year round, but she was proud of it, why not. She was glad that they'd been invited, even though the music now made her sad. She was tempted to take a glass of champagne in each hand, remembering how Rachel had once walked through a black tie affair, drinking champagne, wearing nothing but an old black bow tie.

She noticed Philip talking to an older woman. He looked as if he were made to wear evening clothes. He even looked comfortable in them. She saw how he excused himself, opening his arms to her slightly, inviting her to dance. "What do you think?" he asked, meaning the party, "lots of interesting people," and she realized that even he wanted to receive some praise, wanted his generosity acknowledged. Every man, even Philip, she thought, wanted unabated love to flow over him, like that first most magical mildness.

"It's perfect," she said simply.

"I could dance all night," he pulled her up to him, and she came gratefully into his arms, trusting his direction, and they danced close, his strength firm, sure, commanding, and she liked his height, just slightly taller, and she pressed her cheek against his, wanting to kiss his neck, his ear, but instead she leaned back, smiled at him, and said, "I love your teeth." He held her a little closer.

Then he seemed to have a sudden idea, and in the middle of the song said, "Come with me." He led her through the dining room, into his study, shut and locked the door. There was a Francis Bacon hanging over the fireplace. She considered the work, and as she turned to talk about the image he took her in his arms and kissed her, really kissed her, pushing the juicy stalk of his tongue deep into her mouth, and her hands went up to his face, and held his head as he kissed her, not wanting it to stop, for he made her feel like antique velvet, soft and smooth no matter which way you rubbed it. "You're fabulous," he whispered, his hands still feeling the material that wanted to slide from her shoulders, "the most beautiful woman here. Did you know that?" But she couldn't say anything, silent. "Let's take a look at the snow," he suggested. The music was still whirling around inside of her, and as she touched the coolness of the tall French windows, he leaned up close behind her. The night outside seemed to bounce and play, big thick flakes of illuminated snow. The entire world seemed to be rising around her as lightly as the snow fell, as if her equilibrium had been turned upside down like a crystal snow ball swirling, those bubbles of champagne, rising in her as well, and she felt so high, so glad and good, as he moved to collect her again, kissed her again, even harder, pressed up against her and moved himself, and she wanted to feel his weight, his tongue, his arms so strong around her, and carefully, she too explored his form, his back, his arms, his shoulders. His body was too thrilling, and she knew now that he was serious, and then she had this wonderful notion, that this whole event, this evening, had been built around their embrace, and it came as a terrific gift. She didn't quite know what she could give in return.

She opened the doors, and they both stepped out, lifting their faces to the flakes, catching some on their tongues, relaxing into laughter before he pulled her back inside, pressing the doors closed against the night, and he brushed the flakes from her curled blond hair, her shoulders, dress, and told her, "I've got to break you in."

I can't believe that you're my friend, you're such a jerk!" Kate teased her over the phone, and Julia felt a silly kind of grief— how could Kate say that, even joking? But Kate felt she had to shock her friend with warnings, admonishments, help make her aware of what she was doing. "Think of your children! Just think about those boys!"

Julia didn't want to shame their friendship, in a small town like theirs, so conservative, but she felt that Philip and her children were in two separate worlds that hardly touched. She wouldn't let it go any further. She knew Kate would stand by her no matter what, remain loyal, but Kate might also do something drastic— like approach Mark and say, "Do you know what's going on?" in an effort to wake up the situation. Rossie was Kate's godson.

"If you take this any further, you're going to be kicking your marriage in the balls, and I don't think it would survive this time. Don't you remember what he's like!"

Unfortunately she remembered. The blow to the inner ear, the bruised cheekbone, the swollen head, the cracked wrist.

"But I haven't *done* anything!"

"You've got a mind to," Kate said, knowing that her lectures would do no good.

She called him "Melissander" in front of his girlfriend of the week, and he looked a little hurt, thinking she'd called him a salamander, but she was just warning this girl out loud, and herself too, that he had a honied tongue, and this woman joined in the spirit of camaraderie and said, "I know *exactly* what you mean."

He didn't like them ganging up on him, but he deserved it, trying to ride with two women at once. No other girlfriend had ever ridden with them before, and she couldn't help thinking—who is this chick, moving in on my turf.

All of a sudden, Julia felt like seconds, as Philip called out to her, "Lindsay, come on up here and ride next to me." They were going through Farmer Watten's dense pine forest, and she hated seeing him take Lindsay's hand, hearing him use a line he had used in the exact same tone with her. Hated it! How dare he do that in front of her. She wanted to kick him with her riding boot.

Lindsay was a skinny, affected little thing, who contorted her mouth as she spoke, but Philip thought she was "gorgeous." It hurt Julia's eyes to even look at her.

They galloped along an open field, Lindsay and Philip leading, and he looked like he was all eagerness. Julia hung back with Frank and tried to chat. When they brought their horses along behind, Philip turned and said, "It's so nice to ride with people you like," and Julia went, "*blanh blanh blanh.*" Lindsay and he both laughed.

Maybe Julia could cut his butter, butter his bread. Maybe he liked it when she kept him straight, which was almost never. Lindsay was obviously wealthy, and he knew how to handle the rich. He pampered when necessary, when she got in a huff, when Frank did the ole charge-from-behind routine, and she announced, "Some people do not like that!" Julia turned to Philip and suppressed a guffaw. Philip thought it funny also, but he was concerned that she not be upset.

He knew how to coddle the delicate egg. He knew how to make the right turns, took the right trips, had the right leather baggage and the best blankets, silver plates and toasty fires, the bachelor's bathroom, and the well-chilled mousse, his thoroughbred and Austrian saddle. Someday he would have to have his own stable, with a dark green carpeted tack room and handy bar, antique pictures of hunting scenes, maybe even a trophy or two, and there would be a hayloft. She liked the idea of a hayloft, and would want him to take her up there. She would want to smell the darkness filled with bound bales.

No one else would be riding with them that day, no one to get home to, no one else to please, but her, and both of them would recognize what it was they wanted, as he took her hand and led her up those raw unfinished stairs, into the musty silence of bales, and they'd almost whisper, listening, to the horses' heavy movements in their stalls, until she'd give him a playful push, and would climb those bales like building blocks, and he'd be after her, catching a leg to pull her down, jerking apart her pants, almost rough, and she would feel astonished, like a star in brilliant gas, in flame, alight, lit up, diminishing as she fell, like a meteor all but burning out across that second's sky, as he caught her cry between their mouths as she held his plunging closer. "I love your body," he would say to her—

Something inside of her froze. She knew now that she was ruined, that she might have been anyone. Anyone! That these certain words, or phrases, came out of his mouth, as if he'd turned on the faucet of his left ear. He could have said the same thing to a hundred women before her, all of them as gullible as she was, waving their flags of surrender, and each one thought she was special, that she could kiss him in front of the others. But he never liked that. He didn't want anyone making claims. She hated the fact that she was no different, and that she still wanted him too. And that he was delicious, delectable, *damn*, driving her almost crazy.

Frank had kept Philip's horse for over three months, had paid for its feed, overseen the shoeing, called the vet, babied that thoroughbred, but now he was almost fed up. "I wish I'd never taken that hòrse," Frank said at one point. "It's going right back come April." He'd been patient about his pay. Philip had paid him in full the first month, but now it had been nine weeks, and whenever Frank asked he was put off. Frank's pride was badly hurt. "He knows what it's worth! I'm not going to chase him down." He started counting what was owed, out loud, keeping that big horse fed, especially now that snow was on the ground, and Philip was even afraid to go riding, too slippery, too cold. What she had feared, the end of their season, had come. And now he was shrugging off his responsibilities to Frank, and in a sense, even to her. She forced herself to call him.

She always felt funny, being the one who had to call, leaving her messages, leaving her eggs, leaving her jar of quince jelly. Her readiness, her stupidness, her soul. She thought that perhaps he did take that, for now she wondered where it had gone. She had given him a taste of her love, and he'd eaten it like angel food, that confection of petrified honeycomb. He might have replaced it with something.

When he finally answered the phone, and she suggested that they ride that afternoon instead of the following morning as arranged, he didn't think so. "You don't need me to ride," he said. She was shocked by this answer, insulted, silent for a moment. But then she persisted in trying to convince him that it would be safe to ride, that it was going to get warmer that afternoon. But he believed it was dangerous. Bob Metford had told him so. Everything had its season, and now it was time to ski. "I thought we were going riding

54

tomorrow morning. Tomorrow would be perfect," he said.

Perfect, she wondered, why perfect. "Tomorrow's supposed to be windy and cold, ten degrees," she said, "but this afternoon it should be in the high thirties."

"Maybe if the weather warms up next week. My horse isn't properly shod." Then why would tomorrow be perfect. What was he trying to pull.

"When are you going to pay Frank?" she asserted.

"Why are you so mad?" he wanted to know, suddenly nicer in tone. "You know I'm going to take care of that."

"Well you haven't. And I have to listen to him whine." She was beginning to whine herself.

"We'll all get together next weekend," he promised. "Now you go and have a good ride," so patronizing she couldn't bear it. "Don't be upset."

"Well I am," she said, clicking the receiver, dropped into a stupefied rage.

Philip tried to call back, but she had disconnected the phone. So he got in that luxury car of his and took a mad drive over to her house. But she had already left for Kate's. Kate wasn't there. Philip drove by old Frank's place, but Julia wasn't there either. She stopped there minutes after he'd left, shocked and flattered that he was looking for her. She had made a fool of herself.

Frank said, "He came and stood right here, but do you think he offered to pay me?"

She didn't know that Frank had told him, "Oh, you can pay me anytime."

"I don't want you getting involved, Julie. It'll ruin your friendship." Which was exactly what old Frank hoped for, because he preferred the good ole days, when they rode alone together. But she had Frank write down what it was Philip owed. The figures were scrawled and vague, the addition inaccurate. She said it had to be businesslike.

"But that was never how it was going to be! It was all supposed to be up front. He knows he's getting the best price here. Just let him find somebody else."

When she got home, Mark said, "Philip Mercato called. He asked us for dinner."

"You're kidding. When?"

"Tonight."

"Tonight?" she repeated. She thought Mark might be testing her.

"Do you want to go?" he asked.

"What did you say?"

"I said, sure, if you weren't too exhausted from running around." She was exhausted, but a hot bath revived her. She wore a new winter skirt, a beautiful full viyella material, slate grey plaid, a cream-colored silk blouse and a soft blue vest made with a bulky flecked yarn that looked French. She felt lovely, peaceful, relaxed.

They were going to be the only ones there, just the three of them, which felt a little odd, but they began to drink wine right away, and she tried to make light of that morning's scene, saying to Mark, "Tell him how great the riding was last winter. Frank and I were perfectly safe, weren't we."

"If suicidal is safe," Mark said, and Philip winked at her.

They had a parsnip soup, followed by veal marsala and wild rice, a green salad with an extra splash of pungent vinegar — he had her smell it — from his own vineyard — almost a bright splashy smell, wine and still more wine. They all liked it, and he had a lot of it, and she drank too much of it around him. It made her want to make out.

They talked about Paris, polo, teaching and books, then resorted to silly jokes. Mark was getting pretty drunk, but the men seemed to like each other. Philip even invited Mark to go cross-country skiing the following weekend, and Julia raised her eyebrows.

They shifted back into the living room, where a fire was

lit in the hearth. The joking went on as they drank more Calvados, putting their feet up.

Philip wanted to know about their courtship, and Mark was quite loose and eager to spill. "You should have seen me pull up to their estate that first Christmas," he said. "A hippie in hiking boots."

"He didn't even own a tie," Julia inserted.

"And I wasn't too keen on borrowing one either. But you should have seen the letter her father wrote me. He called me a born loser, communist no-count, said that I might be interesting to her now, but that she'd get bored by me in six months and that I could never support her. But we patched things up."

"Yeah, you beat him at ping pong," she threw in, wondering why he wanted to expose all this.

Mark understood that her parents didn't care for him, even if he was educated, because then there was the issue of the draft. They found out that he had failed his hearing test on purpose. You have to have very good ears to pull that off.

Mark overheard them as he approached the breakfast room.

"I certainly would never marry a man like that," her mother was saying.

"Well *you* don't have to," Julia responded.

"I don't think we're talking about marriage here," her father added. "We have to look at reality."

"But if they're sleeping together," her mother said—she felt that they *should* get married.

"I think a year abroad would be just the thing right now."

"But you promised," Julia turned to her mother, and Mark backed away on the carpet, went back up to read on the twin bed they'd provided for him in William's old room.

Mark wondered what he was getting into.

Philip asked her about the wedding. "Did you get married in Wisconsin then?" And Julia recalled the big pink tent, the French horns playing from behind the bushes, an elegant garden wedding. Kate was her only bridesmaid. They didn't have a honeymoon. But then she remembered how Mark had forgotten to feed her cake, and had begun to feed everyone else before giving her a bite. It was almost a metaphor for their marriage—he had never given to her first.

"And I was so young, a mere puppy," she laughed, but that made Philip think of something.

"We were married for seventeen years," he said, "and right when things were breaking up, she got me to go on one of those couple weekends. It certainly didn't help us, but I'll try anything once." He was trying to remain cheery, though he looked a little wounded. "And there was this one evening, when we all had to sit around together, and say what it was that we most wanted, and I said that I really wanted to have another child. I was always pushing for that, for a second child," he went on, and the mother in Julia rose up and wanted to go and put her arms around him. What a wonderful thing to admit in front of a group like that, and it touched her, just as it seemed to touch him now. "But when you said puppy," he turned to Julia, "it reminded me of what my wife wanted most. She was the kind of person who let everything hang out," he made this loose gesture, "and she said—I just want to be naked and get licked by a dog."

They all burst out laughing. "Well good for her!" Philip poured more Calvados, and he went on about his wife, how after she'd left him, after that horrendous two-year scene, she realized that she wasn't getting any younger, and so she found another man, married him and had his baby.

"A setter," Julia tossed out, and he loved that, a setter.

It had gotten late, and they were all tired now. Philip suggested that they take a walk in the snow. It was a full moon, and though bitter cold, she liked the idea of walking down the drive between them, holding an elbow on each side, feeling secure, wanting to be surrounded, the winter moonlight balancing there on the curving slopes of white. But instead, Mark suggested that he and Philip walk, and that she drive down behind them in the car so that then they could just drive on, head home. So she was sent over the squeaky, splintery sounding snow to the red sedan, and though she had wanted to walk too, she did as he told her. They looked casual enough, walking along together, her headlights illuminating them both.

When Mark got back in the car, he said what a good time he'd had. "But that guy's odd," he added. "Do you know what he said? He's got everything, and you know what he said he'd like? To just live in a little stone cottage, just a one room place, filled with old copies of books, like Thoreau, and he'd just live there and read and fuck all night. Do you think he might be gay?" Mark asked.

"I doubt it," she said.

"Strange guy."

The next weekend, when Mark went to Boston, he didn't get his story straight. When Micky, his friend, called to tell her what time Mark's bus was getting in, she asked him where Mark had spent the previous night, and Mick said, "Oh, last night he was over at Buchanan's." And then when she picked Mark up at the bus stop, he said that he'd spent both nights with Mick.

The discrepancy whanged right into the middle of her body, and then rose slowly to consciousness, along with the realization that she now had permission, that he was being more duplicitous than she was, and it felt doubly sordid and sad, for there was Ross, in his father's arms, so happy to be riding on his lap, and Alexander, strapped into his carseat, wanted to hold Mark's hand. Thomas was skiing, but when he got home he would want to play cards with his father. The boys seemed to need him more than they needed her now.

She feared for the lives of her children. As if her very actions might bring harm to one of them. This idea almost sickened her, but the only solution seemed to be total abstinence, and she wasn't ready yet to give Philip up.

That afternoon she skied back into their forest on a cross-country ski trail, and as she went gliding deeper and deeper in, the closer she came to some anguish. This was no way to live. She wanted to change, for she already felt abandoned. Even her angel had fled. She knew she was digging her own icy grave, but she couldn't seem to stop, as if her life and actions had all been turned over, and she was merely playing some part. Anything could happen now. She could run away, get pregnant, she could lose everything she cared about, and never see her children again. This would be the worst. She could move to New York and live in a loft and see her boys on the weekend. She could yank them out of their wonderful school and move to another state, home state, where her father would protect them. She could simply get a divorce, or she could come to her senses, and realize how she and Mark had been managing before Philip rode carelessly into her life. They could maybe just be friends. They could ride when the fields had thawed. She would get clean, get pure, repent. But she did none of the above.

Mark was back in Boston for a lecture series he was giving, and Julia hadn't asked him where he was going to be staying this time when she dropped him off at the bus. He liked the bus because he could read and relax, prepare. Mark was always preparing, as if life itself lay somewhere in the future, on the other side of his desk.

She had gotten a babysitter, curled her hair, pulled on a pair of black velvet pants, a creamy cashmere sweater before driving over to Philip's house. He was waiting, and as he kissed her hello, he murmured that she looked spectacular. They were going to the movies, a theater in another state, and it felt thrilling to be going out with him, to take his arm, the thick navy wool of his coat, to ride in his classy car that still smelled of leather. Her car had kid junk all over it, and smelled vaguely of ketchup. His car was clean, immaculate, as well organized as his life, which seemed to be without flaw or complication.

But life with children was complicated. He didn't realize what she'd been through, just to get out the door — making dinner for her three boys, pasta with pesto, frozen peas, the quarrel over who got which plate. "He touched my fork!" And then Rossie spilling his milk, Thomas making him cry when he yelled, "You baby," Alexander mauling his dinner with his fingers, and when she tried to shower, they started pelting peas. She stepped on one, disgusted, refused them all dessert, sent them up the playroom, where they could get undressed and take turns in the great big tub. Alex and Rossie, first together, made the water cruise back and forth in such gigantic waves that she could hear it splashing over the rim, and then Thomas squirted cold water on them and they screamed. Rossie wanted revenge. Alexander bumped his toe. She got them into their p.j.'s, made sure they had brushed their teeth, and said, "I'm going to get Emma now," their favorite babysitter. "I'll only be gone for ten minutes, but I want you guys to behave. If you don't, you're going to be penalized."

"What does that mean?" Rossie wanted to know.

"Punished," she said.

"Oh," he seemed relieved. "I thought it meant — cut off your dick!" And they all screamed with laughter. Even she had to chuckle as she descended the stairs, but when she returned with the babysitter, they were chasing each other with magazine perfume, and *Def Leppard* was on full blast. It all seemed to be getting away from her.

What a relief the adult world was. Even if the roads were icy. Riding in Philip's car, she felt like a daughter on a date with her dad, just for a moment she felt that. But later she wondered if he had taken advantage of how susceptible and trusting she was. Did he like imposing his stronger will upon the quite strong will of another? How did he get what he wanted. How did he make his choices. Was it simply instinct, a visceral response? Or was it partly an unconscious drive to repeat a pattern, for Julia was thirteen years younger, just as his own mother, also an artist, had been thirteen years younger than his father. Philip was now the exact same age his father had been when Philip was conceived.

There was hardly anyone in the theater, and no one, thank God, that they knew. When the film began and the room was dark, he slipped his arm around her, collected her to him, and she reached for his hand, sank down to the side so that she could lean against his shoulder, happy as high school, her sweetheart. He even reached around, feeling the softness of her sweater, and rubbed against her breast. He fed her Jordan almonds, and then took her chin and kissed her, and she put her hand on his leg, moved her fingers up and down. It was as if they had come all that way just to kiss, to sit this close to each other, but he also wanted to hear the Italian, *"Ti voglio molto bene,"* while she felt inspired by the hallucinatory, vibrant color.

Coming out, arm in arm, they saw the snow was falling fast, and there were drifts pushing out onto many of the roads. His car warmed quickly, and he played Handel as they drove, chatting easily, her hand on the neck of his collar, feeling the recently trimmed hair line above his Oxford cloth shirt. She rubbed his neck a little. She could tell that he liked it, but then he took off one glove and held her hand before looking over at her.

When they got back to his place, he said that his housekeeper was away on vacation, and she saw that her car was half-buried. He asked her in for a drink and she said that she couldn't stay long. She had a young babysitter. His house was all but dark. He started a fire in the huge stone hearth. She liked to watch him do anything physical, just the concentrated way he applied himself, the way he crushed the paper, criss-crossed the kindling and lit the match, while she lay back on the creamy colored sofa, that felt like rich velour, and then, once he got the fire going, he flicked on the sound system and turned on one distant lamp. Suddenly she was very tired, but equally glad just to lie there with her eyes half-closed, watching the dance of the firelight, and then he brought out two snifters of brandy, poured her some, and she took a sip, then rested the glass on the floor before opening her arms as he descended, the couch very soft and deep, and it seemed only natural that he would descend and stretch out beside her, moving slowly on top of her—they had waited a very long time—and she loved kissing him, being covered, and it felt completely natural, as he began reaching gradually into her clothes.

Leaving his house that night, halfway out the door, the wind blowing up snow, she was in a hurry, and she thought he had said, "I love you," and she had whispered, "I love you too," or did she misunderstand him. She didn't know, wasn't certain if it even mattered. If he had said it, did he mean it? And if he meant it, why did she want to know. Out loud. Why did she have to tell him too, giving away her power. Or had he even heard her.

"You're not exchanging me for anyone," Philip had said. "I'm just an addition to your life."

"I know that," she answered. "Now that you've had me, you'll probably just discard me, like all the rest." She had certainly seen it happen.

"That's not real," he said.

"What's real?" She didn't know anymore. "Don't forget I live in a fantasy." And she knew she was making most of it up.

Even though the forecast said that it was going to snow four to eight inches that afternoon, she asked Frank to trailer the horses over near Philip's. She wanted to ride by his place.

He said he was bringing up an old friend that weekend, some-one he knew through business.

Just as Julia and Frank rode casually by, Philip pulled into his driveway. He stopped the car, and she got off her horse, and they walked up the road a bit. Frank had waved once, then looked in the other direction, waiting. He couldn't be mad anymore, because Philip had paid him in full and they were all squared away now.

"I missed you," he said, and she acknowledged the same. She tried to kiss him then, made a gesture in that direction, but he pulled back and glanced toward the car. The woman had brunette hair, overdone. She had an urban glamour. "Margot is just an old friend," he repeated.

"Do you want to come with us?" Julia smiled, knowing he couldn't. "It's a great day for a ride." The snow had started to really blow, and she and Frank looked like two on the lunatic fringe.

"I can't," he apologized. "But why don't you come for lunch tomorrow."

"Possibly," she said, leading Bunko back past the car, where this woman gave her an icy look. "I'll call you," she added, swinging back into the saddle with a graceful, easy turn.

The powerful, quiet, *chunk* of his door.

But when she called back that evening, to say that she would like to come, he made her feel like she was inviting herself, and now he was trying to get out of it—his housekeeper might not be back from vacation, and if that were the case, he'd have to take this lovely lady out. She must have been within hearing range.

Instead of backing out, Julia suggested that she bring Thomas, since Mark was out of town. "It would be nice to have another gentleman." But he suggested she call the next day and find out what was up. He wanted to ski the follow-ing morning, and from the tone of his voice he had already schussed away.

She had wanted to tell him about the bees, what had happened during the week. Bringing the double bags of groceries in, she had noticed the white bee box. Something told her to check them. Had Mark replenished their food? He'd been so preoccupied lately. She set the brown bags down on the wooden table that stood in the middle of their cozy kitchen, dim with winter light, and then climbed the little hill to the bee box, opened the lid and gasped at what she saw. She didn't want the children to see this. Their beautiful bees. The corpses were just lying there, the queen bee in their midst. She touched them, their brittle lifeless shells. She scooped a handful up, let them drop like worthless seed. All that life, their honeycomb, all that golden humming gone.

She felt awful as she hung up.

But still, she went ahead the next morning, washed and ironed the clothes she wanted to wear. Thomas took a bath, eager to go anywhere if the house had a television. She waited, using ultimate reserve, until eleven-thirty. Paula answered. She was sweet and calm as usual. Luncheon was on, and he expected them.

She wore a red plaid flannel skirt and dark green sweater which Martine had knit for her birthday. She was in a rather excited mood as she came into his house. Paula walked out from the kitchen, said that Mr. Mercato was still cross-country skiing with the Metfords. Then Margot walked into the room and over to the fire, where she tossed in some paper. Julia introduced herself, but Margot refused to even look at her. She did give a quick smile to Thomas, who wanted to find the TV, which luckily gave Julia an excuse to get away from that cheerless countenance.

"Paula," she whispered, as they walked back towards the study, "did you see how she wouldn't even look at me?"

"Well you are another woman," Paula shook her head. "Don't let it ruin your appetite."

When Philip bounced back in the door, invigorated, robust, Julia came out of the study, and Margot was there on the couch. He said to her, "Have you met Julia Chapin?"

And she said, "No." So he introduced them again.

Paula had held up lunch for him, so they sat right down. Julia was eager to drink as much wine as politely possible. Philip seemed grateful now for Thomas's presence, now that he was at the head of the table in this kind of invisible trap between two women, a trap of his own making, granted, wincing at the words she shouldn't have spoken, "So you're both friends through business?"

Margot turned to him with this adoring, longing look. "Is that how you described our relationship?" She seemed unnaturally good-humored and possessive when regarding him.

What could he say. He shrugged. Julia geared the conversation back to her son, his wonderful school, his reading habits. Because they had no TV, she had to go to three libraries to keep him stocked in books. She spoke about how well he could ride. "But he had a scare last summer, riding with my father."

"Julia comes from a very influential Midwestern family," he mentioned to Margot, and Julia thought — you don't have to legitimize me.

"So do you like to ride now?" Philip asked Thomas.

"Sort of, sometimes. My grandfather bought me this horse."

"Much too big for him," Julia put in, "a huge jumper. Tell him what happened last summer."

"My grandfather's horse kept refusing this fence, so mine decided to show him how."

"And Thomas was on top of him. But he stayed on."

"An then got off, for good," Thomas punctuated that story.

"You're terrific," Philip announced. "You look a lot like your Uncle Winthrop."

"Actually, more like William," she corrected.

"What do you think of your uncles, Tom?"

"They're o.k.," he shrugged, "when they're sober."

Philip thought this was hilarious. They needed some comic relief. The haricot beans were slightly undercooked, but everything was described as "marvellous" by Margot, who kept dishing up these adoring smiles. Spinach simmered with black olives, a delicious rosemary pork. Thomas took seconds, then thirds of that, poor meat-and-TV-deprived child. Julia excused him from the table so that he could go back and watch, with his piece of "chocolate death" which Paula had made for dessert.

Philip suggested they take a walk after lunch, but Margot pouted, "Couldn't we take a little nap?" Her meaning was obvious, suggestive. It was clear to Julia that she hadn't used the guest house.

Margot didn't look like the type who savored braving the cold, but she didn't want them to get away alone together either, so she came, hatless, and Julia started to run ahead, skidding on her smooth boots down the drive. She could almost hear Philip saying, "She's no one to get jealous about, happily married, a painter." How they occasionally rode.

As Julia turned to wait for them, she saw Margot shiver, shaking her fox fur shoulders. She was heading back for the house. So Julia went back to join him, and when she tried to take his arm, he held back. She couldn't bear his reticence. "Did you know your name means lover of horses?"

"Really? No. I thought I was named after Philip Augustus."

"Royalty, eh?" King of the Dips, she thought. "Why did you tell me she wasn't your lover?"

"She's not. That's part of the problem. A lot of anger there. We used to be together, after the divorce." Julia didn't know what the truth was anymore.

She tried to kiss him again, but he refused it, glancing back toward the house. Now she felt rejected, and in her own anger pulled away. "I'm not going to get addicted to you."

"Good," was all he said. And they walked on in silence for a little while, not touching. "I can see you next weekend," he mentioned, but he seemed so strangely reserved. "You know Margot's a multimillionaire," he said, as if that excused everything.

Julia gave a little laugh, "I'm impressed."

But these things mattered to him. Perhaps every move he made was basically financial. Maybe he wrote off these weekends as a kind of business expense. New and old clients, snowed in. She felt herself getting nasty. She didn't want to dislike him. This was the world he lived in, not unlike her father, and she had never really blamed *him,* a world in which Philip had to perform, which he couldn't let slide just because he was fond of her, which he hung onto, climbing, because of the endless effort it took to get to where he was, because of the losses, the wife who walked out, the unadmitted bitterness, because of the only daughter he was determined to spoil to make up for his absence, because he was way way up there, but still could see far above, because there was no end to this climate. Still, she wasn't impressed.

"That was quite a ride we took yesterday," she changed the subject. But he didn't seem interested. "It ended up being a blizzard."

"I know."

"I was totally covered."

He looked over at her, as if he couldn't say what he wanted to say.

The snow storm had collected around her and Frank, as if to obliterate, to eliminate them from sight. It felt like a whiteout, wild at first, as they hooted in the midst of the snow, until it really started to come on, sticking to their hats, their shoulders, brims, eyelashes, melting on their faces. She sang out loud, sang fiercely. At least she'd had a glimpse of him, a cool but cordial reception, but it was beginning to sink in, and she was sick at heart, which made her over-jolly, laughing and singing as if to deny it, when she wanted to cry and howl.

Frank was as happy as a youngster, amused by the wildness of the weather, mainly glad that he had her all to himself and that Philip was out of the picture. He grabbed her hand and squeezed so hard he almost hurt her. He wouldn't let go, as he said for the fiftieth time, "Don't ever let me down. Just don't ever leave me."

She reassured him with a nod but didn't soften. "Let's ride on up to the mound." She led the way, a nice slow canter. "Frank," she said, "don't crowd me."

The huge round uncollected bales of hay scattered across the curving field looked like huts on some arctic desert, left there in the blur of the blizzard, buffed out to a lustrous fade, a sueded grey of sky, keeping their vision minimal. The dark green trees across the field were shapes now more than color. As they picked their way along, encrusted with snow, cheeks blazing, she suddenly felt a kind of freedom—that she didn't need anyone at all. She belted out, "The Yellow Rose of Texas," which seemed incongruous, and the tune sprang up like a rebel shout against the hills where his house sat, as if she could alert him to her whereabouts, to the volume of her madness. Then heading back up the road, which the horses did know well, she let Bunko move into a canter, then a gallop, and the snow was whipping at such a slant that it stung, and she couldn't see anything, so she simply closed her eyes and let him run, which wasn't wise, but none of this is wisdom, for there was nothing to see in that blinding whiteness, and she believed that she didn't care.

She cared. And she wished that she didn't care. If she didn't care, she wouldn't have been there to begin with, she wouldn't have had Frank trailer over, she wouldn't have ridden past his house, she wouldn't have called, nor come for luncheon, she wouldn't have taken this charming walk they were on.

"Maybe we'll ride next weekend," he offered.

"Don't say that," she came back. She just wanted to go home now, to be with her boys. There he was in his cross-country ski clothes, the right sport for the proper season, his woman of the week warming herself by the fire, and Julia was simply certain that it was over now, that whatever little tension they had shared was over now for him. She wanted to kick him with her winter boot and scream at him, You Reptile! Why don't you fucking speak. I don't give a shit if she *is* your lover or not. I just want the truth from you.

The evening was the coldest it had been. "I think we're going to leave tonight. I don't trust this weather."

"It's going to drop to thirty-five degrees below tonight, with the wind chill factor," she said.

But he wanted to know what the exact temperature was, "Skip the wind chill factor."

She wanted him to at least break down and kiss her good-bye, and he did, on both cheeks, pulling back from her even as he did so. Thomas got the door, and she put her arm around her son as they walked quickly for the car.

Maybe he did have feelings which she simply couldn't decipher, something he couldn't express. Maybe he just had to protect himself. Maybe he actually cared, or had a frozen capacity. She tried to remember how good it had been to lie down with him. He was off in Italy now, then France, skiing with the Metfords, business and pleasure both. And all she could do was paint. Picture after picture, as if it would replenish her. Maybe she hadn't behaved herself. After all, there were certain rules, and she rarely obeyed them. She had an authority problem, remember? Remember the mad old lady who raced out and yelled, "You should know better!" But she never did. She never knew better. "And I still don't," she told Kate.

PART TWO

It wasn't often that they got off alone together without children, children who always seemed to perk up and listen when their mothers' voices dropped to a secretive hush. Julia usually told Kate everything. She could trust Kate, but lately, Julia had been holding something back.

"I want an update now," Kate grinned. "Any more smooches from Mr. Mercato?"

Julia's heart started to slam. Her stomach felt queasy. Kate's eyes widened, for she took in Julia's expression — a kind of contortion about to become words — Kate's adrenaline starting up too as Julia just let it slide, "I'm afraid things have progressed. It's gone way beyond that now."

Kate blew out, opening her hands, gesturing slightly, as if she were ready to receive the waterfall, let the crash of realization pound down on her, and as she breathed back in, it looked as if she knew she'd have to hold her breath now for a long, long time.

They were sitting by the window, and Julia turned her gaze to the parking lot, away from the rest of the restaurant. "I think I might be pregnant."

"Oh boy," Kate breathed.

"It's the worst. How could I? I just wasn't figuring right."

The wave having hit, Kate recovered. "Listen, nobody has to know. You could have an abortion and I'd go with you. I'd be right there."

"We'll see," she said.

It didn't seem like Kate to suggest abortion. Neither of them took it lightly. She had told Philip, "Be careful with me," but maybe he had wanted to get her pregnant. Maybe she wanted his child.

She had been hearing this name, "Antonio," receiving it in an odd, almost indescribable way, as if she had woken from a dream with that name whispered over the outer rim of consciousness. With her eyes still closed, she had groped for it, as it went floating by, and she'd scooped it out of that river, and listened to what she'd received, "Antonio." She liked the sound of it. But then she had to jerk herself back, as if ducking the impulse of the angels.

She thought of Martine, who had been trying to conceive for so long, her nest so finely prepared, but empty without that lullaby—like a lovesick bird, calling from its solo and silver cage, calling for some child to hear that song—why did nobody come? Why were things cast this way?

It seemed that everything should have meaning, but if this accidental pregnancy had meaning, it came as a lesson in the grown-up school of hard knocks, where that one slip, the fraction of an inch or hour, had become her educated panic. And yet it was also seductive, "Antonio." The name rolled over her tongue, a beautiful name, but no. The mere idea was not even something that could be considered. Nor could she fathom the alternatives, going through with it, lying to Mark, deception on the deepest level. It seemed easier to run off to Italy, where the name seemed to want to lead her back to that land of dark eyes and dark hair, the olive oil complexion, extra pure, extra virgin green.

"The chances are that you probably aren't, right? So cheer up. And let me eat that if you aren't going to. You're going to be fine in either case. But boy! How could you hold this back? I don't believe you. When did all this happen?"

"I just didn't want to burden you."

"Forget it." But Kate did feel anxious. She was trying to keep control over a nervous condition that had been getting worse during the past few months. "So," she asked, "how was it?"

Julia looked up, startled, then smiled. She wanted to praise him, wanted to describe, to convey, how wonderful, how experienced he was, how erotic it had been. Even that slight mention, "How was it," brought a flush of recollection pulsing back inside her.

"Oh no. You're in love with him, aren't you."

Julia nodded yes, but then the good feeling swung back away from her and her fears rushed in, because she didn't believe he really loved her. She should never have given in to him.

Do you think Kate's becoming religious?" Martine asked on the phone, not understanding it at all, not trusting it, as if it were a sign of weakness. And maybe it was, and maybe that was a good thing to admit.

Rachel, Martine and Julia had always considered Kate the strongest of them all—even the way she walked, full of stride, the firm placement of her feet and the brisk, sure direction, her long red-golden hair fanning out behind. They always felt that she could cut through anything, that her response could always be trusted. Nothing could really shake Kate. Nothing could knock her down. But perhaps no one is what she seems. The most strong, determined woman, might also be the most feminine, which the cunning, kittenish gal might actually be the most ruthless. The maternal-looking woman might be no good at mothering at all, and Kate's strength might also have been covering up her weakness.

Two years before, Julia had flown into Massachusetts, with her father piloting his two-prop plane. She knew Kate would be waiting at the little airport in the valley, close to the house she and Conrad had built. Julia was bringing all three boys, while Mark drove their Volvo from Berkeley. They sailed down safely onto the small runway, climbed out on the yellow wing of the plane. Kate and her daughter, "Atea," were waving.

Julia's middle son, Ross, had been born on the exact same day as Galatea, which was always cause for continued, mutual awe. They even looked like celestial twins, thin, slight, blond, but Atea was shy, while Ross was a bit brash. She made up for her shyness with a gigantic voice, "Why did he SAY that!" And then Rossie withdrew, hunching his shoulders in glee, glad at having upset her.

"You look like you could deliver tomorrow," Julia said, hugging her friend, quickly realizing, too late, that no one in their third trimester wants to be reminded of her size. But Julia wondered if Kate might not be mistaken about her due date, or if it were possibly twins, she was that huge.

"We're going to have to be patient," Kate said, with a calmness that seemed unusual for her.

Kate had located a farm house for them to rent, and when Julia saw it from across the field, the large white house with embracing porch and big red barn, like a boyfriend on the side, she gasped. It was perfect. Terribly grand, yet comfortable too. They fell out into the yard in their travel daze and looked up at the mountains, incredulous, as if their eyes couldn't dilate wide enough for the surrounding views, ripening apples, field of cows, but above all — the serenity, the quiet.

Kate suggested that they get together in the morning, go swimming in the river, and it was then that Julia saw how extreme the stretch lines were across Kate's belly. Her skin looked bruised, rippled with the tautness of having to give beyond the normal dimensions.

Instead of giving birth that month, as expected, Kate's pregnancy went on, beyond the due date, until she was sent to the closest hospital for a stress test. She just wanted to keep calm, to let the baby come on its own schedule without their stupid interference. She wanted to be left alone.

"You know Rachel was three weeks late for both her babies, and they were totally normal," Julia said. "Everybody's different. I know some women who have full term babies at eight months." Kate had been a week late with Atea, and so that probably was her rhythm. "You won't believe how much easier it is the second time around. There's no comparison."

"Just keep telling me that," Kate grimaced. They were

heading for her appointment, and the atmosphere seemed full of moisture, buoyant, almost like being at sea. Kate felt like she was out on some ocean, sailing into preliminary labor, though it was mild, very gentle.

Julia glanced over at her friend, and saw that tickled smile Kate kept half tucked in like a hanky, and she admired Kate's wholesomeness, the golden red of her coloring coordinated with this season of stain and flame. What a liberating feeling to be zipping down a glorious autumnal valley road, with the maples glowing like huge unearthly lanterns. It felt like they were off on one of their college adventures, which had been so regular fifteen years ago.

It was a time of convertible driving, Orange Crush and Mounds bars giving the brain a rush as they tested each other on geology, "O.k., so what's a coprolite?" Excess laughter and beginning Russian, Old Golds and Blackjack gum, raving happy trips to Williams with the radio turned full blast. They had their first legal cocktails at "sour hour," where the boys from surrounding colleges crowded in to assess the goods. Kate never went back after her first experience—some guy from Union went under her skirt and goosed her amidst that crowd. She had spilled her drink on his head, but laughed like a lunatic later. They went dancing at The Golden Grill, an all-black bar, and when "Pointy-head" asked Julia to dance, she could feel *it* pressing against her. They sang out loud to "Tenderness," ready to travel anywhere with Otis Redding on the radio, basically conservative but wanting to feel wild.

After freshman year, they drove to the Southwest—Taos, Santa Fe, and then Albuquerque, splitting gas money and tuna fish sandwiches, wanting to look like hippies with their long, streaming hair, but then Julia found herself a real, live, New Mexican foothill hippie with an actual beard. "Does that itch?" were her first words to the man who'd become her husband.

"Where?" was his response.

She wondered if that were dirty. He looked like he might have a dirty mind, the way he'd brushed her ass when she passed before him in the theater. Kate and she were crashing a student film series. "You girls aren't from around here, are you?" he asked.

"Why do you say that?" Kate answered.

"Your style," he grinned. "My name's Mark. Mark Mason."

"Sounds more like a preppy than a hippie," Kate whispered as the film began, but Julia liked his looks — big, majestic, craggy blond. He wanted to teach art history, and was slowly working on his Ph.D. "Another perpetual student," Kate commented, but soon they became a touring threesome. Kate didn't seem to mind, but actually she did. He didn't make her feel included. It was hard being the only one not in love. She found herself a kitten instead, and immediately named him, "Igneous."

Mark stayed in New Mexico when they drove back east, the little tiger kitten sitting up on the dashboard batting at the feathers hanging from the rearview mirror. Kate was glad to be leaving him behind, and Julia was glad to be leaving the sauna-like intensity, but they had both come to love this landscape, the bony ridges, the spare expanses where the eye could travel all the way out. They made a pact that they would come back someday. Maybe they would even rent a ranch, and Julia could have a horse, and Kate would turn that dust into a bountiful garden.

They took Route 66 as far as St. Louis, and Julia couldn't stop talking about Mark. "You know Mark got arrested on this road for indecent exposure," she said.

The endless conversations about Mark wearied Kate. "What was he doing, mooning out the window?"

"Just taking a pee, in the middle of the desert, and then this cop shoots out of nowhere and handcuffs him."

"Must have a pretty dangerous looking cock," Kate said, and Julia laughed.

"Do you think I'll be with him forever?" Julia mused. The sky was a streaked watermelon color.

"Why don't you see if you can live with him for a year. He *is* a difficult man." Kate thought Mark didn't give much of himself, awfully self-consumed, but Julia thought she was jealous. Kate thought it was a sexual thing, that he would never make Julia happy.

It turned out that Mark was the jealous one, and it angered him to feel that way. He drove back to New York State later that fall to visit, and he was certain that Julia was seeing an old boyfriend from Williams. He yanked her so hard she dislocated a shoulder. Julia was afraid of his temper, but the intensity of his love excited her, and they seemed to thrive on the tension.

He was trying to finish his thesis and this frustrated him, and her prodding maddened him, and the draft board was looking for him, and the cold weather didn't agree with him, and he thought he might head back west, which made Julia even more urgent, while it made him more aloof.

Once Kate came racing up the stairs to the third floor looking for Julia, because her brother, Winthrop, had just called, offering to have them both down for a big Yale weekend. Kate knocked hard, then hearing Mark's, "Yeah, come in," she pushed the door open and found them both in bed. She was mortified.

Walking into Mark and Julia's bathroom years later, finding Mark standing there, stark naked, shaving, she had been reminded, saying—"Whoa!" before making her retreat. "Boy Mark, you have made my day!"

Things don't change so fast, or maybe they change so rapidly that time just blends together, and remains on some other plane, where all tenses merge and equalize, the comings and goings, the goings-on, the partings and reunions—all smoothed out in time's efficient blender.

Sitting there in the doctor's office, Julia realized that she had known Kate even longer than she'd known her husband. It was a comforting thought, continuity. This evening, after the appointment, they were going to go out and have "Confusion Pizza," just the two of them. Julia wanted to urge Kate to overeat, believing that it might bring labor on.

Kate had asked her to be there for the birth, and even Julia was getting anxious, always waiting for that phone call. Dr. Horder tried to dispel Kate's anxiety, coming out to greet her. Julia noticed how well Kate carried her weight. She hadn't gained a lot in other places. The rest of her looked normal. But as the appointment was winding down, Julia could hear the urgency in Dr. Horder's voice, "I just won't be confident about a home delivery unless you have another stress test." He was having trouble hearing the baby's heartbeat through the preliminary contractions. She was in the beginning of mild labor. "I'm sorry you have to go through all this again, but I *do* want that test done tonight."

Kate looked concerned, as if she were in a hurry. "Looks like postponed pizza," she said, but Julia only cheered, how wonderful that it had begun, and of course it was best to be on the safe side, to have another stress test. Kate borrowed the office phone to call her husband, Conrad, and there was a controlled panic in her voice. "Everything's *fine,*" she emphasized, "mere routine!" She was unsettled, being so late, and now being hustled about.

"You know this whole process, the birth, all of it, has started to seem unreal to me," Kate said in the car as Julia drove. "I haven't even felt the baby kick in a couple of days."

"I used to have long periods like that too, with Rossie. He was the most placid baby inside. I can remember thinking that Ross was a girl, just because he was so inactive."

"You just wanted a girl."

"But I'm glad I've got boys. Your baby's so big and engaged, he probably doesn't have any room to move."

"Don't say *he*. I really don't want to get my hopes up."

"You're going to have a boy, a big healthy boy, I know it."

"Julia, your baby predictions are *always* wrong. Look, my breasts are even leaking."

Julia had liked how nursing made her breasts so large and juicy, and now she almost envied Kate's milk. All that was over for Julia.

Kate put her hands on her belly, and began to gently blow. "It's so hard and tight."

"That's good. Just go with it." Julia slowed by the little country cemetery where they would take a left, but it was only after she began to pull out, accelerating, that she saw the huge truck barrelling down the hill right at them. She gunned the engine to make it across, while the truck swerved like something on ice, whirling by, horn blaring, as their hearts lurched and Kate grabbed at the dashboard. Julia headed slowly up the hill. Kate sat frozen, tears locked behind her eyes. All her nerves had been brought to the surface, and they were now collecting in the hard contracting ball of her belly. Birth almost seemed pointless to her at that moment, as if life were just an accumulation of instants like this one, which made death seem as clumsy as a fast truck, sudden as a bad decision.

"Call me," Julia said, dropping her off.

Kate saw no one was at home, and she felt spooked. A gust of wind slapped up, and the bell chimes gonged in the pear tree. The air seemed pre-torrential, beckoning, threatening, pushing and pulling. She turned on all the lights. She wanted grated carrots. She wanted to taste their wet and juicy orangeness, mixed with lemon and oil, sweet and tart, until it all contracted and Conrad drove up the drive, thank God. He had taken Atea nextdoor. He seemed very up, light of mood, in a good humor about it all, giving her a kiss on the cheek as she stood leaning against the counter. But she brushed him away, "Let's go."

"O.k., my sweet, let's roll 'er onto the road."

Kate had grown serious now, fighting back her fears, and when the rain began to pour, splashing over their car, she felt as if they were all being baptized. She rolled down the window, stuck out her hand, wiped the wetness across her brow. "Hurry," she said. "Can't you hurry?" Though the labor wasn't urgent.

The beating of her belly seemed to have transferred to a pounding in her head. The throb, the beat of blood inside her, couldn't be picked up. The panic of their searching, under the surveillance of machines, slicked to the belly, recording what was nothing, that registered on the face of the nurse who probed, almost prodding, trying to find that heartbeat, but the sound wasn't happening.

Kate read her face and knew.

The nurse looked down, ashamed. She said she'd get the doctor.

Kate said, "It's all right."

Conrad started to cry. His knowledge came with immediate tears, until wracked, shaking, and Kate held Conrad's hand and tried to comfort him. "It's going to be all right. It's really all *o.k.,*" knowing now that the baby was dead, that it wasn't alive inside her, and yet she felt illuminated by some larger grace, some force that was moving through her, that still had to deliver her, and she felt the peace of it, the calm before the shock hits, unable to absorb what had actually happened inside her. The true impact of that would only come much later in much fuller force than anyone could feel right now, like a tidal wave, internal, to knock her down, to bash her down, to hold her there, under the churning blackened water, until she could hardly breathe, to hold her, pressing down with the force and weight of tonnage, as if she too should die, but that realization hadn't even dawned yet.

The doctor was in the room. His expression was like that of a basset hound, she thought, mournful, and yet amusing to her. His serious, clean hands. Everything about him seemed overly neat and tidy, and she wondered why doctors were so immaculate when life was such a mess. She shut her eyes and pictured him with a shining, silver spade, standing on the top of a garbage heap, gulls whirling overhead, making gull jokes about him, as if he could find anything worth keeping here, on this heap of rubbish, in his expensive, clean, pressed clothes.

But now his hands were in her, testing. The chill of the iron, the smooth cool silvery parts of the bed, the rails, she hung onto, the tiny delicate wallpaper like some fine, fine emotion, some fragrance on the cheek of her grandmother Baba, some buttercup of life, denial, crushed underfoot, the tiniest little flower, smashed, intentional, No — this couldn't be.

Conrad's face was streaked with grief. And the doctor took the stethoscope from his ears, as if he'd heard enough of that music, and he was saying what was obvious, that their baby wasn't living. The perfect heart was silent. But still in there. Mild labor. And very large. An extremely large baby. But not born. And it still had to be born. The slow, powerless labor. They agreed on an injection. And he looked concerned about her. He looked at her oddly. But she didn't feel that she was the odd one. All of *them* were odd. Outside. Outside this fact, looking in at her, as if through the nursery glass, while she was at the center, still, poised, perfectly at one, inside the eye of the cyclone, the funnel through which she'd pour. She held their baby in. It was hers, a part of her. But she was strong now. She would give it birth, give their baby birth, and then the medication took hold and the contractions became very real, and she was unable to think about anything else, but her hair seemed in the way, and she snapped at Conrad to DO something with her damn hair, "Pin it UP!" And then she told him to stand back. The energies were releasing the cool grey infant coming — pushed, as any other, pushed and pounding against the quickly dilated cervix, splitting her then, huge, the head, she felt it with her hand. So strange to feel that hardness, head, and then to feel the rest, inside her, coming—she moaned, again, the shoulders, the body being born, pulled up by the hands of the doctor in his rubber gloves, all greased, and the body was a slithering mass, with very real hair, dark brown, and she laughed, and then gulped as she saw, "A boy," and she reached down, completely herself without pain now, and the doctor, bless him, helped her hold the baby in her arms, before the placenta had even come, but on the next contraction it did, and he was so large, and healthy looking, perfect, "Conrad, look at his hands," and his toes, his feet, so perfect, "My God," and the nurse was standing there saying that it was time.

"Wait," she looked up at her husband, and said plainly, "Isn't he beautiful? The most beautiful baby boy." But this started Conrad crying again, bawling, almost like Atea, she thought, so extreme, his anguish rising to the surface so quickly, like their daughter. Kate had no need to cry. She just wanted to hold the baby. "Just one more minute," she said.

The nurse waited with a cloth in her hands. They always wanted the mother to hold the baby, to know that this was something that had actually happened, that this was death, not life, that this was silence, not screaming, that this was actual, not breathing, but not to let her hold the child too long. "All right now, dear," the kind nurse said, for this time it was not a question. So quickly those attachments bind, so firmly they remain, fiercely bound, forever, as he already was, but she handed the baby over, and they wrapped him, and took him, and her eyes lunged after—How she had wanted that baby!

Kate hadn't called by nine-thirty, so Julia left to go get groceries. What a crazy, stormy night it was.

As she walked back into the kitchen, her arms loaded

with damp bags, Mark came to greet her, and she saw a kind of curtain flutter over his face.

He waited for her to put the bags down, then embraced her, but she pulled back. "How's Kate? Did she call?" Their boys were all asleep, and the house felt uncanny, quiet.

"Kate's baby is dead," he said to her.

"No," she backed away from him, back across the kitchen. Her hand made the gesture to stop, stop it. "No, I can't believe it."

"They asked you to come tomorrow." The wind clapped, and banged and blew. The rain seemed to whip the windows from every direction. "I talked to Conrad, and Kate is fine, but they want you to call Rachel and Martine."

"Oh my God," she said.

She waited until twelve-thirty, when it would be nine-thirty in Berkeley, and hopefully Rachel's children would be in bed and they could talk. She asked Rachel to go over and tell Martine in person. Martine would take it the hardest, and Julia felt Martine, who lived alone now, should have somebody right there, not to hear it over the phone.

"It was a boy," Julia said. Just what Kate had wanted. Kate should have had that baby.

"How could this happen?" Rachel wanted to know.

"They said it was post-maturity syndrome. The placenta just gave out."

"How will they ever survive this."

"Maybe it wasn't meant to be born. Kate was so abnormally large, weeks ago, and the baby was huge. Something might have been wrong that the doctors can't even understand."

"But what if they had induced? That baby might be living right now. And healthy. And normal! That doctor must be out of his mind. I was tested every other day when I got that late. I just can't bear this. I *will* go over and tell Martine, but this is going to be terrible. You just have to keep her together, o.k.? For all of us. And give them *all* our love."

But as Julia lay in the dark, trying to sleep, she was jolted by this clammy fear that something ominous was hovering. She pictured the four of them, linked in a circle, holding onto each other's pulse beats, but something heavy was inside each one of them — the heaviness overwhelming. She knew there was no understandable reason why Kate's baby had died, that one could not even use human values in responding.

Kate's words came back to her then, "God's value system is so much different than our own. Sometimes He gives the hardest trials to those who were meant to know more of Him." It seemed horribly true at that moment in the night, that deep grief, great illness, suffering, loss, could work more of God's character into a person. But what a price, what a terrible privilege.

Betty, Kate's mother, went to the hospital early the next morning. They wanted Julia to come in the afternoon. They would need help coming home. But what could Julia do now? She decided to go over to Kate's and clean, just to do something. She vacuumed the entire house, scrubbed the tile floor in the kitchen, the tub, the basin, even the stove and fridge. Why was grief giving her energy? The work distracted her. She picked up blocks and books that Atea had left about. Kate would tell Atea, "The baby went back to the angels," and Atea would accept that as simply as — it's raining today, we can't go out. Julia arranged the dolls and toys, tried to tidy the piles of projects that were strewn about the big open living room. Kate was a bit of a slob, so unlike her inner nature, which was clean as a whistle from a grass blade. Her physical surroundings were haphazard, artistic, colorful, with a scattering of baskets — yarn, cut paper, embroidery thread, glue and scissors on the table where she and Atea had been preparing birth announcments. Julia picked up the clothes that had been dropped by the stairs and walking up, she stopped outside their bedroom.

There was the hanging cradle with its wicker hood, the interior draped with soft pink cloth, hanging from the slant of the ceiling, and there beside the cradle on the wall, was the watercolor that Julia had done weeks before, a flying horse swimming through colors of air and light and water, a soft and hazy horse at a rocking gallop, with a star blazing from its forehead, like a beam to see, and a star in the sky was descending as if in answer. Where had that star gone?

The candle holder Conrad had carved was there on the changing table, a beeswax candle, the clean wick, the matchbook even beside it. To change the baby by candlelight. Who else would be so considerate? The cotton stack of diapers there, and the two pins stuck in a bar of soap beside the woolen soakers, everything ready for weeks now. The freshly stitched pink silk doll lay on the creamy lambskin which lined the basket, and there too, above the handknit blanket, folded back, was a little outfit, tiny, delicate, yellow and white, the little silken cap. Julia knew not to touch these things. Not to remove them, not to rearrange. Kate herself would have to take them down.

But how. How down. How go through those motions, those movements of loss, without shipwreck. How take anything down. Or maybe you never do, she thought. And the rest of the life you live, you keep seeing it all set up, as she was seeing it now, and every day from then on was a kind of cover-up, for you never really took anything down.

Julia waited on a metal chair down the corridor from 395, Kate and Conrad's room. She was almost afraid to face her friend, afraid that she'd be of no help. But then she saw Kate's mother come out of the room, and Julia stood, as if it weren't too late, as if this had all been some absurd mix-up, but she could see that the tears were now splashing down on Betty's face as she opened her arms to Julia, hugged her, sobbing, "We'll never get over this. We never will. I'm just too old." And they hung onto each other, and just allowed it. Betty finally stood up straighter and said, "Well, I'm glad you're here." Kate's mother was a good Catholic, yet very realistic, down to earth. She'd had eight babies of her own, and two had been lost in miscarriage. "Kate hasn't been able to cry yet," she said with a knowing look, a grey look of fear for her daughter. "She hasn't even begun."

"It'll take a long time," Julia said, "even years."

"It will take her the rest of her life."

Kate was lying back on the pillows of her cranked-up bed. "Oh babe," Julia said, reaching for her, and Kate patted her back as they hugged, as if Julia were the one who needed comfort. Kate looked beautiful. Julia had never seen her so radiant. They were eating chicken enchiladas, and they both seemed to be in a good mood. Julia's emotions arriving on the scene seemed out of place, the birthing mood still high. The doctor said that Kate could go home. She was eager to see Atea. They drank the white grape juice that Julia had brought, and Kate talked on, describing the delivery, the episiotomy, the details about the baby, how big and beautiful he was.

They ate in silence then, and suddenly the mood seemed to change in the room. They could all feel the coolness. It was as if a cloud had passed in front of the sun, and with it the realization that the baby would not come home. Kate appeared to be listening, but there was only the passing murmur of nurses in the hall. Finally she whispered, "I don't want to leave him here."

When it was time to go, both Conrad and Julia helped her into the wheelchair, and she saw Kate's eyes travelling over that room with its tiny flowered wallpaper, the metal drawers, and Kate's eyes began to widen, as if she were being forced to leave a place she loved very much and would never see again. Julia wheeled her down the corridor so they could talk alone for a bit, and she saw that Kate was pinching her upper lip, as if to control herself. "Listen," Julia leaned over her, "it's good to cry. Just go ahead, if you can," but Kate put her whole hand over her mouth, afraid that if she started she would never stop, until she came to those tears one gives at the very bottom, that make you feel like something found when the snow melts, ruined on rescue.

Rachel wrote Kate: *How can I begin? My heart hurts and the tears well up. I am trying to sit here calmly, but it's as if I'm sitting in the dark, trying to see — why? How could this happen? A shadow has sliced through all of us, this shadow of birth and death. More than a shadow, it has cut the continuity of time and etched our lives. The moment is long, but the insight must give us all greater vision. And yet I feel that a star has left our earthly constellation, left an enormous hole in the sky. I just wanted you to know that I think you are incredibly courageous and a true inspiration to all of us who are lucky enough to know you.*

Martine wrote Kate: *We are all stunned, as if all sound had been shut off and we were in some vacuum set apart. It is terrible being so far away. I want to stand beside you, take care of you. If you'd come, I'd do all the little things so that you could stay in that stunned, quiet place for as long as you needed, a place where you could soothe your wounds in total privacy. I love you so very much. It is the one absolute in my life. But there is so much sorrow inside of me right now, I can hardly move, barely breathe. Would I be any comfort if I came? I really think it would be better if you could just rest somewhere different for a while. I can already feel my hand slipping into yours. I'm the one standing just behind you in case your knees give way. It might be just what you need. Just what I need too.*

And so he went, ashes to ashes, Emmanuel, for she had finally named him, not christened him as her mother had wanted, but given the memory of his body a name, so that she could think of him as someone. Emmanuel, the gift of God.

Returned to them in ashes. The box was heavy. Conrad carried it up the hillside, behind Kate and Atea, just the three of them, up behind their house, over to the other side where he had been clearing pine trees, and they stood on the slope that overlooked the pond, and he read a verse, and then lifted the box, so much heavier than he'd expected, not like wood ashes, light and airy—these were solid, ashes of stone and bone, like crumbled brick, and when he opened the box, Kate took them and scattered them and wept. Conrad didn't cry now. She tried to sing a song as she scattered them, but nothing sounds so stupid as someone crying when she tries to sing. She could not be consoled, wouldn't hear of it. Shook her head to be left then, for she missed him terribly, missed him more than anything, for he was irreplaceable, absolutely without any chance of ever being with her again, and she wanted him so badly, to be there in her arms, and on her breast, which hurt still, engorged for him, wanted him there in a bundle of blankets, asleep in the crook of her rocking. "God, Oh GOD, what are you doing to me!"

Atea had wandered away, gathering leaves, talking and chatting to her father, undisturbed, and Conrad led her back to the house now. Kate could hear her daughter's eager voice, "I can get Mama some tissue," completely matter-of-fact.

Atea seemed so distant from her now, rather than the other way, how she might have imagined, clinging to her daughter. Atea's constant chattering and presentness almost grated on her, though she didn't outwardly show it. Kate had a temper, but she rarely used it on Atea, and Julia had always admired her control. Kate was so patient, even and calm with her daughter. She let Atea turn their whole downstairs into one big playroom, overturning chairs and covering the table with a blanket to make a house. Conrad had built her a wooden stove, and it was covered with sand, littered with seeds and herbs, the flaking petals of flowers. Atea was able to invent the game of life out of anything, amusing herself for hours.

90

Julia had brought Atea two old wooden telephones she'd found in a thrift store, and immediately Atea got to work and set one up inside the homemade house, arranging the other so that Julia could answer it. Kate whispered, "Do you know how many questions she asked me yesterday? I counted them up. Just guess."

"Seventy?"

"One hundred and twenty-two. Things like—why are there holes in these crackers? Sometimes I think I'm going out of my mind."

"Aunt Julia, are you talking? Can you hear the phone?" Atea called from inside her house. "I'm having a party, and George is here, and Susannah is asleep, and we're having gumbo. Do you like gumbo? George does! And cake. Mama, what's gumbo? But I guess we'll have to wait to blow out the candles, because this baby is asleep. Aunt Julia, will you call me back? When can you call me back?"

"I'll try you in half an hour, o.k.? After I visit with your Ma?"

Kate had never liked to talk about herself before, never offered anything up unless asked specifically, and that had always made her appear to be a good listener, but Julia realized now that everyone, at some time, really needed to be heard. Now Kate had this urgency, and had to talk, had to repeat in detail, a continual verbal bath, as if speaking meant breathing, to see it over again, to tell it, so as not to feel it at any deeper level, sweeping and sweeping the same surface, for if she stopped, the floor itself might turn into mud, and then that too would give way, and there would be nothing to stand on.

"I just keep seeing that hand, that little dangling hand, when they took him."

Julia tried to assure that it was only natural. Yet nothing seemed natural to Kate now. Everything was tainted by some slightly unnatural shade, *Emmanuel.* It was more like a prayer, an ash, a wish for him, a whisper of wind, the name that had never breathed with sound. No sweet white breath of clover, ripening its bud in the warm wind. She kept listening, as if she might hear that breath begin, but all she received was a hollow sound, and all she knew was that she had to get pregnant again, immediately, as soon as possible, as soon as the doctor gave the go ahead.

"Don't you think you should try and work through this first, before conceiving?" Julia asked her.

"I can't wait. I don't feel like I can see anyone. I don't even want to go into town. People just look at me, and I know what they're thinking, and I hate them feeling sorry for me. The other day a woman rushed up to me and said—Oh! Was it a boy or girl?"

"What did you say?"

"I said a boy, but he was born dead."

"Hmmm," Julia responded. "Maybe you should take a trip. Go visit Martine for a while."

"I just feel trapped, all day, and even at night. I keep waking up, and it feels like I can't breathe, and then I just *lie* there in this *state,* and I just don't think I can face anyone until I'm pregnant."

"You know how much Martine would love to see you."

It was true, out there, in California, no one would know, Kate thought.

Julia didn't trust using another pregnancy as a remedy for this. She didn't believe that another child would fill up the loss of the one she'd never taken home. But it would help, in time, another child would help.

Because of Kate's loss, two years before, it was hard for Julia to consider abortion, hard to conceive of willing that in her own life, but what also terrified her now was how quickly her own maternal instincts were taking hold. She, who had firmly wanted no more children, was suddenly dreaming about holding a baby. She caught herself humming songs that she used to sing to her boys, and she wondered if she should tell Philip. Would he be furious, or would he want her to keep the child. Mark would insist on abortion.

It seemed as if all she knew and loved could be taken away from her. Philip might even reject her. Or maybe he'd take them under his wing. She had been wrong that he was finished with her, that it was over.

Her silence had created an urge of hot pursuit in him, and yet she still feared to displease him, to create a complication in his life, not to mention hers. Yes, not approaching him when he returned from his trip was the wisest thing she could have done. Not calling when she knew he was home. Not writing when she was tempted, when she was dying for some word. Not leaving a message with his answering service, and even when she saw the note left by her babysitter — *Philip Mercato called* — she still didn't pick up the phone. What reserve. What brains. Because it was aloofness which aroused him. He was excited only by his own initiative, when a plan was his idea alone. When he finally got through to her, he sounded so urgent, "Can you talk now?" His intensity impressed her. "I missed you, darling. I really want to see you. Why didn't you call me back? That's silly. You should feel free to call me anytime. Just call collect. I won't let it go this long again. Can you come for dinner Saturday night? Well then, how about lunch on Sunday? I'm bringing up an Italian friend, an older woman. She's a famous urologist, but just a friend, an acquaintance. Her daughter and son-in-law are coming too, and I think you'll like them. Then we'll ride after lunch, all right?"

She knew the more she held back, the more he would come forward, but given this much encouragement, her emotions lunged on the line, wanting to get to him, wanting to walk into his big embrace. She was so happy, and glad when she was around him, almost euphoric, but she always paid for that later, the reality of balance.

When she entered his house, the son-in-law, Michael, was sitting by the fire, an attractive thirty-year-old man, reading the *New York Times*. He gave her an open grin as she swung in wearing her thick cherry red sweater and turquoise scarf, her hair even blonder now, blown back, light and fluffed and her heart pounding. Philip came out of the kitchen and held her tight in his arms for a long time, repeating that he'd missed her, that it was great to see her, how fantastic she looked.

"Come meet Adrianna," he said. He took her back toward the kitchen. Adrianna turned from the *salade niçoise* she was making. She was a very lovely woman in her late forties with dark, wavy hair, dressed in a sophisticated sleek outfit, a tight, longish skirt. She took Julia's hand, and it seemed her whole being poured through her eyes, and they instantly liked each other. Philip mentioned her villa outside Florence, how gorgeous it was, but she insisted that it was "nothing like Philipe's, so splendid."

"How would you like a cassis?" he asked Julia, but she declined.

"Now you two go sit down," Adrianna offered. "Paula and I are taking care of this little luncheon. Send Michael in to me," she added. "Michael!" she called, "I want your company," and Julia understood that Adrianna was giving the two of them privacy, and having it, Philip moved over next to her, slipped his arm around her shoulder, pulled her up to him and wasted no time in kissing her. It had been so long, six weeks. The mere touch of him floored her, and she could feel the icy covering she'd let harden on the surface just shatter from the impact, the splash of it all coming back, so quickly that it scared her.

They were going to go riding after lunch. It was going to be a simple, light meal, which was all she could take. She knew that she had to eat, but she wasn't exactly hungry.

Adrianna's daughter, Mia, came in from a walk to join Michael. She had her mother's same warm eyes and smile, an aura of feminine sensuality, a soft sensation of giving about her, which Julia always found appealing. Rachel had those same qualities.

Julia liked this whole family very much, and they had an excellent meal, getting giddy on the conversation, feeling instantly intimate, exchanging lists, and she begged them all to speak Italian. She didn't know the language, but felt that she could almost understand what they said. They lapsed back into English, admiring Julia's sweater. She said that she liked Michael's. Adrianna offered to get her one just like it. Julia thought that if she could have chosen a mother, she might have chosen this woman. She was at least as old as Philip, but so lovely. He insisted that they were just friends, and that he wanted to keep it that way.

Frank had gone to a wedding out of state, so Julia and Philip had the horses all to themselves. As she was getting her tack down, he came up behind her, pulling her to him with his hand low on her belly, the other hand sliding down over her groin, and she instantly responded with a rush of wetness, but felt nervous and said, "Not here."

"Why not?" he said, pushing the saddle back up on the rack. She wanted to ooze and collapse right there, but it didn't seem right, and she held him off, but she loved feeling him move on the outside of her blue jeans, over the zipper which he slid down, sliding his hand in, moving his other palm up to collect a breast, to twist the nipple almost hard until it responded. "I just want to touch you. Lie down," he instructed, and she did lie down, watching him proceed as she lay spread out on the old green carpet, which was thrown over the unfinished floor boards. He pulled off her jeans, leaving her thick red sweater on, and descended on her with his fearless mouth, pulling her underpants sideways, until she just wanted to flood. She felt so close, but didn't want to come yet, wanting him there inside her, so she pulled him up and he fucked her gently, fucked her on and on, for it seemed he could hold it forever, and she wanted to keep on going, she wanted to fuck him like this forever on the floor of this

95

dirty old tack room. He was pushing her across the floor with his thrusting, and she was almost under a bench, "Where am I?" laughing as she slipped him out, and moved his hand down to her bush, and indicated that he should just touch her there, for she was so close, and he rubbed and said, "So you like that," and she started to come, and she came so deeply, so fiercely, it seemed that she wouldn't stop, and she pulled him back inside her, and it kept on coming, sucking in on him, endless, the waves of it coming and filling and shooting, and she moaned in his ear as if she'd never get enough of this, and then he got close, "You're still coming," he said, "I can feel it," and it was exceptionally long for her, and good for her, and "Yes," she said, "I want you," and he asked if he could give it to her now, how he wanted to give it to her, "Now," she said, "come in me," and he shouted out as he came, and she gripped him hard and pressed his ass and squeezed his every drop.

Two weeks later they rode alone together again. She had ridden with Frank during the week, and explained to him that she had some things she wanted to talk to Philip about, and that sometimes they would all ride together, and sometimes she'd ride alone with one or the other. Frank didn't like it, but he claimed he understood. "I know you're young. You don't always want to go with an old fool like me. But that guy, he's a homo! You should hear what people in town say." She gave him a look that said — cut it out. She was almost sure she was pregnant. Her breasts were tender, and she felt slightly nauseous. She had stopped drinking coffee and craved meat. She couldn't fathom how she would deal with this, but now she had to hear Philip's response.

As they rode up the hill Philip took her hand and kissed the back of it, and they chatted and walked and then trotted their horses, slowly, warming up. Despite the confusion, she was glad. The early spring forest had come alive with strange shades of red, as if the buds themselves were pulsing. The new green was translucent, while last year's bleached out grass rose up the mound. She would always remember this time, in particular, as the moment when the pussy willows sprang from their neat, grey sleekness, almost nubile, into something light and airy, that pale and fluffy yellow-green. The vibrating quality of the air seemed to sail the birds in tandem, and she too wanted to be swirled up high, coming down into his arms.

They were up on top of the mound now, and Julia didn't know why she brought up Renata, but they had started talking about the past and other women in his life. She knew he still saw Renata in New York, but he didn't seem crazy about her. "I just feel comfortable with her," he said. "We have such similar backgrounds." Julia flinched. His eyes looked tired that morning. He seemed older than usual.

"Do you think Renata loves you?" she asked.

"Yes," he answered, quite confident. "She even wanted to get married," he added, "but I'm not ready for that. Six months ago it all came to a head and I told her quite frankly that I had to concentrate on my work. She's really too old for me. I told her that she shouldn't waste her time, that we could break it off, or remain friends."

"So what did she do?"

"She broke it off. But by the next week she was back. A very good friend," he laughed.

Julia recoiled. She felt she had too much pride for this. She wondered out loud why she felt monogamous. She didn't understand his desires, and he said, "Most women are monogamous. But you know Adrianna? She has four different lovers in different European cities, and she likes it that way. She's a very passionate woman."

Julia stopped her horse, looked over at him. "I thought she wasn't your lover."

"She wasn't," he said, and Julia withered. "It was later, back in New York. It just happened."

Stunned, she turned her horse, kicked him and started

galloping away, tears flying from her eyes — Get away from me, get away, *away,* just get me away from this man! She could hear him galloping behind her, but she wouldn't stop and kicked her horse, but he was up beside her now, and she kept her eyes turned away from him, her face down and away.

"Come on, talk to me," he took her hand, but she still wouldn't look at him. "Julia, what is it."

"Don't you know that I'm in love with you!" she blurted out. "It's very hard for me to take this. To hear all this."

He waited a moment, then said in a soft, kind voice, "That's the first time you ever told me that."

She kept walking her horse away, not wanting to talk, wanting her distance. What would she do. She wiped her tears from her face as he spoke. "It's not unrequited you know. I love you too. I love your spirit, your art, all of it, riding with you. But there's a difference between loving someone and being *in* love."

"I'm aware," she said.

"You're the most important person in my life," he added. She was supposed to be grateful? She knew she fulfilled a certain function in his life, as riding partner, nature slot, while he was everything to her. She felt like hurting him now. But she knew that he couldn't make himself feel what wasn't there. She had let herself fall for him. She had gotten pregnant because of it, and what did he feel? Fondness, basically, a fondness. And that wasn't enough.

"Listen," she said, stopping her horse, "I have to talk to you." But then she couldn't speak.

He had to coax her, "Come on, what's wrong." He always seemed amused when she was upset.

"I haven't gotten my period," she said.

He didn't seem disturbed by this, only excited, amazed. "Do you actually *know* if you're pregnant? Have you had a test?"

"I just don't know what I'm going to do. I could never lie about this to Mark."

"What does he know now?"

"Nothing, really. He knows I look forward to seeing you, riding with you every week. He even asked me if I wanted to sleep with you."

"Just deny it," Philip said.

But she couldn't keep this baby and deny it. She felt a rising panic. She had made an appointment with her gynecologist to talk about her options, and maybe she would never tell Philip what had transpired. Maybe she'd just say, I got my period, an early miscarriage, and she would take care of it. She wondered if she had to have her husband's permission for an abortion, if she could drive herself there and back, how long it would take to recover, how much she would bleed, would she need medication, how bad it would hurt, would she fall into a depression, regret it for the rest of her life, be haunted. It didn't feel like the right thing to do, but screwing her life up completely with a man who didn't even love her wasn't exactly smart either.

Riding back toward Frank's place, they took a dirt road around the marsh and started to gallop. He was right by her side, but she made her horse go faster, leaning forward to race him, and she was out-stripping him, *yah-yah,* taking the lead as he galloped beside her, but then he yelled out, "I love you!" And again she started to cry — the tears flew out of her eyes, as she sat back in her saddle as if crushed, defeated.

"You don't have to tell me that," she said, and he could see the fallen expression on her face. He wanted to lick the tears that streamed over her cheekbones.

"But I mean it," he said, with such tenderness that it almost seemed believable.

"You won't love me until I'm gone."

"What?" he joked. "Leaving already?"

She managed a smile. "I'm sorry," she said, "maybe I'm just premenstrual."

"I bet that's it," he took her hand and wouldn't let it go.

To everyone's surprise Kate agreed to go to California. She would stay with Martine, where she could really rest. Martine's apartment was tiny, but she had an almost Japanese sensibility, and her rooms never looked cluttered. "You're going to be here at *the* most beautiful time of year," Martine exclaimed, "the height of spring!" Colby Street was lined with ornamental fruit trees, and the air in late February was honied with an almond scented sweetness.

Because Martine was teaching an evening class, Rachel offered to pick Kate up, and met her at the airport with a long bough of white plum blossoms. Kate was surprised to see that Rachel was getting a few grey hairs. She had also lost a lot of weight, and looked older somehow, though still radiant, especially when she talked about Richard. "You know I don't think I've ever had a real man in my life before," she said.

"A mensch instead of a dredle?" Kate responded.

"Right," she laughed. "He's a brick. So dedicated. He's setting up this center for abused kids, and he wants us to all move in together." As they walked out of the terminal, the benign quality of the evening air swept up warm, enfolding, such a contrast to the freezing blankness Kate had come from hours before.

Those same pale blossoms were like confetti on the dark sidewalk before Martine's place, a big old Berkeley house that had been converted into apartments. "You're going to have the royal treatment," Rachel told her. "Martine's been getting ready all week."

This made Kate uneasy. She didn't want anyone making a fuss.

"You know this building has a hot tub in the back," Rachel went on.

"Outside?" Kate shrank from the thought, because she would never strip down in front of anybody. Her loose stomach was still badly stretched, and the little scarred pouch just hung there. All of a sudden she felt like a stranger at the wrong party, come to the wrong state, born into the wrong body.

"It's great before bed. You get so relaxed, you could sleep forever."

Everything reminded Kate of death, even a fairy tale phrase like that.

Martine had just returned from her class, minutes before, and she heard them coming through the side gate. She came clip-clopping down the back stairs in her wooden sandals, throwing her arms around Kate, squeezing and hugging her, "I can't believe it! You're here!" Martine pulled back to look at her. "And you *did* cut your hair. I *like* it." Kate's hair had been cut stylishly short and it made her look nifty, boyish.

"It looks like it *feels* so good," Rachel put in.

"It was great letting it go." Kate ran her hand through it. She felt dirty, sticky from travelling.

"Hair is one of our major subjects these days," Rachel said. "I'm thinking about getting mine dyed. Richard's so tall he looks down on my roots."

Kate and Martine didn't respond. They seemed so engaged with each other. "Do you know how long I've been trying to get you out here?" Martine grinned, pulling Kate up the stairs, trying to jolly her up, and Rachel followed a few steps, then decided to head home.

The tiny bedroom where Kate would sleep was filled with jars of flowering branches, and the scent overwhelmed Kate as she stood there. Tears came into her eyes because it was such sweetness, but trapped inside, with nowhere to go, the petals falling around the vases with a dusting of yellow powder, and she was afraid she would never be able to sleep in that room with all those flowers, and she needed to sleep so badly. In the middle of the night, she threw the flowers out through the bars of the window.

Just before waking, Kate had a nightmare. She was lost in a blizzard, and it was so icy white, that she could barely see, but she was looking for someone out there in the blizzard. There was a woman buried somewhere in the snow, and she would freeze if Kate didn't find her. She was digging with her own raw hands in the snow, and her fingers were numb. She was panicked. This lost woman had made a small tunnel through the snow, so she could breath and survive a while longer, but the whiteness was so vast, and Kate was afraid she'd never find her. Then she felt something under the snow, and she cried as she dug with all her might, and found herself there, curled up, but trapped in a case of ice. She had to crack the sheath of ice with her fist and then found herself breathing, warm, almost like springtime, and she was so happy and relieved that she woke up laughing and weeping.

Martine told Kate about her own longings for a baby. It was almost an obsession. "If I could only find a decent man. I don't care about getting married. I just have this biological *need*. It's almost like a craving, to have that baby inside me."

"It'll happen," Kate assured her, but all of Martine's talk about pregnancy made Kate feel desperate to get home, to get on with it. At the same time she tried to enjoy this warmth, this lightness of air, being without responsibilities, surrounded by all of Martine's gentle attentions. They took long walks through the neighborhood, and Berkeley seemed so livable, with its small fecund gardens, dripping and shining, relaxed as a cat sunning on a windowsill.

Chatting easily as they went, Kate almost forgot what had happened to her, but then, in the middle of the block, she heard those wind chimes, blowing gently from somebody's porch, the same set of pentatonic chimes that Martine and Rachel had given Kate and Conrad for their wedding, and which had clanged so hard on the night of the birth. It was like a brilliant, vivid postcard of remembrance. The low haunting clang of those bell chimes was so sweet and yet incredibly painful, and the inevitable feeling of loss came up in her and everything was altered.

But the next day was Saturday, and Martine had decided that Kate needed to go to the ocean. They all piled into

Rachel's stationwagon, twelve-year-old Vergil, and Lianna behind, Martine at the wheel because Highway 1 made Rachel uneasy, twisting and turning as it did above the coast, past Stinson Beach and the bird sanctuary, on towards Bolinas, where they parked at the end of the little town road, sat out in the sun and drank coffee, while local children rode by on their ponies, bareback. The flowers were already everywhere, growing up wildly all over the small, Victorian cottages. Vergil sulked. He wasn't sure why he had to come in the first place. Bolinas was boring. Rachel ignored his fussing and sent him off to buy gum. Lianna started to whimper because she also wanted to ride. Rachel said, "Let's go draw a heart in the sand, and we can watch the waves erase it." Lianna sped ahead of them all because she had heard— race it.

They walked past the shallows of the inlet, out along the sand, down to the moist edge. On around the bend, they were surprised by two women playing a game with a ball and paddles, both of them stark naked. This shocked Kate, and Vergil too. He didn't want to look as hard as he did. Kate thought it was too chilly to be showing off like that. Their bodies weren't even that beautiful, but Rachel said to them, "I bet that feels terrific," laughing her deep dark southern laugh.

"This air feels wonderful anyway," Kate announced as they moved on. "It's the best I've felt in so long, I can't tell you."

"Why don't we sit right here for a while," Martine suggested. So they kicked off their shoes and dug in their bare feet. Vergil climbed the lower cliffside with a couple of local boys, and Kate lay back, making a little pillow of her sweater, while Rachel sifted small handfuls of sand down Kate's bare legs. Kate asked Lianna to cover her. She wanted to feel that warmth pressing in on her from all sides, holding her there, while she breathed the kelp and seashell saltiness. Slowly handful by patted handful, the dry warm sand upon her, she began to feel quiet, peaceful. She just wanted to listen to Rachel and Martine as they talked, for they always loved to recall, and their memories made Kate smile, took all of them back, transporting Kate to another, safer time.

"Remember how Rob used to come sauntering into the cafe and order a huge dinner, and then have no money, and we'd have to make him do the dishes?" Rachel said, and Martine grimaced.

"He just wanted to get behind the scenes where he could grab my ass."

"Well it worked," Rachel chuckled, and even Martine liked to remember this, their early, feisty love.

Thirteen years before, Kate, Martine and Rachel had all worked at a small vegetarian cafe, Best Friends, where they had concocted some sumptuous feasts, giant soups, immense lasagnas. Kate could almost smell that mountainous pile of green onions, the huge quantities of grated cheese, the immense laughter of those days.

Together they had swum in the Rio Grande, and covered each other's bodies with mud, letting it dry before diving in again. They'd all come to love hot food: chili rellenos and stuffed sopapillas. Together they had gone out to the Jemez Pueblo when the poplars along the river bank were glittering yellow and the sky was big and sparkling. They had joked about the underlying carpet of dust that always coiled beneath every throw rug, creeping into their mail and their minds.

And then there was all the gossip behind the scenes at Best Friends. "You know that wild man who works at the produce store whipped out his ugly whanger again," Martine confessed. "Is the water boiling yet?"

"God that thing is green. We need ten onions, sliced," Kate said. "But how does he get away with it?"

"Does anybody care in this town? Indian poets pass out on Central Ave and junkies clean out another neighborhood." Martine always sounded like she was in charge. "I really think we should talk about security for this place. Oh look," she said,

"Conrad's here." She ran out front to kiss him, and then led him back into the busy kitchen. She wanted Kate to meet him.

Martine had been Conrad's lover before Rob came along with his six-gun intellect and sense of rotten humor.

Martine always had an abundance of men hovering about her, as if she were some exotic flower and they were but a swarm of hummingbirds.

Martine hung a vial of that sweet, red juice out for those emerald birds because she loved the way they whirred. It reminded her of sex, and she loved to play at that sport of sports, and she was good at it. Once she had shocked Julia by admitting that she could come in a minute if she wanted, but she also complained that she had to lubricate herself, while Julia was always juicy. Kate didn't talk about sex, and Rachel was fairly discreet, but everyone knew that Rachel had a grand capacity. She might not discriminate much when it came to men — she could fall in love so easily, but all of them agreed that she had the most perfect, womanly body. Men always noticed, and she liked to flaunt it, leaning in close, taking an arm, very sensual.

One bright Albuquerque afternoon, Julia was painting on the front porch, waiting for a phone call from Kate. Kate was coming out for a visit, taking the train from Massachusetts. The train should have arrived, but then she thought she saw Kate rushing up the walk to their place. She threw open the door, but it wasn't Kate. It was Rachel.

"I'm trying to hide from Cliff," she slipped in, and looked through the curtains out onto the street. She was wearing an African print skirt with a slit way up the leg. "Cliff drove by and saw me lying in the park with Willard. I'm afraid we were rather entwined," she lifted her eyebrows and laughed. "He screeched off yelling something, that he'd be back to get me, ugh."

Cliff had a pitted face and the physical bearing of a

fascist, while Willard was almost slight, blond and gorgeous, with a softness about his mouth. He was also a poet, and they seemed to be a perfect match.

"You know what Cliff said to me last night?" Rachel went on, making a face as she made herself comfortable. "*You don't know how to treat a man,*" she mimicked him, "But I said— show me a man and I'll treat him like one."

"Boy, I bet he liked that."

Julia wanted to be encouraging about Willard, but her vision of fidelity was confused by all this, and even Rachel, with all her glowing southern darkness, confused her some.

"I think you and Willard would be good together. You certainly sounded good together," Julia said, referring to the poetry reading they had given a few months back. Julia had been stunned by Rachel when she first heard her poetry. Her poems were long and streaming, but she didn't rush them, and almost mesmerized the crowd with her lilting, Georgian accent. Julia sat on the floor beside Mark, who'd been dragged along. Rachel had pinned her long dark hair behind her ears, and her bright blue eyes flashed about the room. Julia thought almost instantly—this woman will be my friend. Mark's only comment after the reading had been to say, "That wasn't much."

Whenever he saw Rachel coming, he promptly got up and made himself some tea, shutting himself in his study.

"How's Bluebeard," Rachel whispered. Mark thought her a seductive type, the kind of woman who used her sexuality to get approval and attention. Julia thought he might be right, but so what. Rachel had the warmth of the hive. She loved that Indian summer heat, loved to take her clothes off in the sun and lie there, her breasts full, perfect globes. She packed them tight into whatever she was wearing and stood up straight, unashamed, and did unusual hippie-like things with her clothes and hair, flamboyant.

So they sat there in the living room, lounging and talking about these various men, about Cliff, and how she should get away from him, and Julia voiced her approval of Willard, who would someday be the father of Vergil, Rachel's first child, but not the father of Lianna, her second. Rachel spoke about her flamenco class, and Julia urged her to demonstrate, so she did a few numbers on the hardwood floor, clapping fiercely, above her head, turning like some demanding, strutting bird of paradise. Just then, Kate's phone call came. She had just arrived at the train station, and Julia ran off to collect her, part of her exuberance spent.

Kate lived with Mark and Julia for several months, working at Best Friends, sleeping on their little front porch. She never showed how lonely she actually was, but she often felt chilled on that sagging, single bed, especially when she heard Mark and Julia rocking away at night. She often cried herself to sleep.

Kate told Julia about this years later, and Julia wondered what Kate was hiding from her now.

Now Kate felt another kind of sadness, that more impersonal sadness for the loneliness of all things, each human being, and she felt it like a weight, so heavy she could hardly move. The weight and mass of being. Into the world, that baby. Was there any way out of such heaviness? She lifted an arm, a leg, breaking out of the casement of sand that enclosed her, then scrambled to her knees, wiping the sand away.

"Let's drive back along the ridge," Rachel called from the water's edge. Rachel knew of a special road that climbed up through the native pine and scrub oak, up to the top, which seemed as bare as the moon, with unnerving views on either side. Kate felt as if she were up in space, and it made her feel almost dizzy. It made Martine feel high.

"Isn't California amazing!" she said. "Sometimes I can't stand Berkeley, but as soon as I get out into the countryside, I realize how majestic it is, how lucky we are to live here."

Rachel felt the same way, and had disliked living in New England. It had seemed puny to her, rigid, safe, too white and cute, ordained. But Kate felt resistant to this grandeur.

Rachel stopped the car at the lookout point, where hang gliders were setting up, two men and a woman, and the kids insisted they watch at least one take off, "Just one, Mom, please!" Vergil begged. The wind cup-caked under Lianna's dress, and Vergil seemed so tall and thin, quite nervy, climbing like a goat onto the top of a leaning rock. The three women got out of the car more slowly, and walked down the steep hillside. Martine and Rachel sat together on a smooth bare boulder, waiting for the wind to come up at the perfect pitch. The flyers kept dropping little handfuls of grass, which indicated the movement of the shifting air. They waited interminably it seemed to Kate, who was somewhat removed, almost clinging to a cypress, trying not to look down, down to the curving strip of that shuddering beach, which seemed as far away as forever, as distant as unadulterated bliss, freedom from terror, from clinging, and though part of her was glad, and wanted to be there with her friends, something else felt basically wrong, and she wondered—will it ever feel right again?

She was almost afraid to watch that hang glider take off. The woman pilot was first in line. The wind hadn't appeared to change, but when the children gasped Kate did look up, and saw her leap, holding the bars to these immense wings, bright red and yellow, and as she leapt she was carried right out into nothing, and Kate felt her stomach rise and leap also, as she stood, hanging onto the tree—part of her wanting to fly out too, and that terrified her, as she watched this woman sailing out, swinging away out into the air, her feet secured in a pouch behind her, circling lightly, turning, light as a bird, off into the distance, while Kate groped her way back to the car, wanting to get back inside herself, inside the car and home.

Julia realized, riding alone with old Frank, how disgusting it was to be loved when you yourself don't feel like loving, especially when the one who loves is deluded to such a degree that he believes the sentiments are returned. But what was even worse for her was realizing that she might be making Philip feel the same way, because of her clamoring and wheedling, and this simply increased her disgust, through the fear of being disgusting.

It was a grey, cool Saturday morning, and she wished that she had worn gloves, windy up there on the hill. She didn't feel like talking or singing or listening. She would have preferred a silent ride alone, and when Frank kept crowding her horse with his, always trying to stay exactly alongside, keeping up his steady banter, and then reached out, "Let me warm those hands for you," she was almost to the point of repulsion.

In the past, she had felt great affection for Frank, a kinship of spirit, but he persisted in another vein. "It must be love, Julie, you and me." And then he'd ride his horse up close enough to brush his leg against hers, and she felt trapped. She had wanted to be affectionate but her simple gestures had been misconstrued, and now she didn't even like riding alone with him. Frank knew that Philip had changed things between them, "I could say something about that man, but I guess I better keep my mouth shut."

"That's right," Julia admonished him, but at least she gave a smile, a nice big smile like breaking sunlight. Maybe love itself could best be had at a gallop, yelling out loud before the instant ran out. She would not bring the same ruination to their rides, and would keep it light from now on, there on the level of impulse and action, on the surface of the skin.

She imagined riding alone with Philip, heading down an old, abandoned trolley track, through a dense pine forest. Though the day was warm, the juniper and hemlock kept them cool. The floor of the forest was padded with silence. But then off to the left there was an opening of light, and they found a small patch of grass in the sunshine. Bushes sprang up around the edges, and he said, riding up, "Let's get off," and she lifted her leg up over the pommel, and slid off her horse in one movement, her hair, especially golden, light and clean in that sunshine. As he came up to her, she leaned back against her horse, and he started undressing her slowly. He undid each button on her blouse, and let it hang open, for she wasn't wearing anything beneath it. Then he undid her belt, and let the buckle dangle, before he pulled down her jeans, her peach colored underpants. She knew he had something special in mind, and she smiled when she saw him undoing the girth, pulling the heavy western saddle and blanket from the horse, warm and wet where it had been covered. He wanted her to get back up there, and he helped her up onto the high backbone, where she moved a little back and forth. He looked at her ass as he stripped. He knew quite well that she wanted him. She was very excited and hung onto the hair at the base of the mane as the horse, on its own, began a slow easy jog, and she sat right with it, feeling the hairy soap of the horse's lather sticking to the inside of her thighs, but now Philip was moving toward her, and she rode to a stop with that honey-laden smile upon her lips and gracefully opened her shirt more. He ran his hand right up her leg, took a handful of mane, and swung up behind her, cupping her mons, his straight, hard cock against her back, and he touched lightly across her belly, before he pushed her down and held her. She leaned forward on the neck of the horse, tilted her ass so that he could slip into her, and as he lodged inside her, the horse began to move forward, walking, as he fucked her, with the same slow rhythm of the horse, moving forward as he fucked.

What was hardest for Julia, was that she couldn't talk to Kate about this now. It just made Kate too upset. Julia had noticed her reticence on the phone one night and asked, "Kate, would you feel better if I just kept all this to myself?"

Kate answered, "Maybe. I realize it's one of those things, but it does make me feel awful. When I call and Mark answers, or one of the boys—I just can't deal with it."

"I know."

"Maybe when I'm stronger. But I do feel badly, because I know it's such a big part of your life."

Well, what are you going to do. Julia had been right—it *was* a burden for Kate, having to keep her secrets, guarding the lies, a burden Kate couldn't contend with in her present state.

During the past few months, Kate's nervous condition had become aggravated. She hadn't been able to conceive again, and the symptoms of burning hands, numbness and dizziness were diagnosed as clinical symptoms of depression.

Kate had to protect herself from stress of any sort. It seemed like her tolerance had been lowered to such a degree that she could only bear sailing on a still and silent night, rather than risk the slight shifts and punches of wind that life blows with it. And so adrift, phone unplugged, Kate became more and more isolated, more focused on what was happening to her, watching her own growing list of symptoms— headaches, shooting pains, wandering eye, ringing in the ears—until she was sure she had a disease, though her neurologist told her over and over that it didn't add up to anything, that she needed to get a job.

Martine recommended therapy. Kate responded, "That isn't the answer for everyone."

"Just think about it."

Kate did. She kept the idea lit, like a candle left burning in daylight. "I'm really worried about Julia," Kate changed the subject. "We don't discuss it anymore, but—"

"It hurts her not to talk to you," Martine said, and it was hard on Julia, having Kate withdraw, even if she realized that her own frantic passions, her violent ups and inevitable downs, her pregnancy hysteria, her euphoric sexual highs and subsequent exhaustion, were like a religious maniac's schedule of feasting and fasting—way too much or way too little, and Kate couldn't take such imbalance now. Julia understood, but she didn't. She felt she should be the exception, for she had hung in there and listened to Kate, heard out all her nightmares, listened to the blow by blow account of all her terrors and fears, and when Kate began therapy, Julia asked to hear every detail. It helped Kate to remember, to relate what she'd been through.

It was a dripping, cold, end of March day. Entering the Center for Psychosynthesis, Kate felt an overwhelming anxiety. At least no one else was waiting. She might have gotten up and left if Stephanie hadn't walked in at that moment. She led Kate into the room where they would work together. It was all very restful, tidy, with an upholstered mattress on the floor, matching pillows and curtains. It was remote, quiet, safe, and Stephanie's face had a moonlike calmness. Her eyes were searching, sympathetic. She said how she liked to start a session with a quiet meditative time. So they sat there facing each other with their eyes closed. Kate almost felt like she was holding her breath. She could hear Stephanie's slow, deep breathing, and she clutched feeling suddenly hot. The tears rushed up in her, and stopped eye level. She gulped them down, feeling ridiculous. She couldn't start off this way. What was wrong with her. Why was she being such a baby.

Stephanie came and sat beside her, put her arm around Kate, and that helped, strangely enough, less confrontational. She knew about Kate losing the baby. They had talked about that on the phone. She encouraged Kate to cry, handing her Kleenex, but Kate was still fighting it, hot in her face, tense in her body, wanting to cry heavily, in downpour, a great need to cry and grieve, but blocked. She felt the rigidity of her false strength, her great need to present a strong front constantly. Strong jaw, strong will, but a weakness, a fragility just under the surface, like a fake floor in a concrete building. She was really sad. But she couldn't quite reach that sadness.

She began to sense an old nightmare, the physical sensation of a well-remembered childhood nightmare, which made her feel nauseous, which seemed to do with pregnancy and death—a swirling of greys that pressed down with the weight of a tomb, crusty and yet simultaneously smooth, a nauseating heaviness swirling away, and then pressing back down, sickening. She had had this nightmare often as a girl, had woken and screamed for her mother, who thought she was such a "scary child."

Many tears came then, each sob swallowing a sob, like ripped out knitting, unkinking, coming in yanked out rows, skeins of emotion, little girl sobs, left alone on that bed to just cry and cry. But when she wondered out loud about it, that great pressure that was smooth and crusty at the same time, she thought maybe it had something to do with shit. Why shit? But then she thought of her father, drunk, passed out on the toilet. The way her mother had gasped, then yelled at her to get out of there, as if Kate were in the wrong. "Just go to your room." And she realized that shit was merely a metaphor for all the negativity she had had to swallow her entire life, sitting there taking it in, as her father had downed his bourbon. How she had swallowed her anger, as he swilled his.

She remembered him calling her "Daffy-down-dilly," and she suddenly felt a great love for him. But then she thought of the tyranny he held over their family, making her mother angry, making her want to hit him. It was an eggshell way of life they had to lead, for he might drop the basket any time. He might not bring home his paycheck. He might even get belligerent.

When she rushed up to give him a kiss, she found the smell disgusted her. She then turned and ran to her mother, "I hate Pa—he's a pig!"

Her mother had reached out and slapped her, "I never want to hear you say that. Go to your room. And don't come out until I tell you."

As she felt those same sensations of the nightmare pressure coming down, Stephanie had her bend low, head to feet, knees out, feeling his liquor nauseating her, and she pictured a toilet overflowing, and Stephanie had her make vomiting noises. She even brought over a wastepaper basket, just in case, and they laughed and mock-retched and kept getting it up, but when asked, Kate felt she still needed to keep a little of it inside her.

She imagined herself then to be her father, how he had felt when he had this need, when he succumbed to his sickness. And she felt the weight of his life, all his children, the money problems, the tedious work, the mortgage, the church, felt all of it, between his wingbones, pressing him down, pressing his head down until he was forced to take a drink, and then how he couldn't help sliding down into that river, floating away on the only relief he could find, unconscious of it all. She heard Stephanie ask this father how he would feel if his daughter, Kate, stopped swallowing the penalty he had paid, stopped swallowing the shit that had made him sick, which was making her sick as well, and he said from the deepest part of his soul, "I would be glad if she stopped taking it in."

"Why would you be glad?"

"I would be glad if she stopped," Kate said, "because then she would break the chain."

Kate changed positions and was herself again, facing her father. She kept her eyes closed, but could feel a crack of light opening in response to him, a distant love light softening her, not an embracing, merging love, but compassion. If she made room for love, she could feel a greater peacefulness inside herself—she felt it in her breathing.

Still fear suffocated her at night. It crept up like a big black hand and squeezed. Sometimes while she slept she saw a tunnel dropping beneath her, and she'd fall or her baby would fall, endlessly down into this cold black bottomless pit, and she'd wake up in a sweat, with the fear still crawling on her back, but it was also like a rusting hole beneath the body of her car, which had become her nighttime vehicle.

Every night, awakened, she'd have to steal into Atea's room, make sure that she was still breathing, and the fear hung onto her like a growth, with its claws in her shoulders, until she felt like an emotional hunchback, carrying her load of symptoms. Maybe she deserved to get sick and die. Maybe the mother who can't keep her baby alive deserves it.

Julia thought she should be checked by another doctor. It worried Kate even more to see others worrying over her. Better to keep the burning hands, the tension in her jaw, the pain in the back of her head, to herself. But sometimes the fear overwhelmed her.

"What about bio-feedback?" Julia suggested. "If it's just nerves and tension maybe they could help teach you how to relax. You might be able to learn how to control your own responses, I don't know. Why not give your neurologist a call?"

Kate tried reaching her neurologist, but he was on vacation. So she called Dr. Ryder, who worked with bio-feedback. What did she have to lose. It was probably just a kooky California thing, but it might help.

Dr. Ryder was incensed that the neurologist hadn't recommended him sooner. "If you're just suffering from stress, this is the perfect means of dealing with it, and I can't understand why he didn't send you to me months ago. From the sound of your symptoms, you could have any one of a number of diseases. But I can check that out."

Any number of diseases. Kate couldn't believe this. How dare he! Just because he wasn't recommended. No wonder why. But how dare he. Then—what was wrong with her. What didn't she know. What were they trying to hide from her. She drove out into the moonless night in her old VW, screamed at the top of her lungs, "Fuck YOU! You shit, you bastard puke head, FUCK!" She stopped the car on the gravel road, no houses in sight, just farmland, got out, and then ran along the road, screaming at the top of her lungs. She barked and grunted, kicking out at big clumps of dirt left by the grader. Stopping breathless, she screamed up at the sky, at the stars, the moonless night, "You aren't going to ruin My Life!"

We haven't talked much about what you feel your higher purpose is," Stephanie said. Kate was at a loss for an answer. She used to think it was teaching, showing children how they could make something beautiful out of anything—every gesture, each arrangement, a picture, but now she wasn't sure what she believed. What she had to teach. She wanted to believe that the loss of her baby had brought her closer to God somehow.

"Are you angry at God?" Stephanie asked.

"I don't think so," Kate said softly.

"Can you say to me — I'm not angry with God?"

No, she couldn't. She had trouble saying it, as if her mind were reluctant, fighting this today, but she tried to mouth the words.

"How do you feel when you say that?"

"I feel a tension," Kate said, "in my arms, as if I want to hit somebody. I want to beat it out."

"Use the broom." Stephanie quickly moved to the corner of the room, handed Kate a broom, threw a pillow on the floor for her, and Kate sprang at that pillow and beat it with the broom, beat against her mother, who had never allowed her to get angry, who had slapped her anger down. But this was Kate's answer now, and she was furious, furious. "PIG," she yelled. She was furious with God, with injustice, all of it smothering and extinguishing her, and she beat and beat that pillow, pounding and bashing with the broom, until blisters actually rose on her hands, but she still kept on, empowered.

Her anger, which had never been allowed before, had turned itself into despair and walked behind her as a thing called fear. But she wasn't going to have it in her life anymore. She was sweeping herself clean, whacking it out, until finally she felt too tired, and sat down on the bed, then lay down, looking at her hands, and Stephanie said, "That was excellent. Good work."

Kate gave a little laugh, and the laughter became slow tears. She just lay on the small day bed, as Stephanie rubbed her temples, smoothed her hair. "You really cleaned house," she said.

Kate had to smile. "I guess so."

"How do you feel now?"

"Tired, but good. What a relief," Kate answered. She just shut her eyes and felt peaceful. Then she sensed that some higher form of goodness wanted to embrace her, all of her, even her anger and her darkness. Having entered into the depths of her anger, something she'd always considered evil, she was actually making room for this brightness now, the possibility of warmth and acceptance, and she pictured this wonderful angelic being, so large and soft, who encircled her in such a loving, compassionate way, but when this essence of light tried to come closer, Kate felt herself harden, as if to reject. She turned a cold shoulder, became hard, like rock. She pictured a small stone baby, and this being picked the baby up, and she felt the infant inside her soften. She felt herself surrounded, and gave in to it. She let herself be held. And then she saw a flower unfolding, like a lily opening in her brain, and it shot upward, out of her, skyward, and a pearl shot out of the top of the flower and then became rain coming down all around her, and the nourishment was pulled back up, back into her sex like liquid seed, and she saw herself as this happy infant, sitting in the sun with a small bare body, but no, she was a boy now, also. It was her, but it was also him, and he was throwing up his hands and waving, laughing in the balmy air.

They were off, sailing in their old VW toward the ocean, and in four short hours they were on the Cape. She had forgotten how much she loved the sandy expanses, how easily one could float in the warm salty water. They had rented a beach shanty for a week in the Audubon Bird Sanctuary, and Atea was in her element, making sand castles, decorating them with shells, swimming up a storm with her big black inner tube. Conrad fished on the shore. He also loved the relaxing warmth, the ease they all felt together.

Kate had to smile as she watched Atea roaming about with her tin bucket, picking up shells, running earnestly to her father to discuss them. Suddenly she handed him the bucket and ran off to a little group of children, dangling around, hoping to make some contact. Kate sat back on her beach chair and worked on the baby quilt she was putting together. Nice to have a project, and it was turning out splendidly. She sewed until her fingers felt pricked and tired.

Kate wrote Julia: *I do wish you were here with us, eating culls and corn on the cob, everything dipped in butter. Such gluttony! Tomorrow we go for the long drive to Nauset Beach for the day. Today is gorgeous, uncrowded, nice clear water.*

Had a huge panic/anxiety attack the evening of our first full day here. Can still see it as my pattern to have my nerves go whacko. But I see more and more that we live by habit, and we are fools to think our "personalities" are important. What happens happens through accretion and erosion, and it's so striking to me how powerfully we all delude ourselves dozens of times daily. The only way to work with this is through creating habits of being which are healthy . . . slow, hard work, but it seems to me to be such a clear and obvious fact.

I found that drawing you did down here last year, the oil pastel of the two women on the rock by the sea. I enjoyed seeing it again so much. Atea asked, "Which one is Aunt Julia?" And I said—"The one holding the basket." We will always share and stand on that rock, by the sea, together, I know. Meanwhile, Atea uses the doll umbrella you gave her every evening. She opens it up in bed, and she and her doll, Julie, sleep under it. "To keep out the dark night," she says.

PART THREE

I thought it might lead to this," Rachel said softly, "but tell me, go on, I'm here."

"Boy I miss you," Julia blurted out. She remembered what Rachel had written at the end of her last letter, *Fais gaffe,* which meant — Be Careful — but she hadn't been careful enough, and now she was turning to Rachel, just as Rachel had turned to her four years ago.

Rachel had been just a few weeks pregnant with Lianna when she'd called in a virtual fit. Paul was having a stupid fling with some little coed, and when she found out, she destroyed everything he'd ever given her, all of it, the pictures torn, the silver heart necklace and ring both smashed — she burned his letters, left all of it in a pile in the middle of their apartment, there for him to see when he came back to get his pre-arranged "things." She was broke. Vergil was miserable in school, and she despised the east. It was so damn cold, and people were unfriendly. How could she keep another baby in such a situation.

"You can," Julia said. "I'll help, I promise." Julia offered to let them live on the third floor of their old Berkeley house, until Rachel could find a job and her own place.

Rachel had already had two abortions, and maybe that was partly why she decided to keep this child. She did fly back to California with Vergil, hoping that might wake Paul up, but it only relieved him further. She shipped all their belongings, and they did move in with Julia and Mark, Thomas and Rossie.

It was like a continual house party. Rachel and Vergil shared the one big attic room, with its porthole windows and skylights. She slept on a king-size mattress, flat on the floor, while Vergil got the bunkbed. Sometimes Thomas was allowed to join him. The boys loved having each other, the long backyard where they could play catch and run with Juba, throwing her tennis balls. Ross was too small to keep up with them, and seemed to look forward to the baby. He'd stick his juice bottle up to Rachel's big belly, as if he could give that little unborn baby some nourishment.

"You're really a generous guy, you know that, Ross?" Rachel would say, hands on hips, and he'd smile at her. "This little person already likes you. I can tell. I'm getting a signal, a *liking* signal. Feel," and she'd take Rossie's astonished hand, and he'd feel that bump, which was awesome. "You know what?" Rachel said.

"What," Rossie wanted to know. Ready for something big.

"You're going to be like a big brother to this baby. Do you like that?" He didn't answer, but hefted his juice bottle up, and glugged it some, while looking her in the eye.

Rachel felt so good and healthy when pregnant, but she was still overwrought about Paul, and her marriage. She missed him. He called, but he'd joined a hard rock band, "just a temporary gig," promising that he would join them in a month.

Finally, he did come, two weeks before her due date, enough time to settle in, but not enough time to relocate. The dynamics of the house changed, and Mark was uneasy about the whole situation.

Julia tried to leave the two of them alone for the first few hours of labor, but when she came up to the third floor room, Paul seemed nonchalant. Julia timed a few contractions, and they were coming quickly, one minute apart, then forty-five seconds apart, suddenly only thirty seconds apart. "Rachel, you're in transition," Julia said, shocked, then quick to him, "Come on! We've got to get her to the hospital."

"Wait," Rachel cried, as another hit her, and she leaned wildly against the door, as if she might pull it down.

"Paul!" Julia commanded, "We've *got* to get her in the car!"

124

They maneuvered her down those stairs somehow, out-side, as far as the fence, where Rachel collapsed on all fours. Thomas and Vergil were hanging out the second story win-dow, eating popcorn and waving. Julia yelled, "Get back in-side," for Rachel was howling on all fours now.

"It's coming," she cried. "I can feel the head!"

They lifted her onto the front seat of the van. Julia fol-lowed in her own car, both of them running all the red lights down Shattuck, up Ashby to Alta Bates, both horns blaring and headlights flashing, as they squealed into Emergency. She jumped out. A gurney appeared beside the van, and they were unloading Rachel, who was moaning and pushing. Julia bounded into their van, raced to park it across the street, flew back into the hospital, just as Lianna Raphaella Lazar was being born, and as the small perfect body came shooting in-to the hands of the doctor, Julia batted her mouth with in-credulous excitement, and when the baby came, pushed forth so quickly without a tear, into the white dazzling light of the emergency ward, with its flimsy curtain and close-call mood, Rachel was hysterically up with the vigor and rigor of this fast one. "Just look!" Rachel laughed, her eyes flashing, "Let me hold her. Have you ever?" Rachel wasn't even bruised. She held the little wrapped form, and then Paul held her too, carrying her up to the maternity ward.

Rachel had already told Julia that she would be the god-mother. This was her first godchild, and it was the closest thing to having another baby of her own. When she held Lianna for the first time, she wanted to give some kind of blessing. "Sweet girl, gumdrop, grow big and strong, and never be heartless," thought Julia. "I wish for you the strength to meet the wounds of this world—Go with grace and forgiveness, Lianna. Be loving, have heart, and let go of all bitterness, hang onto your own true soul. May the heavens now cover and bless you, as you make your own way, sweet Lianna."

Lianna was the beautiful flower that had sprung up in

this garden of boys, wonderful, energetic boys. But she was something different.

Rachel wrote Kate: *First time I've touched these keys since Lianna's birth. What a complete blessing she is. How I adore her. How her father (classically) cuddles and coos and is unwilling to leave her side. An amazing bundle. She is so mysterious. Who is she? She is strong, attentive, but still in a peaceful sleeping state most of the time. Vergil always so reminded me of a duck. Lianna comes through from a woodsy deepness — chipmunk, squirrel, badger. She is lovely and we are thrilled.*

Vergil is an excited big brother, with a few testy moments, mostly in reaction to Paul who can be gruff with him. Oh, that's so painful for me! Living with Julia is a godsend. Her generosity in friendship is a marvel. The only consternation comes from Thomas and Vergil's relationship. Thomas's frustration and violence bewilder Julia. We've spoken of it some, but it's so delicate. I tend to be over-protective, and Julia, under-critical.

I can acknowledge that a marriage to Paul affords me many features of single life. I think he was afraid of losing his youth to a situation he was not ready for. We could accurately call him an obsessive, endlessly working with the drums. He hopes to dedicate the next year FULLY to music. Some suggest therapy as his next investment of devotion. Anyway, at this moment in time, I'm feeling fit and fiddling, and it looks like we might just make it through this period.

Martine wrote Kate: *Everyone's astir about baby Lianna. She is truly one private, delicious package, and Rachel is looking fabulous. So why does it make me feel bitter and mean. I feel like a shadow of sorts. Can't exactly enter in. Rachel doesn't know how I suffer, just being around a newborn. It all comes so easily to her and Julia, and sometimes I think my heart is being turned into some kind of hateful solid. The other day when I saw that Julia had received a letter from you, I was seized with jealousy. You're the only real mother I've ever had, the only person I can trust. It's so strange feeling like I need to be held and babied, and then I turn that inside out and believe it's a baby I want in my arms. Which is true? When Rachel and I took a walk the other day, she had Lianna in this African sling, and she let the baby suck on her while we were walking along. I have to admit I was fascinated, but also disgusted by her nonchalance. I pictured all the care I'd be taking and I wanted to scream, but then I pictured my own baby screaming and what would I do with a crying baby? It helps to write to you. You're so important to me, you give this Shadow Lady some human form again. Do come visit, even if it's just to be nice to this wayward, decrepit soul.*

Paul's added presence in the big old Berkeley house made their situation crowded. It wasn't the baby. The baby was simply a gift. Everyone loved the baby. The boys took turns rocking and amusing her, and Julia spelled Rachel when she wanted to go out. She too felt bonded to this baby, but now the balance seemed off with Paul refusing any real work, only endlessly practicing his drums, day and night, up in that attic room. Even when he just used the sticks on a block of wood, that rattling rhythm permeated the house, that constant rackety-rack.

But then one day, Rossie found a hypodermic needle in the garbage. He had accidentally tipped the can over with his Big Wheels, and he brought the needle to his father, asking if he could shoot water out of it.

When confronted, Paul said it wasn't his, but Mark didn't believe him.

"Well you can stay here for another week or so," Mark said, "but then I think you'd better find your own place."

"Sure man," Paul said, sauntering away. "We need our own space too."

All of this had happened on the spur of the moment, and Rachel was thrown. She knew that Paul's presence was getting on everybody's nerves. Little squabbles over food and cleaning had begun, and it was odd, because they'd been so harmonious before, but she was defensive. "That needle wasn't Paul's!" She lit out at Julia. "I just can't believe you didn't talk to me first. Am I your friend, or what? Do you think I'm some sort of freeloader?"

"Of course not," Julia said.

"And what am I supposed to do with this baby? I thought you cared about her."

Julia had never received such a tirade from Rachel before, and she felt clobbered. "It's not you, or the kids, certainly not the baby, but Paul just makes us nervous, and I'm sorry that Mark said something before we had agreed on anything."

"And who gets to agree? I guess I have no say. Not even two damn cents."

"Rachel," Julia said, "Don't! You *know* I'm sorry about this."

"Well that's easy, to be sorry when you've got it all. Try it from the other side once. Just try!"

"Even at the beginning I said you could stay until you found your own place and a job."

"And I'm supposed to work, with a four-month-old baby?"

"Maybe *Paul* could find some work."

"Paul *is* working. He's a musician. I know you don't like him. You're jealous."

"He's a fuck-off Rach, and you know it, and he's probably into drugs whether you know it or not."

"Well I guess I'll just go pack," Rachel stormed out of the room. Vergil slunk through the kitchen, and Julia felt terrible that he might have heard. She walked out into the yard and pulled old dead roses from the bushes that lined the fence, throwing the petals on the ground.

Now Lianna was four years old, asking, "What's a blizzard, Mama?"

"It's something unexpected. And very cold," Rachel explained. "Let me finish talking to your Aunt Julia, and when I get off the phone, I'll tell you all about snow." Rachel then turned her voice back to Julia, all the way across the country. "Snow in April," she said, disgusted. "How can you stand it?"

"I know, but it'll melt by May," Julia tried to make light. Rachel was in bed with a fever, and Richard had not been nice to her lately. "Doesn't he know he's dating Rachel Lazar? Doesn't he know what he's got?"

Rachel sighed, "Only in this narcissistic way. I mean, I *have* to be terrific if I'm dating *him*."

"But does he make you happy?"

Rachel couldn't answer. "I just feel too old to be doing this."

But it was a joy to Julia, just to hear Rachel talk, turning everything into a smile. Richard hadn't seemed that special. What did he want, if not Rachel?

"You know when he gets nasty," Rachel sounded amused, "he reminds me so much of Mother, I can hardly stay in the room. I've never been in love with a man for so long and not lived with him, but maybe it's for the best. The other day, I arrived at his apartment in the city, unexpectedly, and he was just returning from this conference in Tucson, and I walked in with the kids, and he just *looked* at me, as if I were the Plague, with my two little plagues."

"Do you think it has anything to do with your father? Not being there?"

"Actually Paul was a lot more like my father, artistic and out of it, ineffectual in the world, one of my favorite combinations, those failing qualities, but Richard is so damn brilliant and moody. I don't even know if I'd *want* to live with that."

Rachel had gotten her tubes tied after Lianna, and now,

because of Richard, she was considering a reversal. He was indecisive about marriage, and she didn't want to have the operation unless they were sure, but then he wasn't certain that the operation would be successful, and he didn't want to marry someone who couldn't have his child. "It's the same old story, the same old question," Rachel said, "which came first, the chicken or the Huevos Rancheros," but Julia didn't laugh.

She had spent the entire afternoon in a horrendous state of not knowing, waiting to hear about her pregnancy test. Even though she was almost certain at that point, she hoped science would prove her wrong. She had had to wait until four that afternoon to find out, and she felt like she was going to throw up, having to wait for that answer. She had felt like she was standing by some drop-off, dizzy, about to lose it, when the phone rang, confirming her suspicions, "Positive."

She hung up, and looked out the window. She could hear the boys. But couldn't see them. She saw that the snow was softening. She felt like some old rag of clothing, the color of dirt, found when the snow disappears.

"I just don't know what I'm going to do," she told Rachel. "What *can* I do."

"First of all, you can always keep the baby. Things will work out." Rachel sounded optimistic. "Maybe not like you expected, but you know you'd love that child." These were almost the same words Julia had used when Rachel was pregnant with Lianna. "But you know I went through two abortions. I was between marriages, and couldn't afford another baby." That had always been a source of discord between them, that Rachel couldn't, but Julia always could, afford it.

"But it's not Mark's child."

"I see," she said, quietly, as if she were gathering something in with a large net.

"I'm thinking about abortion." Even the word, coming out of her own mouth, horrified Julia. Maybe if she said it out loud, over and over, it would lose its dreadful power. "Is it possible to tell me, can you tell me what it's like? I know it must be horrible, but I don't know what else I can do. You're the only one I can talk to about this. I need to have some picture."

"Well I wish I could be more encouraging. I think you want me to be honest, right?"

"Of course."

"Well, it's worse, in many ways, more painful even than childbirth," Rachel began, "because you know, you really know, gut level, what's involved. I mean, what you are doing."

"Yes," she understood.

"And they literally suck you out, with this vacuum machine, this pump-like thing that sucks, and they have to get it all out, or there's danger of infection. It hurts *like hell*. It's the worst."

Julia was glad she had said it, the worst. Though she also knew that Rachel had had a terrible experience with her second abortion.

She had walked into that clinic alone, young and unmarried, already on Welfare with one small child. There had been no question in her mind about what she had to do. She was being evicted from her apartment. Willard had left her and Vergil to their own devices. But what she hated most was turning her life and the perfect fruit of their now rotten love over to those machines. She tried not to think about that, tried to believe that she was in the hands of some greater reality, protected in some other way.

They gave her a shot that struck the bullseye of her body, deadening her cervix, before they dilated her, and then the sound of that machine, clicked on—like water rumbling through a tunnel long distance, and Rachel squeezed her eyes shut and felt herself jerked, sucked through the vacuum, as it pulled on her, then nothing—blacked out.

The next thing she knew, there was a bright, white light,

131

faces in a circle, like a medical show, and she was bleeding, bleeding badly. They were worried, she could tell by the urgency in their voices. "Get the gauze pads! Hurry up!" A perforated uterus. She remembered how they wheeled her out to the ambulance. She was lying on this gurney, but then she felt herself — drop, as they collapsed the bed with a simple movement and slid her in like a slab of meat. The ambulance siren on the way to the hospital, proceeded on its own bloody music, and she thought of Anne Frank. Sirens always made her think of Anne Frank. The horror of flesh. Pried open.

But now, in surgery, she had to sign a paper. It gave the doctors permission to remove her uterus if they had to, and she didn't want to sign, but she was bleeding. Finally, a nurse held her hand, "You're going to be all right," and the loving firmness in her eyes made Rachel give in. "Just try to relax," the nurse said. "Try to place your mind elsewhere, somewhere nice, outside in the sun."

Willard, she kept thinking of Willard, and she didn't want to think about him, but her will was gone. Her mind was holding her hostage, forcing her to take that trip again with him.

They had driven to that mountain pool, north of Taos, late afternoon. They'd slipped out of their summer clothes, and breathed in the dry heat of the chaparral hillside. She stretched her arms, and sighed, then tested the cold water with her foot. He came up behind her and hugged her, making a valentine shape on the dark valentine of her mons. He wanted to fuck her on the grass by the hard slide of granite. "No one's going to see us," he said, but she almost liked to think of someone watching. She lay down and embraced the weight she was eager for, quick to respond as he moved on her. She wanted to take this whole man in her mouth, to cover every inch of him with kisses, turning him around on the spit of her love. She wanted his hardness inside her. She reached her arms up above her head, taking hold of the wild grass in both hands, as his cock rubbed both inner and outer, making her quiver like leaves in a fit. She felt herself taut — to the peak of her limit — until it sprang out and his rock hit her pool, and she clutched him and pulled him, deep, hugging him into her, lifting her legs to take him more down, and his fuck yell exploded against the granite enclosure, and he lay there quiet until his member slipped out.

He turned upon his back, and she cuddled on his shoulder, wanting him to cover her large breast with his hand, to touch her some more, but he was gone to the world. She kept on caressing, all over the smooth blond surface of his skin. She licked lightly over his lips once, his warm lips, closed and silent. She moved on top of him, letting the wetness of her cunt pat the wetness of him, and little shocks of afterfeeling pulsed gently through her. She knew that she shouldn't be the first to say, "I love you," but she did, and she could tell it increased some heaviness in him.

"I love being with you," he answered.

She got up and dove into the water. It was shocking. She had to catch her breath, and paddled, going nowhere. He followed her in, swam up and kissed her, his face cool and wet. They both swam apart. She dipped under as he moved further out. He could take it. He liked being shocked by cold water. She swam to the ledge, and felt chilled right through. She had to lift herself up. She wished she'd kept silent. Maybe she didn't love him like she thought she did. Maybe she only loved his sex. Maybe she didn't need any man in her life. Maybe she hated his soft, blond shoulders. Maybe she was angry at his reticence. Angry at her father. Gone, like — *pffft* — maybe no child would ever come to her. She wanted a great warmth to impregnate her. Maybe their physical love was all she could expect. She hadn't expected Vergil.

But you know," Rachel went on, "it's also this incredible relief. Both times, afterward, I felt this huge thankfulness. And sadness of course, a sorrow, but I really believed that tiny being would understand and be patient. I wanted to convey, maybe just to myself, that I would have loved, if it were possible. I mean, it's a terrible time, but you get through it. I wish I could be there with you. What about Kate?"

"I can't involve her now. I don't think she has the stamina for it."

"But you're going to need some help."

"Am I?" she asked. Could she ask Philip? Or would that implicate him if something went wrong.

"Don't be afraid to ask for help," Rachel suggested. "People sometimes have a lot more to give than you think."

"Not around here," she said.

That night, lying in bed beside Mark, she dreamt of kissing Philip. She was passionately kissing Philip with her whole mouth and tongue in a way she never kissed her husband, and Mark had been startled awake by her unconscious passion, and liked it, but he wondered — who did she think he was, and the next morning when he brought it up, she was embarrassed. How could she bring another child into such a state of confusion.

She made the appointment, arranged an all-day babysitter, determined to drive herself. Her hands were sweating on the steering wheel, arms almost shaking. She didn't allow herself thought, sentiment or emotion, but kept her mind in the grey.

The waiting room was anonymous, an insipid country print on the wall. She had to try and control herself as she gave her name. "But I want to pay cash," she asserted, as a young woman came out, sobbing, being held together by her very young biker boyfriend. The nurse looked disgusted, as if she hated her job, hated the women who kept her working full time.

Julia got undressed. Her body felt clammy, no longer hot. She smelled sour. She tried to lie down, to breathe. Just relax. The nurse said that she would be back. Julia nodded, lying there, looking up at a "Smile" poster on the ceiling. She hardly felt like smiling, even if the worry would soon be over. Or would it be over. Might she not repeat the same mistake? Or would she put a stop to it now. Was she up to that? She remembered what she'd said to Philip, "You won't love me until I'm gone." I won't love this baby, if he's gone, she thought. Gone forever, and all of it over. Her love for him would be over. She could hold on, and love this baby, if she wanted. It was all up to her. She didn't have to expect anything from Philip. She didn't have to be married to anyone. Though she believed, deep down, that this baby would make Philip love her in a way he couldn't even imagine right now. She pictured his face, entirely proud, holding up his baby son.

Julia sat up. It was as if someone had slapped her out of an hysterical mood, and suddenly her mind was wide awake, and she was clear. She saw the faces of each of her children. She felt fiercely protective. She imagined their brother, this baby inside of her, strong and yet peaceful, how he had chosen her, chosen Philip for his father, for some reason she wasn't able to discern, but how it was wrong for her to interfere now. What had occurred had already happened, and something good would come of it.

I won't do it, she said, shucking off the paper robe. She started getting dressed, and when the nurse came to the door, Julia announced, pulling on her second boot, "I've changed my mind," with such conviction, that the nurse pulled upwards, astounded, and then actually looked impressed as she said, "Congratulations."

She ate an apple as she drove, turned on the radio and sang. She felt sure she was doing the right thing, even if she didn't know what would come of it, what would happen to her. Even if she had to pass through some tunnel of pain, even if it hurt beyond belief, she knew it would turn out, somehow, and that she would never regret this decision.

She drove slowly, very slowly. She felt that she was very small, moving, drifting along in this much bigger picture, like a dot on a billboard, as if someone else were describing the picture to her mind, showing her where to go, taking care of her direction, guiding her slowly, without her even being aware, and she felt thankful for this inner assurance, thankful for the baby and for her three growing boys, for her life, and her love, and now she experienced what Rachel had described as the big relief, and it was wonderfull to feel it washing over her, leaving her these few brief moments of calm.

God, I'm so glad you called," Martine said. "If you hadn't, I would have written one of the longer letters of my career."

"And now I'll only get a postcard?"

Martine had gotten Julia's last letter just two days before, and she was curious to have more details. "I think it's great, what's happening to you. You're happy for a change. I bet you didn't even know that, but I can hear it in your voice."

"I do, I feel — inspired."

"More paintings than the walls will hold?"

"More than my life can hold. But you know I've always thrived on excess. I'm in a state of almost constant eroticism."

Martine laughed, liking that.

Julia didn't mention the pregnancy. The subject was too delicate. "It's great to talk to you. I can't to Kate right now."

"I know. It's just — you've got to try and understand, and just hold back. It'll pass. But you can tell *me* everything."

"I don't know where to begin."

"Where do you go? How do you manage it?"

"Well, he has this little guest house," Julia began. "It

136

looks like a Fellini set, like an overgrown dollhouse. You'd love it. We rode our horses over there the other day, tied them to some bushes, and he took me inside."

"And you wanted to move right in, right?"

"I fell in love with the place. It has a fireplace, and leaded windows, and this tiny bedroom with the most beautiful big old wooden bed, painted white, like a piece of wedding cake."

"Don't forget, you're already married," Martine said.

"What's odd, is that I feel married to this man. Something about us just fits."

"I can imagine."

Julia was thinking about how he had leaned against the footboard of the bed, and how she'd gone down his body, freed his cock, and kissed him, for he liked that, how she had sucked him sweet and low and long, and fondled him while she worked it, like a pump with endless patience, wanting to give him pleasure, which meant giving herself great pleasure as well, for she loved getting mindless in this way, and she was coming to need his body, and felt their connection as something beyond articulation. It was more like a total sensation of warmth. She could hear the horses up the hillside as if she were hearing their hooves underwater, and a smile splashed over her face as she thought of the little round garden outside, where only blue flowers grew, and she loved that just as she loved this man, and perhaps this was where she would sleep someday, on his big white bed piled with pillows, awash on a sea of blue flowers.

Julia asked about Tibor then, and Martine was eager to talk. "It's so different living with him. You know how the wrong kind of man always had the right effect on me? Well, Tibor put an end to that syndrome." He was a lawyer with a conscience. He brought her flowers when she had cramps, that kind of guy. "But it's so odd being in this big house. We just sort of rattle around."

"Well one of these days you're going to have a baby with real rattles raising the rooftop."

"That's the only kind of music I want to hear," she said.

Martine wrote Kate: *I'm feeling like some broken down machine, or a toy that a fat-fingered kid has split open to see if he can figure me out. Another fertility test. This one included radioactive oil squirted up inside me, and I wondered if I would light up like a neon sign, flashing —* Nothing, Nothing, Nothing. *The only word I read these days.*

Tibor helps me continue. He turns everything into a game. Next on our agenda is a delightful afternoon date to DO IT. *Then we'll rush on over to Dr. Tightass, who'll pluck the gunk from my nether regions and see if the spermatozoa are making the trek, a bit like climbing the internal Himalayas in the pitch, black dark, and sometimes I feel so alone. Wish you were right here with me!*

Tibor has hinted recently that this has all become my obsession and he just happens to be a necessary tool needed to repair my psyche. I never would have even considered having a baby with anyone else! I know I've been totally absorbed, but I hope not self-absorbed. Anyway, I guess it's better to be craving something with a man worth loving than to be in Rachel's shoes. I'm sorry, but Richard is so limited. He won't last long. To deal with him and Rachel's "mutha" in the same week . . . Puhleeze! I got to treat her to a terrible tea party where we all had to listen to her tell us about being a beauty queen and all. Then she lit into Rachel about the minuscule lines on her forehead and her two grey hairs, while Rachel took it as sweetly as a mouthful of Milk Duds. Why can't she get mad?

It's horrible when you see how some parents simply can not be kind, how friendships can sour and fall apart, and love affairs turn into mushroom dust. I have such a great desire to give! I do wonder how long Rachel will continue to fool herself over this Richard. I'm amazed that he gets along with Vergil, but I guess they're about on the same level. Maybe someday we'll all wake up and realize it wasn't men we needed, or even children, but each other.

Martine loved the colors and textures of yarn, the surprise of working a pattern. She'd made a hat for Julia's third son, Alexander, using a very fine, blue-green baby wool, with angora to soften it. She'd worked yellow, rose, lavender and aqua into the design, and it was gorgeous. People stopped Julia on the street and asked her who had made it. But one afternoon, Mark took the baby out in the stroller—they were living in Berkeley at the time—and when he came back from the walk, the hat was gone. Julia had gone out and searched, but never found it. She never quite forgave Mark for his carelessness, for the hat had almost come to symbolize her last baby's infancy. It had stretched as his head had grown. The colors were his colors. It had made him even more beautiful.

Two and a half years later, Julia and her family now living in the Berkshires, Martine was walking through the northside COOP, picking up a quart of yoghurt, when she saw the hat. It was on the head of a little dark-haired girl, and the mother appeared very pregnant. The hat looked like it barely fit. Martine walked over to take a closer look— unmistakable. In her delight and surprise she said to the pregnant woman, "I made that," pointing to the little girl's head, and the child gave Martine a worried smile. "I made that for one of my best friends, for her baby, and she lost it. Did you find it somewhere?"

"My mother gave me this hat," the woman responded.

This answer set something off in Martine, equally assertive and possessive.

"I'm a knitter," Martine continued, displaying the patterned sweater vest she had on, "and that's a one of a kind hat. I made it, and I would really like to have it back."

"My mother's up at the check-out if you want to ask her about it," the woman started pushing the cart along fast, and the little girl hung onto the bar. Martine followed, as the pregnant woman went up to the front of the store, all in a huff.

Martine assumed that that was the end of it, but no, now the grandmother came up to her, short and chubby, with frizzy grey hair.

Martine said, "I'm sorry, but I did make your granddaughter's hat, and I was just wondering where you found it. I made it for a friend's child, and the father lost it, years ago actually."

"I see," she paused. "Well, you know I run a daycare program, and some little girl came in one time, and left it. So I just passed it on to Teensie. We'd be happy to return it."

Martine could hear the pregnant mother telling one of the check-out tellers, "She wants to grab the hat right off my baby's head." Martine looked away, and waited, while the grandmother tried to talk sense, "She can't help it if she lost it."

And then suddenly the pregnant woman flashed up and threw the hat into Martine's shopping cart, and just as instantly disappeared. Martine took the hat up in her hands, that same familiar softness, such tiny needles she had used, though it looked like it might have been put in the washing machine. She would wash it again by hand, pull the pills of wool from the delicate pattern. She slid the hat into her purse, embarrassed by the scene she'd created.

Moving to the express line with only six items, she noticed *The Enquirer*: BABY FOUND INSIDE 86 YEAR OLD WOMAN. The fetus had calcified, and never been born. "How gruesome," Martine said out loud.

"Glad you got your hat?" the teller asked, beeping the items through.

For years Martine had been picking up baby clothes, little girls' dresses at yard sales, in thrift stores, precious items gleaned from the free box, booties from Verona, hand-smocked shirts. She kept a box in her closet, thinking maybe someday, but then occasionally she'd go through it all, and send off this item or that to Rachel, Julia or Kate. They always marvelled over her terrific finds. She wanted to participate with the children, but it wasn't her world. She kept toys on her bookshelf for when the kids came over — a Chinese metal acrobat, chattering teeth and stacking blocks, a slinky, a balsa airplane and a set of nursing piglets. But one time Vergil and Lianna stretched out the slinky, leaving it useless as some discarded snakeskin. Neither child took the blame. Martine assumed Vergil was responsible, and should replace it. Rachel stepped in, "It was probably the baby's fault. I'll get you another."

But Martine thought Vergil needed discipline. "Rachel," she insisted, "Vergil was standing right there, and it must have taken two of them to pull it out like that." She thought he should be made to face up to what he'd done. She didn't know how difficult it was to be a single mother, how easy it is to jump on the older child, how hard it is for a mother to be fair and consistent.

"Here's three dollars. Will that cover it?"

"That's not the point," Martine said.

She finally decided to send the hat back to Julia, for she had made it for Julia's baby, and Julia should decide what to do with it now. She knew what a thrill it would give her. She didn't know that Julia was pregnant.

When Julia opened the little padded envelope, all of the tension she'd been holding in, as if holding her breath underwater, all of the secrecy and suppressed anticipation, all of her feelings surrounding this coming baby, and all of the fear that went with it, all of it rose up, accompanied by memories of her three existing boys. She saw their little starfish hands, the way she had held Alexander, his warm, sleeping head, the moist and parted lips, how she had kissed each brow, held and rocked and nursed each one of them — all of it came back, right there in the presence of her husband, who was tearing open the rest of the mail. She started to cry. She couldn't stop it. The boys were at school, so why not.

"I didn't know that meant so much to you," Mark said, looking at her queerly. "You didn't even make it."

Julia just wanted to cry.

"What's wrong with you," Mark wanted to know.

"Nothing's wrong," she lashed out at him. She had been so nasty to him lately. He couldn't say anything without her jumping on him. "But nothing is right either. Nothing is right *or* wrong. Everything is just nothing."

"Listen, Julia, what's going on here," he took her shoulders in his hands, and seemed awkward yet concerned. There was a tension in his touch. He had felt her drifting away from him. He could tell she no longer wanted him, but they were married and that was that. The little hat in her hands made him think back as well, made him feel the slight guilt he'd felt when he'd lost it that time, and he had been sorry, but it hadn't seemed so important, and now, what did it mean to Julia now. "What's eating you, anyway?" he asked her, standing up.

She hung her head. She actually wanted to tell him. Why not. Why not get it over with. If not now, when. Never? It had to be sometime. He wanted to know. He was big enough to handle it. She had had enough. She didn't love him anymore. She couldn't bear for him to touch her, that was it. "I'm pregnant," she said.

"Oh no," he answered, his voice dropping, then quickly picking up again. "How far, second month?" He sounded hopeful.

"It doesn't matter."

"What do you mean?"

"It's probably the end of my first trimester." She realized she couldn't get out of it now. She couldn't stop now and turn back, and not say.

"Well, it's not too late," he said, turning from her.

142

"Too late?" she repeated.

"Not too late to abort."

"But I'm not going to," she said.

"I thought we talked about this. If it ever happened again."

"I'm not going to, that's all."

"Julie honey, we can't have another baby. It's crazy. I promise I'll have the operation this time, I swear, but . . ."

"Too late," she interrupted.

"But it's not too late," he insisted.

"It's not your baby."

He didn't answer her. But his hands rose and tightened. His eyes changed. They retreated into some density of maniac brain, and she could feel the energy rising up through his body, hardening him. She could almost feel his heart pounding down through his body and into the floorboards, thudding over and up into her own double heart beat. She crossed her arms and tried to stand away from him, the hat scrunched up in her one hand, protective of her belly, her little belly that didn't look like it held a baby yet.

"You cunt," he whispered through his teeth. She didn't look up or answer. She was numb, still as any animal in the woods who knows to hold perfectly still. Maybe the danger would pass. Maybe he would walk out of the house, slam the door. She thought that she could smell his sweat. It disgusted her. Suddenly he pushed her, shoved her so hard, she lost her grip and hit the highboy. It had started now, she knew, it had started — whatever it was that was going to happen was going to happen right now, and then it would be over. "It's over," she yelled, and that gave him permission to strike her across the mouth.

"You want it, don't you. You really want it this time."

The baby, she thought, would he hurt it? She thought she could run, out through the kitchen, but he caught her as she turned, by the collar, took her shirt at the collar and yanked so hard it burned across her neck. Her hand went up to feel it, before she felt the backside of his hand, that smacked her head before he asked, "Whose is it." He was demanding now, and she felt the warm sweet looseness of blood on her lip, her chin, her shirt. "Whose fucking baby is it!" He kept shoving her back, further back, as if each shove gave him energy, made something bigger rise up, and he was determined, each line a threat jab demanding, until she was backed into the dining room.

She felt her own anger rise. "It's my baby, mine! And nothing else matters."

"Nothing matters? Three children and fifteen years don't matter to you? I *moved* here because of you."

She was horrified by the finality of this. "I'm sorry," she said.

"You're sorry!" He looked crazy, looked as if he wanted to violate her in the most basic way, tear her limb from limb.

"Don't touch me," she uttered. "I mean it, don't touch me!" she screamed, as he yanked her around, snatching up the pink cotton skirt she was wearing. He tripped her onto the floor, yanked her underpants off — she was struggling, face down, to get away, not that she had much power under his weight. Her head felt wobbly, swollen, and his big dumb hands were squeezing her neck, and she knew that she had to give in to the bastard — "o.*k.*" she gasped, and he rammed himself into her, but she didn't let herself feel it, didn't move one ounce, didn't grip or respond, as he plunged there inside her, face down as she was. He was long and hard, always easily hard, but he always came too quickly. She lay there and took it, took his horrible, last bit of seed, and didn't move or speak as he got up. She was lying face down, under the dining room table. She felt him standing above her. She wondered if he would drop something heavy on her back. She could hear him panting. There was a terrible pause, and then he kicked her, hard, between the legs, and she rolled to the side with a reeling agony she couldn't get away from, until she heard him at the door, "You better — not be here —

when I get back with Alexander. I don't think you'd want him to see you."

As soon as she heard his car start she tried to move, and felt a sharper pain, yet she was lucid. She figured everything out. It was over. What to do now. The boys. What rights did she have. And where would she go now. Yes. She stumbled, got up, lurching forward, grabbed the hat from the floor, put both checkbooks in her purse, went to the bathroom and groaned. Who was she? That face. Looked smeared across her mouth, and her neck, her groin. Should she go to the hospital? Actually call the cops? She pictured little Alex seeing that flashing light in the driveway. She had to escape this. She took a suitcase from the closet, started tossing clothes in wildly, jamming them in. She had clean laundry on the bed, in little piles for each member of the family. She took her pile, stuffed and zipped the bag. It was over, the end, thank God, at last the deceit and all was over. She called Kate, who was there in five minutes. Kate looked stony, in shock. But Julia didn't have time now. With sunglasses, makeup, she could pass. She would have to leave the boys until things were decided. She would get a lawyer, the best. Kate drove her to the airport. She would fly to California. Kate would call Martine.

Flying out of Hartford, Julia sat alone in her row, holding the soft angora wool hat. She wanted Martine to teach her now to knit. She would make a blanket for the baby. Philip's baby. She took out his picture hidden in her wallet. Her eyes kept returning to his profile, as if every direction of thought led back to the same location. And now she was flying away from him.

She hoped to get custody of the boys, and believed that they would be able to join her. She knew that no one in Berkeley would judge her, and that Mark, in the long run, would be happier too. He could never handle the boys alone.

145

Part of her life was over, a precious, awful phase. Maybe even Philip would change now, for she was not only flying away from him, but her energies were also rechanneled. Soon she would feel the quickening, that first slight shift of movement. The progress of a pregnancy came back quickly, familiar. She could tell that this pregnancy would be a good one. No nausea. Her two hands filled the hat.

Martine, Lianna and Vergil were all there at the airport. She didn't know who to hug first, but Vergil leapt forward, surprising her with the intensity of his greeting. How wonderful that Martine would bring them, yet it made her wonder where Rachel was. "I'll tell you later," Martine said, as they headed toward baggage. Martine held Lianna's little hand, and the child kept looking up at Julia with her blue, almond-shaped eyes, same color as her mother's. Such lovely honey-colored hair. "You've gotten so big," Julia complimented her, but Lianna reached up as if she wanted to be carried. Julia did pick her up for a ways, and Lianna asked, "Are you going to the hospital, too?" Julia realized that her face must look awful, but that wasn't it.

"We're going to stay together tonight," Martine announced, "and we'll see your mother tomorrow."

"What's wrong?" Julia whispered, but Martine didn't say. They could talk once the children were in bed.

Martine and Tibor had bought a big brown shingle on Bonita, so there was lots of room for all of them. Julia would sleep in the downstairs bedroom.

"Your face is really a mess. Nice work, Mark," Martine said, bitterly. She hated Mark for this, thought that Julia should have done something a long time ago.

"I just feel sorry for him, for all of us, at this point. Sorry about everything but the baby."

"Let's hope it's o.k." Martine didn't want to delve into that subject at the moment, her own longings and disappointments too close to the surface. She went up to put the kids to bed.

"So what's happening with Rachel?" Julia asked, when Martine came back downstairs.

"Paul, it appears, has hepatitis, a really severe case." Martine poured each of them a cup of tea and sat down at the kitchen table. "He has a very high fever, and lost all this weight. I don't know why everything has to happen at once, but it was drugs, dirty needles, or something. I can remember you guys thought he might be into that. I guess it started when Rachel left him back east, and he got in with a bunch of rotters. Anyway, Rachel is up in Sonoma, visiting him until tomorrow."

"Poor Paul," Julia said. "I know he just sort of dropped out of her life, but God."

"And now this. He wants to see some weirdo doctor. He was always so strange, never sent a penny for Lianna, and when you think of the family he came from." Martine noticed how tired Julia looked. She was exhausted but also wired from travelling and wanted to talk.

"Tibor must think he's inherited one hell of a family," Julia said.

"It would take a lot more than this to shock Tibor," Martine answered, "with all he sees in Oakland." Tibor was a people's lawyer, advising the poor about their housing rights. He often didn't get paid, and they could use the money, but Martine admired his priorities. "You know I've never been with such a loving man before." He didn't believe in the institution of marriage either, but they had decided that if it helped with the adoption they'd go through with it. "I just hate to kill the romance."

"Is that what does it?" Julia wondered, blankly. Or was it simply time.

It's Philip Mercato," Martine said, looking across the living room, "and he wants to speak to Julia Chapin." Julia's heart began to pound. It had been twelve days since she'd left.

"I'll take it," she nodded upward, "in the bedroom."

"You found me," she almost whispered, before he could say *darling,* and they embraced with their voices long distance.

"I've been so worried about you," he continued. "I had a very bad scene with Mark, but denied everything. He wouldn't tell me where you were, but then I called your friend, Kate. She almost wouldn't tell me either, but I convinced her."

"How did you do that?"

"I've got my ways," he laughed. "I just want to talk to you, I mean in person, and I'm coming out there in a couple of weeks, to check out an investment in San Francisco, and I wanted to see you."

She could almost see him smile, and she understood now that he was happy, that he wanted the baby. "I love you," he said, his voice dropping even deeper.

"But are you in love with me?" she teased him.

"I am," he admitted. "And I like you too, that's almost more important." She didn't know how to answer him. "I'll be coming into Oakland, two weeks from Friday, United #595, at 7:23 p.m. I can only stay two days, so we're going to have to make good use of our time."

She couldn't believe he was coming. "I'll meet you," she said. "That must sound stupid. I just feel like I've been, like my life has been suspended."

"Everything's going to be fine," he sounded so manly, so firm and in charge.

She wondered if he wanted to marry her. She wasn't even sure if she wanted that. And yet this comforting, embracing tone of Philip's wooed her. She wanted him, but in a less demanding way. At this distance from him, she was more focused on her children, talking to her lawyer daily, who was talking to Mark's lawyer, who was filing for abandonment, but that only seemed like a threat in light of the violence. Since she was willing to share custody, her lawyer thought his lawyer would bring Mark around, as long as the financial end was clear. Meaning, she would have to pay. All of this took time.

Kate was allowed to visit the boys, and she called in with information, told Julia in detail how they seemed fine, what was happening in school, with sports, not saying how they did appear more fragile. "Mark even went out and bought a TV and VCR, admitting that it was the best babysitter he could find." Alex especially seemed to be easily upset, and Kate felt that Julia should try to patch things up, end the other relationship and somehow make it work. But Julia knew it was too late for that now. Too late, *too late*, too late.

Martine had taught Julia how to knit, and Julia was working on a bright blue baby sweater, garter stitch, very plain, but now she saw a hole, and had to tear out the last fifteen rows. The yarn looked permed as she pulled it loose, and then once she got the stitches looped back on the needle they seemed too tight. She decided to wait and get Martine's advice. Rachel was proofing her new book of poems, which a small press in Berkeley was publishing. Julia had been asked to design the cover, black and white, and they had decided on something typographic. The title, GENETRIX, would be in hot pink lettering. She dropped the knitting in her basket and picked up her scratch pad.

"I think I'd like to do a series of round paintings, great big round ones, off-center."

"You could call the show, *Toujours Enceinte,*" Rachel kidded her. Always pregnant. "I almost called this new book, Always In Love. I think a woman *should* always be in love. Socrates said he was."

"That wasn't very wise of him. Have you heard from Paul?"

"God, Paul. You know I had forgotten how much I really

care for him," Rachel said, looking up. "I mean like I might have loved a younger brother."

"Do you think he'll be o.k.?" Julia asked, regretting that she'd brought him up, not wanting to bring up the old buried subject of the needle in the garbage, how he might have exposed them all to AIDS.

"I'm sure he'll pull out of it. It's just a matter of time. And Marcy isn't much of a nurse. She's only eighteen."

"I never liked to nurse anybody either," Julia admitted. "It's a good thing my kids are basically healthy." But this made her eyes suddenly fill. She felt now that she would crawl a hundred miles for any one of them, just to kiss a sore knee, or feel a forehead. "Shit," she covered her face, and Rachel came over to her, put her arm around Julia and stroked her hair.

"You really miss them, don't you. It must be hard."

Julia had always felt mothered by Rachel, and it was comforting to be there alone with her friend, the children at school. She could always count on Rachel to make her feel better, unlike her own, real mother, who had only left her dangling. Perhaps she had leaned too much on Rachel in the past. Possibly that was why it had been so upsetting for Julia when Rachel and Paul left Berkeley for the east years before.

Rachel had given Julia a stone baby for her 28th birthday, and it had always rested in Julia's garden, so much a part of the setting that it could hardly be seen. This grey stone baby was bald and unearthly, sitting relaxed with eyelids closed on the world, in its own little shade beneath the fuchsia amongst the ivy. Perhaps Julia was the only one who noticed it, who knew how well it rested in the place she'd chosen for it. And yet it disturbed her now, and when she tipped it over, the earth beneath was dark and moist, and many small insects wriggled down in for protection from the sun.

Now that Rachel was moving away, Julia felt like she was carrying a stone baby right in the middle of her gut. Thousands of miles was the thought in her belly, there with the stone baby. When there was talk of the future, a visit next summer, an eventual move, the stone baby seemed to groan, as if it knew a story when it heard one.

Rachel had begun to pack everything into cardboard boxes. She packed a box a day, and she'd been doing this for some time. She never realized how many boxes worth she had, nor the value of certain items, until it came time to sort them — the sellable pile, the give-away pile, the cherished, inseparable pile — those Puerto Rican shoes. But Julia couldn't pick any of these piles to place herself in. She felt like she didn't belong. The plants, the rug, the Chevy, the old sock rabbit, were things that had to go. The house came off the walls. But what distressed Julia was seeing her friend's apartment in this state of dismantlement. She forced herself to witness it. The place had held so many before, a gallery of faces, and now there were only walls, and they weren't worth looking at really.

"Come on, sit down," Rachel coaxed her, and so they ate zucchini pizza on the kitchen floor, and talked about the unborn daughters that they hoped for, which they might conceive someday, daughters whom they would encourage, daughters whom they would let go, but the evening wasn't long enough, and both of them grew very weary. Both of them were sad, but both tried hard not to show it.

"I want you to have this begonia," Rachel said that night. She loved the large begonia which she'd started from two leaves. Rachel asked her if she would love the begonia also.

"In time," Julia said, "I'm sure it will come to mean much

more than just a begonia." But she didn't like the idea of exchanging her friend for a mere begonia either and yet that wasn't the choice.

Julia was ready for her friend to leave now, but then Rachel wasn't so sure if she really wanted to go. Her reasons, once clear, seemed uncertain now, and she wanted Julia to convince her, and Julia did try to convince her to stay, though she'd had no part in this plan. No matter what Julia said, no matter what she did, she felt she was ony daring her friend to make her so miserable.

Julia thought a decision should provoke a direct and immediate action, but Rachel knew how to linger, and even enjoyed the ambiguous swing of her feelings. Paul was also a procrastinator, he wasn't helping to get this show on the road. It all made Julia uneasy, because her feelings were obvious and yet not essential. She simply did not want her best friend to desert her.

The stone baby had always been alone. Its mother had always departed, and it never did mind. The baby took care of itself. It didn't need water or sun, much less any tender human contact, and yet it was solidly there, and could not be forgotten.

As Julia sat motionless in her garden, she felt that she was the guardian of some unborn thing. Or perhaps the baby was a kind of recipient. Julia liked to believe that this statue actually needed her, that both of them needed each other—the baby to be seen, for it had been made for this purpose, and Julia to behold it, to symbolize it, and thus to understand.

And yet Rachel remained. There were always new, vague reasons for the latest delay. Then one afternoon, Rachel stretched out her arms, and laughing over the music asked, "Julia, will you marry me?"

Julia said, "Of course," and though she smiled, she turned away from her friend. Maybe the grey stone baby wasn't so real to Rachel, but an idea you could come up with or drop at whim. She was afraid of her friend's light heart, that she was simply toying with some other notion of love. Could there be no promise between them?

Julia would never be a man, after all, and marry her friend in that way, take care of her with human seed and a normal home life. Although she enjoyed the proposal, it was also disconcerting, because what she'd always provided, and what she'd received from her friend, lay in another realm, and on another threshhold.

Julia realized that it was their friendship which finally was cheated, because they were both only women and didn't come first. There would always be a man, a child, an acceptable version of love to remind them of this, to reprimand them for the negative space of the not yet born. Why should they give each other this sadness. Because they shouldn't care so much?

In the past, she had never felt so good as when she and Rachel lay back on the pillows of the sofa, warmed by the filtered light that heated the room each morning. Rachel would read a rough draft of some new poem, and they'd end up laughing profoundly over nothing memorable. They had offered each other an available ear, heart, hand, and the other had always taken it. But then the hand, which was always there, was suddenly withdrawn.

Rachel came to hug her friend, to kiss both cheeks goodbye, but Julia felt herself harden. She knew that Rachel didn't see it her way, for she was the one who had chosen. Rachel saw herself as a daughter still, not the mother of a stone baby.

And so Rachel, Paul and Vergil finally piled in, and drove away from Berkeley, California, off to western Massachusetts, Paul's home. His parents had offered them a rent-free garage apartment, close to Kate's school, where Vergil would attend first grade. It was nice that Rachel would have Kate close by. They'd be able to visit New York, and she hoped to find an agent. She had even said that one of the reasons they were going back east was that it would make it easier for her mother to visit.

"Rachel, who are you kidding?" Julia shook her head. "Do you know how cold it's going to be? And who are you going to have coffee with. You're going to be in the sticks!"

Rachel didn't realize that Julia was painting a more realistic picture than she cared to visualize. Rachel didn't know about Sorel boots, or mittens on elastic. She had never dealt with snow tires or woodstoves, icy roads or Price Chopper. She didn't realize that Berkeley was a circus that she'd become accustomed to, and that a social life, a literary life, a constant, chattery, on-the-telephone-all-the-time, in-and-out-of-it life, had suited her sense of well-being.

Rachel believed she would like the solitude, and she did have more time to write, but failed to find an agent. She had believed that it would be good for Paul to return to his roots, but that was the biggest mistake. He became depressed, and ended up with a hammer in one hand, and young college girls in the other. When Rachel found out about that she was six weeks pregnant with Lianna.

Waiting for Philip at the arrival gate, Julia had been so nervous until she saw his eyes searching her out. He pushed past the other passengers, came and grabbed her, kissed her right there in public.

Even waiting for his bag, he kept leaning over her, nuzzling her, "You look so pretty," and she was beaming, for she'd never received his affections so openly before. It had always been overly guarded, discreet.

"I brought you something," he said, gathering her to him.

"What?" she wanted to know. "What is it?" But he was

going to make her wait. He had made reservations at the Claremont Hotel, and they had to drive in separate cars. She hated being away from him even for an instant. The hotel, lit up, was as big and white and grand as a wedding cake, and it made her think of that white wooden bed, their own small slice of sweetness.

There in the lobby, it was as if they were meeting all over again. He already had the key. He had driven even faster than she had. "I can't wait to see you," he whispered, in the elevator going up. "You don't look very big."

"It's only the end of my fourth month." She felt like she could melt and blend in with him. She wanted to be like the liquid coating of love, entirely surrounding.

As soon as they closed the door, he was taking her clothes off, and she stood there, breathless, letting him. He admired the new fullness of her breasts, and kissed them, each, the nipples puffed and sensitive, and then he carefully smoothed his hands down over the little shape of her belly. Her skin was smoother, resilient, and her sex seemed almost swollen. "I love you like this," he said to her, meaning so ripe and round, and her hands were on his clothes now too, tugging at them, and he was aroused, responding fast — at last they both stood naked, and succumbed to that first sweet skin on skin, before he moved her onto the bed, and she wound her legs around his, wanting to pull him in, where he slid, and moved, the consistency of his cock so good, and she could read the pleasure on his face, the mild contortion, eyes held closed, and she took it up inside herself and murmured how good it felt.

He was thrusting slowly into her, wanting to save himself, and she wanted to fuck and fuck all night, wanted him in every part of her, and she slid him out and pulled him forward, so that he was kneeling above her head, and she took him in her mouth then, wondering about her own juices slick on the stretch of his, but it didn't bother her, not at all, she just wanted him deep inside her mouth, and she wormed her way down even more so that she could better suck him in, while he knelt there gently thrusting, and she twirled her tongue around the tip of it saying, "I love your cock," and it was more beautiful, round and engorged, than any she had ever imagined. She felt wed to this cock, and he wanted her more than with just his sex, but with all of himself, and she could feel the difference.

"I want to taste you," he uttered, and he moved his tongue up and down on her which made her petals open, and she pushed her bush up out of his way so that he could lick even higher, and it drove her high up with wanting him, his lapping and sucking and then back down, into her deeper, in there with his tongue, and then back up, until she was close, and he said, "Let go," and she tightened, her legs almost cramping, as she built to the peak, as he mauled her with good feeling. "Don't stop," she cried, as she got closer, and she wondered if she could make it, but he didn't stop and he didn't stop—she imagined his cock, big and straight as a horse's, plunging right into some slippery doll—and she felt herself *there,* as he raked with his teeth, and she wanted him back up inside her, and his face was all wet and he fucked her hard—"You're delicious," he said. "I could feel you spurt all over my tongue," and she gripped him hard as he yelled out loud, with a groaning shout that gave them both sweet deafness, which obliterated the world.

She just wanted his manly large spent weight to lie on top of her then, to cover and bury her down, as she felt the strength of her uterus, tightening and contracting, embracing their forming infant, as if the child were included too, and it must have felt good inside there, within that love-good muscled bag that wouldn't stop massaging.

For the first time that night they slept together. They had never been allowed that luxury before. But she found that she didn't sleep well, and was afraid that she might disturb him. He slept right through and never woke until first thing in the morning, when it was clear that he wanted her again.

156

It felt like the honeymoon she'd never had, and she felt entirely relaxed with it, more languorous, more open to whatever it was he wanted. She took his lip between her lips, and he wanted to kiss, to pass his tongue across her teeth, her perfect pearly teeth, and she wondered where they would go from here, for there seemed to be no beyond.

"I have something to give you," he dislodged himself. She felt pained at his withdrawal, but he pulled the covers up to her chin, and she waited, watching him move, liking to see him now in daylight, how naturally dark he was. She felt like a lily beside him, and he adored her pale, smooth skin, her light blond hair, her cheeks now rosy from roughness, from the blood of that morning's love. He held up a little something in his hand. It was wrapped in yellowed tissue paper. She put her hand on top of his. "My grandfather gave this to my grandmother on their wedding day," he said. "I wanted you to have it." She wondered if she had understood him, or if he knew what he meant, but she slid her hand from beneath his, took up the tissue paper and began unwrapping it. She scrunched up in bed a little so that she could see it better. She was silent. Hesitant, and looking up at him, he nodded for her to go on, and she did, though almost afraid, for it was, "No!" too beautiful, an incredibly gorgeous pin, in the shape of a flower, with a diamond in the middle, and little petals of pearls radiating out from the center. He asked her if she liked it.

Did she like it! She couldn't believe it. He brushed the hair away from her face, away from the tears rolling down her cheeks, as she enclosed the pin in her hand.

"You're so sensitive," he said, in such a kind way. "I forgot how sensitive you are."

But suddenly she missed her boys, and in the midst of this she felt dread. It came out of nowhere, but it made her want to escape. As if she might reject what she wanted most, and the rawness of this feeling scared her. Her emotions seemed so extreme, too loose. Her longing for little Alex was like a rip in the side of her flesh, each boy an inner wound in her, and somehow this man was to blame. This man had taken them from her and replaced himself. No, she couldn't believe that. She would see her boys again soon. Kate had promised to work on Mark. Philip didn't say anything more about marriage, but the pin seemed to be an engagement present, and yet she wasn't divorced. Philip assured her that when she returned, she could stay with him, use the guest house as her painting studio, and the boys could come over whenever she wanted. So he did care about them.

"I love you," he said, and she looked at him oddly, but smiled then, remembering.

"There's a difference, you know," she repeated what he'd said once, "between loving someone and being *in* love," and she felt he deserved this teasing, but he looked worried, and didn't remember the context.

"Maybe you don't know what you want," he said, sitting up.

"I know what I want," she said softly, touching his upper arm. "This bicep."

"Why not this one?" he pointed to his left arm.

"No, all I want is this."

He seemed reassured, as he lay back down beside her. She laced her hands around his neck.

"Even our baby seems grateful inside me."

"What do you think you'll name him?"

"I was thinking about Antonio."

She felt his reaction, like a small but recordable seismic shock that passed from him into her, and she asked him if it seemed wrong, and he shook his head and said, "No, it's fine."

"You don't like it," she said.

"Did you know that my grandfather's name was Antonio?"

No, she had never known that.

"Antonio and Sylvanna Mercato."

Do you think there's any chance you could bring the boys?" Julia asked over the phone.

Kate answered rather frankly, "I doubt if Mark would go for that. You know he just hired this *au pair* girl, Aileen, from Ireland. She's going to school, and I'm not sure it's legal, but she cleans and cooks, and babysits whenever he needs her, and she's good, I think, very even."

"Do they like her?" Julia asked. She pictured this woman, cuddling her boys, reading to them, making them eggs in the morning. She pictured her house, flowers on the table from her garden, the screen porch open to her living room, letting in the summery light, the swing on the hill in motion, the echoing call of her boys from the pond. Would this girl protect Alexander? He still didn't know how to swim very well, and the big boys were so reckless. "What about Thomas?" Julia said. "He's old enough to fly alone. If I paid? Do you mind asking Mark for me, this once?"

"He might go for that. Just Thomas."

Her heart flew forward, stammered, jumped and then burst around that corner, just as he was getting off the plane, "Tommy!"

She ran to greet him, though he appeared cool, acting casual, as if he hadn't just flown across country, but when she grabbed him and squeezed him, he hugged her back with all his might.

"Hey Mom, you're really putting on some weight these days," he kidded her, but she could tell he was embarrassed. He looked so huge, the one way in which he was like his father. They didn't get along, and Mark had been glad to send him packing for a week. Mark was very close to Ross, their second child, identified with him, but Alexander was getting the short end of the stick.

Kate had spared her friend the details. Alexander always seemed to have a cold, or was crying when she came over.

His hair never looked brushed, and he almost clung to Kate. She tried to have him over to play every week, for Atea liked having a little boy around, somebody she could boss.

"Thanks for working this out for me," Julia called her that afternoon. "I can't tell you what it does for me."

"Well things are looking better," Kate responded. "It almost looks like Mark's willing to share custody. That's totally off the record, but I had a long talk with him the other night. Listen, I've really tried to stay on his good side. Otherwise he'd just figure I was snooping for you, which I am, but still, I *am* a godmother, and that gives me certain rights. I've tried talking some sense into him, and I think he realizes it's a bit much for him to handle. He wants to move back to California, sell the house, and he wants you both to share the boys, out there, after this year is up."

Julia felt her heart drop. "He just wants to keep me away from Philip." Philip would never move.

"Can you blame him?" Kate said.

"Any word on that score?"

"Not a peep, thank God." Kate really didn't want to talk about Philip.

Thomas had found the television. She went to him, knelt beside him, watching, then she kissed him, squeezed him again, until he said, "Don't kiss me, Mom."

"Mothers always kiss their boys," she said, tousling his hair.

"Not when they're not around."

She heard him, heard the hurt, wanted to reassure him, wanted to say something, but the sound of the TV seemed to stand in the way. "How's Rossie, and Alex?" she asked.

"Fine, I guess."

"Do they miss me?"

"I suppose," he said, looking straight ahead at the set.

"And you?"

"Mom, can't I just watch TV?"

"Sure," she said, resigned. "It's just that I've missed you

so much. It's like I've been constantly hungry. And now that you're here . . ." But this only made him think of his own eleven year old hunger, his own resentments, and loneliness. Mark took a lot out on him, blamed him when anything went wrong, made him do most of the chores. He didn't know where he belonged anymore. Though he was glad to see his mother, he didn't know what to think about this pregnancy, or what the breakup was all about. He had gotten into fights at school recently, had even been caught smoking. A commercial came on the tube, and he asked, "Is there anything to eat around here?"

That familiar question sounded so good to her, she laughed, "Let's go look," taking him around the shoulder. "If I haven't polished everything off, I bet we can at least find you a small rack of lamb, or a wheel of brie or something."

"When is Vergil going to get here." He seemed impatient.

"He's got All-Star practice, but he should join us for dinner."

"I guess you can't ride when you're pregnant," Thomas said.

"Not now, anyway."

"Frank died," he remembered, stopping at the bottom of the stairs. She stopped too, as if listening, waiting to hear that she hadn't heard right. "He had an accident," Thomas went on.

Frank had been trying out a new stallion. He had always wanted to get into breeding, and this horse was young and strong, pure white, almost without a blemish. Frank had put on one of his old Western saddles and taken him out, urging him from a canter into a gallop, and with that extra exertion, the leather of the girth had snapped. The saddle flew to the right, and Frank had fallen to the side. The stallion had galloped down the gravel road, but Frank had never gotten up.

"His horses were taken to auction. And Dad said he wasn't going to pay for Bunko's feed."

Frank gone? Bunko sold at auction? That meant by the pound, for dog food. Did Philip know? Had he rescued her horse along with Sensation? Frank actually gone?

She wanted to call Philip, to talk to him. But she was afraid of his response, that he hadn't been concerned about what happened to her horse, or even to Frank. He hadn't mentioned it in either of his two rather perfunctory phone calls. He was always in such a rush, and when she told him how much she missed him he only said, "Don't worry." It was his tone that made her worry. Suddenly she was sure that he had taken up with someone else. It was very hard not to call him. Sometimes she just sat by the phone, willing it to ring.

Martine tried to distract her. "Why don't you go for a swim?" she'd suggest. "Do you want to take a walk up to Inspiration Point?"

Julia's look betrayed her.

"Don't call," Martine said firmly. "He knows where you are."

Martine wrote Kate: *Can you believe I might do what I always promised myself I would never do, ruin this relationship with a ring? But it looks like it's necessary for the adoption, and I'd promise anything at this point, say anything, do anything, if it meant getting that babe in my arms.*

I wish I could be more optimistic, wish I didn't feel like a crotchety old lady half the time, yelling at her own noisy feelings to Scat! I wish this lead-colored depression would just go and leave me, leave me alone. I'm so tired of talking to people. People and again more people. Writing, talking, phoning, wheedling, pleading and trying to convince a league of idiots about my capacity to raise a normal, healthy child?

I swear they're poking their noses into every book on our personal shelves. What do we think? How do we breathe? Would we spank? Are we racist? Are we HAPPY? Will we last? How do we feel about not getting to make one of our own? I find this adoption procession one of the least pleasant marches I've been on in my adult years. We shall not count out loud.

So now I'm being forced to dig up that old dead body, memory, in the putrid garden of my feelings. Twenty years later and the past still haunts me, while the future looks pretty bleak. Why is Tibor so positive? Sometimes I think he is simply naive, assuming that goodness will land on us. But most snow jobs turn into slush, and I'm not sure of anything. Ever since I was seventeen, I have believed in one thing only — that nothing is sacred. And now that very belief jangles its bones in front of me as dust flies from its womb.

Martine was knitting Julia's baby a sleeping sack, using skeins of cream and yellow yarn in a lovely wavy pattern. When she finished a skein, Rachel mentioned, "My mother used to knit. I think she knit when she gave up smoking. It was a kind of therapy."

"It is for me too," Martine admitted. "But for some reason I also need *real* therapy *and* smoking."

"She made me this awful navy blue pullover, completely out of shape, but it really impressed me, that she'd done all that for me. It was just this one dark color, navy blue, and a very plain style, but every time she'd come to the end of a ball, my father would announce, that someone on earth had to die. I guess the Greeks believed that when a goddess came to the end of a skein, death happened. There must have been sixteen skeins in my sweater, and I sometimes wondered whose lives I was responsible for ending, but Mama always made light of it. 'Everybody dies someday,' that's how she'd respond. But maybe he was trying to warn her."

"Do you think she killed him somehow?" Martine asked.

Rachel was silent. Maybe, as a child, she had thought that. But now she didn't, no. "He killed himself," she finally answered, and that felt like the truth. She hadn't done it. Her mother hadn't done it. Life hadn't even done it to him. He had chosen to do it to himself. Or was that fair? Life was either very simple, or very complicated. Maybe both. As a child, at least, life had seemed simple. You went along, and you had what you had.

Rachel had been nine years old, playing with pine straw in her backyard on Habersham Road. She was making Bluebell a bed. Bluebell was her favorite, most special doll, the one she needed in order to sleep. Bluebell had a special feature. She was a lovely white lady with silky hair and a satin blue gown on the top, but you could flip her upside down, and she'd be a colored Mammie with a red print apron and big button eyes. Her father was sympathetic to the *schwartzes*. He wouldn't allow the word *nigger* in the house.

Rachel had a photograph of herself talking on the telephone, dark dark eyebrows and sensual mouth. Even at that age she was pretty and slender, quick with her responses, flying through the details, lighting, realighting, settling for a moment, only to be off again. She was a real little princess, her Gramma always said, taking such care with her buttons, her canopy world, already understanding how to pose, and what it took to entertain.

She went where her parents went, moving from one southern city to another, as her father tried this and then that job, unable to dig up any meaning where money was involved. No money where there was some meaning.

They were living in Augusta when it happened. She remembered hearing her mother make that strange noise — it sounded as if she were gargling on fat — and Rachel went solemn and silent to the bedroom door, where Mama was gripping the receiver, a wad of the blue chenille bedspread in her other hand, and then her mother's eyes shrank over her, and a hand went up to that large loosened mouth. Her father had left them, forever. Unutterable silence. Quietly, he had rolled on out of their lives on the toxic fumes of his car.

The butterfly inside her—stuck, with a pin. It could have been the tie pin she found later on the floor of his closet. She wanted to stick it back in through the silk of his stripes, matching the slant, feeling his big tickling arms, getting a ride, getting a song, hearing—"I love you. A bushel and a peck and a hug around the neck." She wanted to make Bluebell *feel*.

So Rachel had an idea, that was more like an action. She felt passionate as she took to it, for it seemed like a solution, though it was work, hard work, scissoring off both heads from her doll. She pushed the pin down deep into the middle of its body, and then sewed the heads back on, so that the lovely white face was on the black black Mammie, and there were big button eyes on her little white lady.

PART FOUR

I don't think you ever get over it. You never forget," Martine told Julia that night. "There's something so profound about carrying a baby, even if you know you can't keep it. There is something always pulling there."

Martine had been seventeen when she fled Santa Barbara for New Mexico, already five and a half months pregnant. She was getting away from her parents, who didn't know, and from her boyfriend, who did, but didn't want to. She took the Greyhound bus to Albuquerque, passing through the summer furnace of Arizona. At least the bus had air conditioning. She stared through the filthy windows, counting giant saguaro — *un, deux, trois, quatre,* trying to avoid conversation with other passengers. Why do mothers always travel alone with whiny children. Why do servicemen always leer, and old women have clairvoyant eyes that see right through you.

Martine called *The Little Chapel of Sweet Mercy* from the terminal. The heat had cooked the grime of travelling onto her skin, but that didn't keep her from smoking another cigarette. When the nun arrived, driving an extra-long stationwagon, she seemed very business-like. "Hello," she said, "I'm Mother Margaret." Then she plucked the cigarette out of Martine's mouth and stepped on it. "You might not want this baby, but someone else will want it to be healthy. We don't allow our girls to smoke."

That was just the beginning. In more ways than one she felt she was serving time. The heat was insufferable. There was a cross in every room to remind her of what she no longer believed in. Born half-Catholic, half-Jewish, she thought of herself as an atheist. Mostly she kept to herself, to her novels and her roommate, a quiet Chicana named Marie. The other girls were generally impatient, paging through magazines, painting their nails and dancing around with their ridiculous big bellies under shortie pajamas.

"Get hip, Martine," the girls teased. "The twist is good for your figure! You trying to raise that baby's I.Q.?"

One evening in the cafeteria she heard a black girl announce, "Martine's just trying to starve herself so she won't show." Martine was much smaller than most of them. She didn't pop out until the end of her seventh month.

When her time came, it was sharp, fast, hard, back labor. She was left alone to flail and churn, helpless without anyone beside her. She didn't have a mother sane enough to care for her. She didn't have a father capable of love, and she wanted her child to have more.

"How was it?" the girls asked afterwards.

"Easy," she answered. "Like shitting a pumpkin."

She didn't want to talk about the loss she felt — like some irreplaceable part gouged out of her. She didn't want to talk about her son — how the nuns had crossed themselves when she signed him over — her dark-haired boy, her love. She had not held him, but she had looked, for one incredible moment — wrapped, red, bleating, beautiful, gone.

This had always remained Martine's secret, until she unburdened herself to Kate. Kate was sworn to secrecy, but eventually Kate told Julia about it, trying to explain Martine's behavior after the simultaneous birth of Galatea and Ross.

Years later, when Martine and Julia were sitting alone in Martine's tiny apartment in Berkeley, the one with the windows surrounded by plum trees in bloom, moonlight on the blossoms, Martine finally told Julia what had happened to her, what she'd been through back then.

"I was only seventeen, and I knew I couldn't keep that baby. It was a Catholic home, and the nuns used to point out the other girls who were keeping their babies. I had to lie there alone, recovering afterwards, with my milk coming in, all swollen, and hear those babies cry. I was desperate to get out of there."

"God, how horrible," Julia feigned a certain amount of shock. Supposedly she knew nothing about this. "How could you live through that. You were just a child yourself."

"And then two weeks later, my mother swallowed fifty seconal and had to have her stomach pumped. But the past isn't so difficult. It's *now* that's hard, wanting a baby so badly, and all of you having children. I can't describe it, but it just kills me sometimes. I want one so bad, it's almost like a craving, a physical need in my gut."

Julia had never realized that a maternal instinct could be so profound. Perhaps she had never felt that, because she'd had her boys early and close together.

"Sometimes I think it's just me, something missing in me, some child need that never got fulfilled or satisfied, and that I have to figure that out first." She offered Julia another one of her cigarettes, and poured them each more B & B. "I love knitting up things for all your kids, but it's not my world, not yet. So you have to understand when I draw back, because it's painful, because it's not mine."

Julia saw now what it was that had stood between them at times, when she was so absorbed by a new baby. "For a while last month, I thought you were angry with me for some reason. I thought it was something I'd done. Or was it."

"No, no," Martine shook her dark brown curls. The curly bangs almost reached her eyes. "But you see how it is. It just overwhelms me sometimes. Especially in the springtime when that baby was born. You know when I left New Mexico last year, I dreamt that I could hear his voice, that he was actually calling me. It's weird, because that baby is now nineteen years old. I could be a grandmother! But that doesn't make it any easier. I get so down every time I get a period, and now with these plum trees in bloom — they're so beautiful, it really depresses the shit out of me."

But Julia wondered if Martine didn't almost have this need to feel unhappy. Martine felt pain more clearly than most people, and yet it gave her dark brown eyes this extra depth, like the shine of a bruise, and it drew men to her, as if they could hold that delicate pain and give her pleasure instead. Her sorrowful, big, dark eyes were a challenge, and her smile was their reward. She gave in to it, because she did find momentary relief inside the arms of men. She took them home casually, and opened her kimono easily. She had the kind of figure most men liked—little but shapely, and then that luscious hair that made one think of a lost lamb, sounding so sweet and lonely, like the little one left on the hillside when the others had returned to the fold.

Martine considered men a challenge to her imagination. She only needed a man to step into the appropriate costume to perform what she wanted from him. She wasn't making love to the real man, as much as she was to this image—and when she closed her eyes, the picture began again, whatever current movie she had going. He was the one who made her come so easily, this dark male image, powerful, aloof and cold, and yet very sensual at the same time, a threatening sexuality. It was a kind of exchange. He never told her he loved her, like the real men did. He didn't care about her, not the real her, he just wanted to use her body, and that's what turned her on.

Martine saw herself in a darkened dining room on a huge silver platter, dressed only in her kimono. The tray was set down at the head of the table before this man, who was hosting a party for his best male friends. There was already the sweet smell of smoke and whiskey in the room, the overflow of seasoned talk, and though she didn't look up, she felt the presence of anticipation focused now on her. She could feel the men assessing her, hear the murmur of approval. He was proud to show her off, slipping the robe open to expose her breasts. He weighed them in his hands and laughed, pulled on them, so that she had to lean forward and let them hang. He slipped the kimono off her shoulders, exposing her skin, which was butter smooth, the kind of poreless, perfect skin that makes a man want to take a hunk and chew.

He took her on his lap then, and held her knees apart

to expose the small dark wedge. He told her that he wanted her to crawl around the room, and take each member in her mouth, that she'd be doing it for him. She moved from man to man, as if his impulse guided her, and they were boisterous in their enjoyment, and she too was well aroused, but only truly passionate when she found her way to him, sitting in the chair at the head of the table. With him she was gone in the blindness of sucking, and he was proud of his own equipment, and his friends acknowledged how hot she was.

He laid her back on the table then, took a decanter of oil and poured a stream over her body, smoothing it over her breasts and her belly, her lower lips, then almost as a second thought, he poured some over her mouth, opened her teeth with his fingers and mushed the oil around, while stroking her, testing and teasing, tuning her up, as she heard the chairs moved out, the men lined up, surrounding her now, as if for some buffet, but then the whirlwind of their hands became like a darkness over her, and she thought of a tornado, that she had been lifted up by that spiralling movement, which was curling through her now, as she felt those engorged organs, those fleshy prods, touching and pushing here and there, as if to test her firmness.

Suddenly she was up in his arms — he was carrying her into the living room, as if on to another course. He flung her on the floor, got on top of her, while the rest of the men were clamoring, watching and urging him onward. She was afraid, but excitement was building amongst this fraternal camaraderie of shared sex, where he'd be the winner — and the hard nap of the carpet cut, as he squeezed both breasts in his taking hands, ungenerous mouth, his greedy cock, which slowed itself inside her, slow, and then even more slowly, like the most delicious, quiet killer, until she felt an end to it all — until she stopped and arched and called, held him, squeezed him as they came, with a splash of liquid poured over them both, and she opened her mouth, released in a heap, as they lay there, fed and perfectly quenched — Love, she said, my physical love, I hate you.

Rob, her ex-husband had worn the wedding dress. He'd hung the veil over his scraggly beard and thrown the bouquet, while Martine wore tux and tophat. Martine had kissed the bride. Rob had been good at performing for her, but he hadn't been good for much else.

She had wanted his child, but he wanted to remain the baby. She wanted his love, but he was a womanizer. Julia and Rachel both encouraged her to come to the Bay Area, and when she finally left Rob in Albuquerque, he followed her to Berkeley, and tried every tactic to get her back, offering a change of heart — how he too now wanted to have children — pleading with her, telling Julia how he'd never find anyone better. Julia agreed. Rachel told him, "Honey, you missed the boat." But he refused to give up, tried tenderness turned to violence, seduction turned to anger, calling her in the middle of the night, threatening suicide. But she had succumbed to his tricks too often, and though she felt sorry for him, she was no longer going to mother his problems. She wanted him out of her life.

There were plenty of men interested in her, and for a while she thought she'd just get pregnant and raise a child alone, but she could see from Rachel's situation that being a single mother wasn't a great solution. Then she found Jean-Paul, a French graduate student, and just when she thought she might return to France with him and have his baby, she met Tibor. She hadn't been looking for a man at the time, and so he didn't have to receive the quality of her need. He just took her in — took all of her, and she threw her passport in the basket.

It had been nine months since she and Tibor had lived together. Nine incredible months. He greeted her on her birthday morning with a tray of blintzes, a vase of purple and red anemones, hand-squeezed orange juice, and a cup of freshly ground French roast. "Eat up my sweet, for today we've got an all day date." He had rented a sailboat to sail them around the bay, out to Angel Island, where they'd have a picnic. That night, he and Rachel and Richard were taking her to Chez Panisse, and he'd pre-ordered a triple chocolate cake with sparklers.

"But first," he seemed so excited and organized, "I want you to open a couple of presents. This one came from Julia. She was smart enough to address it to me, so that I'd hold onto it for you." Martine always opened presents the minute they arrived. It was a tiny golden book, that opened like a locket. Inside Julia had painted a minuscule watercolor of a juicy-looking heart.

"This is too perfect." Martine adored it, and had Tibor hook it around her neck. "You know I never had a birthday party growing up, not once," she confessed to him.

"I can't believe that." He had been an only child and his parents had doted on him. Almost in return, he now liked to give to Martine. There was a rose-colored silk scarf from Kate. She'd done some very fine embroidery on one of the corners, little French knots that looked like a cluster of roses. "But now this one's from me," he said. It was a big book on Georgia O'Keeffe, because she loved that Southwestern land-scape, and then he gave her a peach-colored camisole, silky and sexy. "But are you ready for this?"

"More?"

"Yes. My divorce went through. I'm a free man. Well, I mean, I *am* spoken for, but . . ." She pulled him down on the bed, pushing the breakfast tray aside, and he kissed her, but then, "Wait a minute. I'm not entirely finished my dear, with all I have to say. Don't make me jump the gun." She was already undressing him, which felt a little funny, since he'd so recently gotten dressed. "I have something very important to tell you. Now, are you listening, or are you just wanton."

"I'm deaf with desire," she said, "please." She kissed his neck, moving her hand inside his shirt, but she could tell he wanted to talk first. "O.K., I'm listening."

"All of this was just a kind of warm-up act for the big news."

She couldn't quite figure him out. Why all this talking? His face looked so amused. She couldn't take her hands or eyes off him. He had such strong, manly shoulders, straight brown hair and hazel eyes.

"I bought a house," he announced. "For us."

"What?" She didn't know if she was happy or horrified. "A house?"

"Dan showed it to me a couple of weeks ago. It wasn't even on the market yet, but it's perfect. When I went inside, I knew you'd love it, window seats, and an old tiled kitchen, real homey. A big fireplace."

"A real fireplace?" She had never lived anywhere with a working fireplace.

"It's on a quiet street, and there's a big space in back for a garden, five bedrooms. You'll love it."

"Five bedrooms!" Martine gasped. What did they need with five bedrooms? She'd lose him in such a house. "Why do we need so many bedrooms?" she asked, looking worried. "I don't want to live in a commune."

"No, silly. They're for all those kids we're going to produce, starting right now." He hugged her, and she pulled him onto her, and they made love immediately and immensely.

When they came home from the sailboat ride that afternoon, dazed by the light off the rocking water, a bit sunburned and feeling warm and skin conscious, Martine found their double bed filled with a balloon garden, red balloons tied to ribbons, anchored by oranges, neatly spaced and reaching at various heights toward the ceiling. "Tulips for your two lips," the card read, and *Kisses from Rachel & Kids!* was written in red lipstick on the mirror.

Tibor cornered her again, there in the tulip balloon bedroom, lifting her up, "Into the garden with you, trowel in hand!"

She struggled against him, "Don't," not wanting to upset the lovely arrangement. They popped one as she landed. "Can't we just lie on the floor?" she asked. Already he was on top of her, and she liked his urgency, his power over her, pressing her down against her slight efforts to resist. Giving in to him was heavenly. "This must be a perfect birthday," she started to cry. She was so happy, but she couldn't stop crying, as he rocked her back and forth in his arms.

Martine Brown. She sat in the depths of the blue upholstered armchair, gripping her knees back to her chest, letting her mouth and chin both press, as if she could ponder the immensity of the day, March 14th, her birthday, and no one apparently knew. Such a melancholic expression for such a young girl, but she didn't think of herself as little. She was the oldest and often in charge.

Her younger brother and sister were still finishing their cereal when their father came through the breakfast room without saying a word directly to her. He had other things on his mind. He ran a chain of shoe stores, and sometimes she pictured him with shoes hanging from his ears, like the tiger in *Little Black Sambo,* and she was the one who had lost those crimson soles and crimson linings. She wanted her father to give *her* beautiful clothes like the father in the story, or at least a birthday hug, but he always focused his attention on her brother, "Tickets for the Dodgers this weekend," while she got out their raincoats. Her mother was still recovering. Recovering from her endless inability to perform.

Martine would slip into her mother's pink satin chamber, where the striped material was stretched across the padded walls, shades drawn against reality. She would kiss her mother goodbye on both cheeks. Her mother was not well, her father always said, and she did seem almost stupefied. When she reached out and asked, "Ça va?" Martine pulled away before getting trapped in the suffocating cloth of her sentiment. There was no way to ask — Am I going to have a cake? Do you know what day this is?

Her mother had been born in Lyon. Maybe that's what made her strange. Grand-mère had been quick to send this little Mama packing, when an American man came along, who didn't speak the language, who didn't understand the import of "les crises," and he had been blinded by his feelings — the intensity of which had also been quite foreign, and which hadn't survived the distance.

Martine wrote Julia: *I can't even begin to tell you how much I am forced to cram into one day. You are so lucky you can just stay home with your children and don't have to work. I know you have your painting, but I wonder how you manage to find inspiration when your life is so idyllic. Don't you sometimes long for real pain, true suffering? I think that's what it takes to make great art. Too bad I wasn't born some kind of artist. I could have been a new age Baudelaire or female Frances Bacon. But meat and blood are not my metaphors, they are my daily fare. Having the laparoscopy the other day I got to view my insides on film. If no one steps forward to write my biography, at least I'll have my internal organs on celluloid. Seeing my own guts like that reminded me of the time Rob left a big stinking pot of chitlins on the stove in the restaurant, as a comment on our vegetarian trend, and I think I know what he meant now, life isn't just apple brown betty or a dose of wheat grass juice, it's blood dripping from the sirloin, hunks of liver red meat in your hand. Do you think you'd be able to paint that? Get the colors of loss on the canvas? Maybe O'Keeffe did it in her way through those barren landscapes, so exposed, her life out there alone in Abiqui as raw as the terrain. Are there times when you too long for that kind of commitment and solitude?*

Julia wrote Martine, but didn't send it: *I can't begin to tell* YOU *how much I'm forced to cram into one of* MY *days. Try waking at 5:30 a.m. after four hours of sleep because Alex has a piercing ear infection and Mark has gone to Boston. So I'm single-handedly nursing, cooking, doing laundry and cleaning up, while children either need transportation or medication. Of course having two hours of cleaning help a week keeps me in the lap of luxury, but besides that, let me respond to your presumptions about my art work.*

First of all, I would never use menstrual blood on my paintings, ok? I'm not trying to achieve a carmine red shriek, and frankly, I'm a little tired of hearing about every slimy detail of your insides. Really Martine, it's as if you were the only person in the world to have feelings. You're so wrapped up in your own narcissim that you assume only your pain is worth glorification.

I don't need to live alone on some mesa in order to go on with my art. I paint because it's my life, what I do. I don't have to romanticize it, the way you do "mothering." I'm sure what you're going through is extremely difficult, but raising children is also plain hard work, and I doubt if you have an inkling of what it's like to give in that way, as you continue to indulge your every need. Yes Martine, you might indeed have been the bride of Baudelaire, or at least his inspiration, back in a time when women swallowed arsenic if things got to be too much.

I'm never going to get pregnant like this," Martine complained to Kate over the phone.

"Listen, Martine, you're no spring chicken," Kate said in her abrupt way. "Don't just sit around and wait."

"But I want it to happen naturally."

"Forget it! I know too many women in their late thirties who are having a damn hard time conceiving. It's a whole lot different than when you were seventeen."

"Thanks for reminding me."

"Well if I don't, who will?"

"So what am I supposed to do?" she whined.

"Get yourself a thermometer to start with, and figure out when you ovulate."

"Tibor would make fun of me."

"So what! You've got to get going on this. How can I

make you a baby quilt if you don't get busy?"

"I'm just so tired of getting my hopes up. I can feel it all building, and then everything collapses. It's debilitating."

"I'm sure. But it *is* going to happen," Kate tried to be encouraging, "and then you'll just forget about all this."

"Maybe it was my IUD. Maybe that damaged me somehow. The other day I got my period on BART and I felt like throwing myself from the train."

"It might help to get your mind off the subject once in a while, you know? Why don't you try asking *me* a question about *my* life."

"How's Atea?" Martine complied.

"She's great. She started piano and she's into horses. Julia's giving her some very preliminary lessons. I don't know what it is about horses and girls."

"Julia's not exactly a girl," Martine said. Equestrian sports were a bit too elitist for Martine. "I just want to know one thing," she added. "Will you come for the birth?"

"Yes," Kate complained, "I'll come for The Birth." She sounded teasingly fierce. "But see if you can't start taking some remedies. Go see a homeopath."

"But I'm a heteropath!"

"You know it's going to *take* one of these months, but you have to participate."

"Oh I'm participating all right," she laughed. "Very actively."

Months went by, and nothing happened. Nothing but more disappointment. Tibor agreed to be tested, but he had a high sperm count, and their alkaline/acidity combination didn't seem to be a problem. Martine knew that she would have to proceed with the tests, but she was afraid of that remembered pain forking her cervix.

"At least we know that a full term pregnancy was possible for me in the past," she told her gynecologist.

"But that was almost twenty years ago," the doctor responded, flipping through her file. He looked at her like some used car, assessing her.

"Do you think I'm not functioning properly? Do you think my eggs have gone bad?"

"I wouldn't put it quite like that. Age affects us all, but in different ways. I can recommend a fertility specialist. We do have the best in the country."

And so she went from male doctor to female specialist, from mucus testing to ultra sound, trying trying trying to get there, to make it take hold, in vitro sci-fi, much too expensive, pee in a cup, add powder and wait, for hope to diminish. They tried a new doctor, another, another, with penis-shaped mic and jellied glove, feeling for nodules. They tried new positions, tried not caring at all. The hormones brought nausea, not morning sickness, the sickening clockwork of the dismal drug, working against her, time itself, working against her, robbing their sex life month after month.

M artine wrote Kate: *Thirteen days late last month, and of course I ran to have a blood serum pregnancy test and didn't believe the results even when the test showed negative. I thought maybe it was too soon to tell. Then just before I had to get up to teach a class, the dark red drip. Hatefully tricked into hopefulness again. I wanted to yell at my students, WHAT DO YOU KNOW! They're working their asses off not to get pregnant. And I'm seeing RED!*

Then this red turns to grey then to black, to a loathsome, withering envy. Sometimes I almost HATE happy pregnant women, especially the cavalier ones, who never have to suffer, the ones who like to complain about feeling a little sick or tired or fat. How I'd love to be in their shoes! I don't know how much more I can take, when every month my hopes get flushed and I'm left here totally drained and lifeless.

Of course there are physical complications. My right fallopian tube is crimped, not free floating like it should be, probably due to inflammation, but the doctor has me on this fertility drug now, called Clomid, and it makes me feel uptight and exhausted at the same time. It's supposed to stimulate egg production, but so far, only nausea. I guess the best thing to come of all this is the knowledge that I'm more physically screwed up than psychologically, and that makes me feel a little bit better.

If you were here, I'd feel a hell of a lot better. I'd feel great! I just need to hear you tell me again that it WILL happen. Sometimes I think I'm blocking this out of some ingrained reflex. I guess I've trained my body to avoid pregnancy for so long, now that I want it, I've got nothing but an old dog who refuses to learn this strange new trick. So how are things chez toi?

Tibor didn't quite believe in the tests. He thought that if they began looking into adoption, focused on that, it would happen, would spring some release deep inside of her, and then she'd get pregnant before the paperwork even went through.

She still felt that she wanted to carry a child inside her, that she needed that physical experience. To get back what she'd lost so many years ago. But still she admired Tibor. Rare is the man who is willing to raise a child that isn't from his own proud seed, she thought, a man who is willing to take on some less fortunate child. She wanted to adopt a third world child, and was relieved to shift the focus away from her own body. At least there was something constructive she could do now, and they would eventually see results. No more deadly monthly disappointments, no more funerals in the womb.

But first of all, it looked like they would have to get married. "That seems like a superfluous prerequisite," Tibor said.

"They just want to make sure that the baby is coming into a happy, secure home," she explained, eager to go along with all the rules.

"And marriage guarantees that?"

"You know how I feel about marriage. But that's not the point. We have to do everything we can." Still, Martine thought, if they were to adopt a handicapped child, if they were willing to take on a baby that no one else wanted, maybe it wouldn't matter if they were married or not.

Tibor wasn't so sure about this, but she went ahead, active in the whole process of adopting. Paging through one agency's catalogue of available children, she kept coming back to this one bright face of a little Brazilian boy, Guilherme. Tibor also liked his looks, but the child was two and a half years old and had Spina Bifida, paralyzed from the waist down. This made Tibor hesitate.

"I think we should request a CAT scan, and see if there is any mental retardation," he said. She had a virtually unshakeable desire to adopt this boy. For the moment she agreed with Tibor, that if there was mental retardation, they wouldn't carry through with the adoption. At the same time, she could feel herself ignoring this precaution. She wanted him so badly. He looked like he could even be her son. Tibor saw that she wasn't recognizing her own limitations and asked her, "Wouldn't you really rather have a baby? So much is formed in those first two years." He felt that she would thank him later for not allowing her to commit herself to raising a child if he did have a severe handicap. But she was only impatient.

Then more pictures of Guilherme were sent, and they looked so different from the first shot. His head seemed swollen, enlarged, and she realized that she had partly fallen in love with a photograph of a bright-eyed, loving looking child, but still she wanted him.

When they found out that he was indeed brain-damaged, she was devastated, but said, "I just don't care. I have to have that baby."

Tibor was still open to adopting a child, but held firm, "I can't do something so radical. I think we'd regret it."

"All of a sudden you're conservative? The radical lawyer changes his tune on his own home front? You're just so wrapped up in your own career, you can't see what this means to me! How important it is." But mainly she was angry at herself for letting her heart get so attached, angry that

she hadn't been turned away sooner. It was hard to let
go.

She still wanted to carry on, and kept looking, and Tibor
agreed to follow through with the adoption home study. This
part of the process was not as intrusive as she thought it would
be. The woman asked them a variety of questions, like: "Tell
me about the two people who have been most influential in
your life."

Tibor spoke of his parents, Martine of Julia and Kate.
This led the woman to ask if she'd ever been a lesbian, and
Martine laughed, suppressing the response she wanted to
give—Well I hope so!

"What does your husband mean to you?"

Martine had to explain that he wasn't her husband.

"But we will be getting married soon," Tibor surprised
them both.

The woman looked like she didn't believe this, especially since Martine responded, "Really?"

"Why do you want to adopt?"

He let Martine answer this question, though he said,
"She would make an excellent mother."

"And what about you?" the woman inquired of
him.

"Oh, I'd make a good mother too," he laughed.

"What do you like most about children?"

This question made them feel like children themselves,
remembering their own childhoods. The woman had to guide
them back on the track.

"What do some parents do in relation to their children
which you dislike?"

Martine went over in detail the whole incident with
Vergil and the slinky.

"What is your philosophy of life, in about twenty words
or less. Tell me about everyone in your family. How would
you discipline your child. What is a typical weekend like for
you. Tell me about two crises you've experienced in your life,

and what kind of support you received getting through them. What kind of child do you think would best fit into your family."

When Martine thought honestly about that she realized, "A healthy, small baby, of any color or sex."

"That would be best for us," Tibor concluded.

Martine realized how she loved being interviewed, loved explaining her feelings, hearing Tibor's responses. They had five of these meetings, each lasting but one short hour, and then a social worker came and inspected the potential future environment of their potential adoptive child. Martine pointed out all the extra bedrooms, explaining that they hoped to adopt more than one child. They wanted a big family.

The social worker only stressed how important it was that they should be in complete harmony about the kind of child they wanted.

"This dispute over Guilherme — I must tell you, I don't see it as a good sign."

Martine was quick to respond. "I was being way too headstrong about that, I know. I just wanted a baby so badly, I fixated on that little boy, but I can see now that I was over-extended. Tibor was absolutely right."

"Well there is another couple actively seeking to adopt the child, if that's any help."

"It is," she admitted. It was a lot easier for Martine to let go of the dream on hearing that.

"It really doesn't matter to us what country the baby comes from," Tibor said.

"Or if it's a boy or girl," Martine added, though she secretly hoped for a boy, and she'd heard that girls were in greater demand, "but it would be so nice to have a newborn."

"And a child that would grow up healthy," Tibor put in.

"That's asking for a lot," the counsellor said.

But when Martine imagined her child out there,

somewhere in the world, perhaps in utero, also waiting, she remained undaunted, evidence of the invincibility or stubbornness of her need.

Julia's occasional, whimsical postcards to Philip still brought no response, and as she entered the middle of her third trimester, she felt disturbed by this silence, his apparent lack of concern. How could he be so aloof? She had stopped wearing the pin he had given her, put it away in a velvet pouch, for special times, she thought.

Martine tried to assure her that it hadn't really been *so* long, as they sat up late, drinking Red Zinger out of glasses stirred with honey. Martine insisted that Julia let him call first. "Maybe one of the most important lessons you have to learn from all this is how to control your emotions. Or how to give up control of the situation, and let him take the lead. I know it's hard to wait, but believe me, it'll only put him off if you chase after him." This sounded like what they were all supposed to know.

Tibor walked in in the middle of this conversation. He stood there by the stove, heating up coffee, listening, though rather absently. He was getting tired of Julia and her problems.

"Seven weeks is almost two months," Julia reminded her, "and it feels like years, like an eon."

"You have to remember the kind of life he leads. How busy he is," Martine went on, repeating what Julia had said herself while trying to erect her own defense, her own set of explanations for this silence.

"I think you should call him," Tibor announced. "Why not? You're a liberated woman. Just give him a ring." He made it sound so easy, though she hadn't thought of herself as liberated for a long time.

"Tibor, you're wrong," Martine stuck up for her own point of view.

186

"Well at least she'll know, and then you can stop talking about it."

"Oh to hell with it," Julia said. This was the father of her baby, and she would call him if she had to. He had been negligent in the past, had gone for six weeks one time without contacting her, though he had been travelling for a good part of that period, and his lack of communication then hadn't actually meant disinterest — if anything, it had intensified their relationship. But at the same time, she had waited for him to call. She had remained cool, and that had made him hot to pursue. But how long could she hold out now?

She remembered what Kate had gone through with Conrad, months and months with no word, no communication, how Julia had told her, "Men don't write. They just can't." But then Conrad had finally sent a telegram announcing his arrival, for good, for marriage and for life.

So Julia worked this around and around, and decided that she'd excuse her pride and call him in a week if she hadn't heard. She even went so far as to leave extra change for the postman in the mailbox, since the rates had just gone up and a letter might come under-stamped. Martine hated to see her in such a state, and tried to distract her with movies, dragged her along to a benefit poetry reading Rachel was giving in the city, but Julia fell asleep, always tired at the wrong time. She felt swollen and heavy in the evening, and she had to pee so often — that was aggravating in a public place. She just wanted to put her feet up, to sit in silence and knit.

Rachel and her kids had moved into Richard's apartment in San Francisco, and even though it was only a thirty-minute drive, Rachel now seemed distant. All of Rachel's energy was going into making this relationship work. One week they were going to get married, and then Richard wasn't sure. Julia felt like she was the one who always called, and Rachel sounded apologetic but rushed, "What a run around the pony ring this is, but I guess he's worth it." Martine accused Rachel of never making an effort with her girlfriends, that she was too male-oriented, but Rachel laughed that off, and Julia didn't really hold it against her, since she had Martine to lean on.

Julia had found a wonderful obstetrician at Alta Bates, a gentle Chinese man, Dr. Chou, who was as calm and easy as a midwife.

Julia's father had offered to cover the expenses of the birth, though both of her parents were upset, implying that she should have had an abortion. Her mother thought she was crazy, "Throwing your life away! No real mother would ever desert her children."

"I'm not deserting them," she said. "I'm doing everything in my power, and I love those boys."

"If you loved them, you'd be with them. Like a normal mother."

She had never told them how Mark had beaten her up, how she'd feared for the life of this baby. All she could say was, "It's not that simple."

They didn't want to explore this new pregnancy, which seemed obscene to them. She wanted to tell them about Philip, but her mother cut her short. "You always had very poor judgment."

And her father put in, "I just feel sorry for those boys."

But she knew she loved her children, thought of them constantly, wrote them every day, and drew them pictures, sent them Audubon stamps, little presents—caps, balloons, stickers, funny scented pens, clothes she'd picked up on sale. She called them every other night, for Mark had decided to let her talk, and was almost acting decent these days. Kate reported that his girlfriend came up from Boston every weekend, and the boys seemed to like her. Julia wanted to make a visit back east, to see them, to talk with Mark and both their lawyers, but she was getting so big now. Still, she used the excuse of a trip as a reason to contact Philip.

She waited until after business hours, before dinner time,

to call him in New York. She had secured the privacy of Martine and Tibor's upstairs bedroom. Tibor was out playing the trumpet that night, and Martine was in the kitchen making chicken soup. That comforting smell filled the house. Julia decided to call collect, like she used to do from the country. She'd get a chance to hear his voice, answering, before she had to talk, a moment to catch her breath.

"A collect call for Philip Mercato from Julia Chapin," she told the operator. Even that sounded so formal. She hadn't felt like this since she'd called about her serum pregnancy test, and the baby must have sensed her emotion, felt the adrenalin, for he started to kick and turn, and she put her one free hand on her belly, spreading her legs, as she sat on the edge of the bed and listened to his phone ring long distance.

A woman's voice answered, and Julia flushed from head to hands. Should she hang up?

"This is a collect call," the operator repeated the message, and there was some talking within a pause, an interminable pause in the background.

"He will accept the call," the woman said coolly, "but she'll have to wait a minute."

Shit, Julia thought. So he had to explain to this woman on the other end who Julia Chapin was before taking the call in his study, alone. She felt like announcing her role in his life. She felt like demanding — who was that?

"Hello darling," he said, in his most suave, most New York, put-on, controlled voice, the voice she remembered him using before he felt comfortable, before he relaxed into his own real voice. This was his trained voice, his timed voice, his little white-lie manner man voice.

"Hi," she said, "how are you?" as if she had just climbed fourteen steep stairs and was catching her breath, trying to sound casual. "Just thought I'd check in." Her voice rose, optimistic. Oh boy, she breathed out. "How's the polo?"

"It's wonderful," he exclaimed, "a fabulous sport." He said it with too much enthusiasm. "I guess it's gotten under my skin. It's much harder than it looks, but you gave me some very good training. Remember all those rides?"

Remember? Was he kidding? It wasn't that long ago. "Do you know what happened to my horse?" she asked, her voice quavering slightly. "You heard about Frank."

"That was terrible," he dismissed it. "I sold Sensation too." But he didn't answer her about Bunko. "Now tell me, how are you? How are *you* feeling."

"I'm feeling very pregnant at the moment," she admitted, encouraged by his asking, but afraid that he might not like to picture her that way. "I miss you so much," she blurted out. "I was hoping you'd be able to swing another visit, before the birth. Or I could come back east, to see the boys." She waited for him to offer his place.

"It's amazing that you called tonight," he responded. "I was just beginning to write you a letter this morning. And I'm just wondering . . ." he paused.

"What?" she asked too quickly, trying to read the situation, hating the formality of this bi-coastal distance. "Don't you want to see me?"

"Of course I'd like to see you," he said, "I just wish this letter had gotten to you first."

"What's wrong?"

"Listen darling, to be quite frank," it sounded like he was forcing himself to dive off some treacherous point into a dark and dangerous pool, "I'm going to be getting married. Probably this December."

Julia wanted to laugh. She found herself laughing, ready to throw up. "Are you kidding me?" She laughed some more, the tears rising, spontaneously, as the tone of her voice dropped down. "You're serious."

"I'm very serious," he said kindly, calmly, and now it was his voice. "It just happened, I wasn't—"

"Who is it?" she demanded.

"Someone you don't know. Renata's cousin, actually. A woman about your age."

"Ha," she sneered. "About my age. But she fits the bill."

"Yes," he said. "I'm sorry."

"Well fuck the bill!" Julia said, and then added, "Does she know there's a woman out here in California, seven months pregnant with your baby? Or maybe that doesn't even matter to you."

"I was going to tell her about that tonight," he explained. "That's why this is so odd."

"I guess I should have waited til tomorrow!"

"Things don't have to change between us," he had the nerve to add, to patch things up, to placate her for the moment.

"Yeah, it's always been screwed up, so why change now?"

"I mean we can still see each other. You know I care about you."

I must be out of my mind, she thought.

"Julia?" he asked, but she didn't answer. Tears were dropping on her maternity blue jeans. She felt such hatred, bitterness, violence. She could have destroyed herself and the baby inside her. She could have left the receiver on the bedspread, and thrown herself out the window, let him listen to the ambulance roaring up. "Julia," he said, "are you there?"

She wanted to scream, You asshole! Reptile! Cunt abuser! The temperature radically dropping inside of her, freezing these thoughts, even as they came.

"Come on, Julia, I've got to go. Can't you talk?"

Then in a low and shaking voice she made herself speak. "You'll never see this baby's face." She wanted it to sting like dry ice. "I don't *ever* want you to cross my path again. Do you understand? And I'll send back that stupid lie of a pin." She pictured herself taking a hammer to it, smashing it.

"Wait a minute," he said, trying to resume control. "I want to help you, and the baby." She realized he meant financially.

"I don't want a penny of yours. Not a cent! I just can't believe you're doing this. It's not fair," she was sobbing now, hysterical, almost not breathing, or speaking clearly. She felt she was literally breaking her heart. She could feel it snap inside her, like a piece of frozen meat, as the door to the freezer chest fell, as it all sank into the iceberg. He no longer, wanted, her.

"Is there someone there with you?" he asked, concerned about her in this extreme state."

"No!" she screamed violently into the phone, and then slammed it down, kept her hand on it, as if it might jump at her, then quickly took it off again and buried it under the pillow she clutched, so it wouldn't ring if he tried to call back. There was nothing more to say. He did try to call. But it was busy. And he had to go out.

She imagined how quickly he'd compose himself, how elegantly he would resume another guise, of fiancé, of lover, man about town, while she would never get over this.

She gripped the pillow and sobbed, trying to muffle the sound but it felt like the baby inside her was flailing, thrashing about and bawling for them both.

Martine came and stood outside the door, knocked gently and called her name, "Jule? You o.k.? Can I come in?"

Julia was crying too hard to answer, but Martine came in, sat down beside her, rubbed her back, "That bad, huh?"

She sobbed in response, leaned off the bed, afraid she would vomit, but only dry heaved once, then groaned, "He's getting married. To someone. Can you believe it?"

Martine didn't respond at once, but thought how Julia should never have trusted him. "Maybe it's for the best," she said.

"My poor baby," Julia cried. "I have really been such a wretch."

"No you haven't. You did the best thing." Martine applied both hands and rubbed Julia's neck, which helped to calm her down. "I'm going to bring you up a little chicken soup. You just get under these covers. You've had a shock, and you need to rest. Just think of how you love that baby."

192

What was strange was that she did love the baby even more. They had been abandoned in this mess together. She clung, internally, to the idea of this baby on the way. She felt even more attached for some reason. And when she caught herself thinking — will he look like his father — she realized that she'd have to be prepared to accept that, even if he were a walking, breathing remembrance of the man she'd loved most in her life. She would never say anything against him, in the small child's presence. But she'd make her boy believe that he'd had a prince for a father, a kind and caring man, who had died, for Philip *had* died inside her. She carried his tomb in her heart. She laid flowers there morning and evening, and watched them wilt, replacing them daily, as if that might bring him back, knowing deep down that what was over was final, unmistakable as certain death.

Lying alone, night after night, anger rising and subsiding, her body tense, rigid, her bitterness turned to rage — how dare he do this to her. She wanted to scratch his suntanned face. She put a curse on his family, hoped that *his* daughter would get knocked up. He would never see this baby of his. His name would not continue. She would take her boys and move back to New Mexico. She would disappear with his progeny from the face of the civilized earth. She wanted to torture the remains of her love until it was forced to leave her. But even these thoughts of hatred fed her love and kept him alive inside her.

Sleep was difficult now. Often she woke up gasping, as if she'd been held underwater. She had to sit up, and lean forward, trying to catch her breath. It was hard falling back to sleep after that. All she could think of was Philip, the baby, and then her children. Back and forth, alone. Her mind raced on and she followed where it went, lunging and stumbling like a damaged horse.

It had been a cold, spring afternoon, when she heard that animal's repeated cry, way back in the woods behind their house. She had followed the sound, way off the path, until she saw a fawn, perhaps only five days old, with its neck stuck between a sharp rock and a fallen birch tree. The creature struggled as she approached, and when she lifted the limb, it made an uncertain effort to escape, leaping forward, only to collapse into the wet and brilliant ferns. The greyness of the afternoon made the colors vivid. The animal was so delicate. She moved forward to collect it, the live heart beating terribly in her hands, but she talked calmly to it, and held the legs close, so it wouldn't kick out, and that gentle firmness of touch and voice made it succumb, relax. She carried it home like that, in her arms, and its scraped neck bled on her white shirt. She wanted to try and keep it alive, to nurture it some, before returning it to the wilds where it belonged.

Both Thomas and Ross raced up. They wanted to bring it into the house and Julia agreed, for it did seem to need the extra warmth. It was the kind of day that seemed to pull all of the body's heat out through the soles of rubber boots, and she shivered as she brought this wild thing in, sent Thomas off for wool blankets, Ross for the heating pad and ticking clock. Even Alexander offered up one of his old bottles. Its hooves were so black, no bigger than quarters. Its spotted back was sleek and warm, but the thinness of the ears felt cool, eyes glazed.

She lifted the head and stroked the gullet before trying to tempt the fawn to open its mouth for the warmed, raw milk. It seemed to taste, and waved its flag once, a sign of life the boys encouraged, but it must have forgotten how to suck, or didn't have the energy to draw what it needed, helpless, and content to drift further away. She primed the small mouth by offering and withdrawing the bottle's nipple, and it took a little, but not much. She tested the milk again on her wrist. Perhaps it had grown too cool. Thomas quickly moved to reheat the bottle in a pan on the stove, and then they all stood around, trying to coax the creature back — as if their mutual will made a cradle in which to rock it, but

194

it barely had the strength to open its mouth, succumbing to some inner chill.

"Maybe it wants its Mama," Alexander said.

"Maybe it does," she answered.

She asked the two older boys to make a fire in the stove, anything to warm them. Rossie could crush the paper, get the kindling. Thomas could light the match. Odd having this wild animal inside with them. Also odd for her to feel how on-call her maternal instincts were, ready to flow out to anything helpless. She was willing to sit up all night with it, as if it personified her own vulnerable love, which she'd abandoned to the fickle kindness of the world, trapped as she was, hoping to be freed, and wanting her love to survive, but that too hung in the balance, between the forces of warmth and cold, between the urge to suck and the gradual giving up, between the color of fern and turned sod, between the heaviness of rain, which had just begun, and the slanting of the roof, between her and the great unknown. She had given everything she could.

But as she stroked the long, soft neck, and fed the wounded warm milk — her love died in her arms.

She no longer spoke about Philip. Martine and Rachel understood that the subject was closed, but they still talked about "him" together.

"Obviously a total no-good jerk," Martine summed him up, rinsing the dishes, stacking them in great order.

"Who's a jerk?" Lianna asked, but they ignored her.

"I knew he was a money man, but this is cruel," Rachel added, "or maybe he's just unconscious, the kind of child brain that zooms into a candy store and grabs."

Martine caught the pot from its shrill whistling, poured them all some Mellow Mint tea. The mention of candy made Lianna dig into her mother's purse for gum. Finding it, and then given the nod, she trounced off to watch TV.

"That kind of man's got a cock like a periscope," Martine sat down. "Julia's just too inexperienced. I would have seen it a mile away."

"But how could he do this to her?"

"How could he not, it's his nature. He's a horse trader," Martine blew at the top of her tea. "We really should get together and geld the guy."

That man makes Mark look decent," Martine attempted to open the subject, but Julia just shook her head, and then asked Martine if she'd phone her husband. She wanted him to send the boys out for a visit.

She watched Martine use the way she had with men to coax him, telling him how Julia had been alone and under their wing, indicating bluntly that she was "no longer in a relationship." Julia swung her head, no, to keep Martine from saying anything about Philip, but Martine went on, "You know I really think that Julia is eager to work things out, but don't you think the boys should see her? They all should see each other. Are they worried about her? Well, that's good. But aren't they curious about the birth? You should prepare them for that."

Martine explained to Mark how she was going to help at the birth, how she and Julia had been going to prenatal yoga classes together, and how great it even made *her* feel. "And we're going to a refresher Lamaze class too." Mark seemed so good natured about all this, indicating to Martine that his new girlfriend was also a kind of artist, but that she didn't have such a big ego. She painted *faux marble* and *faux bois* for a living. He was amenable to the plan if Julia paid for the plane fare.

When Martine hung up, she had to translate the entire conversation.

"Why did you say *but* aren't they curious?" Julia wanted

196

to know. Martine couldn't remember, but the boys were doing fine.

"You know he even admitted that it was getting hard, taking care of them with his teaching schedule." Martine could identify with that, and she said how he had almost sounded "generous."

"Sure, if *I* pay for the plane fare. He could always afford to be generous with me around."

He had made Martine laugh a few times, and she had found herself liking his humor — it brought back the old days, when everyone was included, and they used to eat fabulous big Thanksgiving and Christmas Eve dinners together.

"I really don't even miss him," Julia told Martine. "I guess I lived through that phase before I even left him."

But her children she missed violently. Four weeks. They would come in four weeks. Julia wondered if she'd be too big to actually lift Alexander, but she now imagined his face, his sleeping hands. She pictured his Tonka truck tractor, scooping away, outside in their hexagonal sandbox, Ross with his Lincoln Logs, and Thomas working hard with his spirograph set. She drew pictures of her boys playing cards before their Amity stove on the stone hearth corner of their living room, how cozy that room was with its red plaid curtains, New England so far away. She thought of the boys building leaf houses, making a new fort in the woods — how they'd soon be pulling sleds up the drive. She could almost taste those cold, exhilarated cheeks, how Alexander would look clumsy in his snowsuit, Juba bouncing in the background.

Juba, her chow, her faithful one. The dog had not been herself, Kate said.

Julia pictured her cold barn studio, the paintings she had deserted, how Thomas used to trudge out there sometime after school, sit on the stool by the heater and watch her, or make his own watercolors on the floor. How big he seemed now, so much older, a kerchief tied around his neck, the way he sauntered, the secret way he loved her, the little boy inside the big boy frame. He cried more easily than any of them. She cried for him most of all.

She marvelled that they were coming. She would make them sloppy joes, and cream-tuna-noodle casserole, BLT's, their favorites. She would go to the library soon and get out some good books, cuddle them under both arms, say "ding" when it was time to turn the page. She'd show them how she'd prepared a cradle for their baby brother, and she would have to find a way to speak about it — how this baby would need them also, as much as they needed each other. How he would be a half brother, but how they could make him feel included, how she wanted them to come back after he was born. They would look at some of the tiny clothes for a moment perhaps, and then race out to play. She would buy them all new tennies, and Ross would have to have velcro. Even at his age, he was concerned about fashion and what everybody thought. He would be the coolest toward her. Alex would be excited about the baby, because that meant that he would no longer be the youngest, but he would also want her to constantly hold him. He would probably make a terror of himself, just to get more attention, so she would try and dote on him, give him extra helpings. She'd take them up to Tilden Park for a pony ride, and they'd all walk out to Inspiration Point. Julia tried to take a long walk every day, and felt fit, strong, and healthy.

Rachel had settled into Richard's apartment in the city, but what was odd, was that he had just been offered a job in Albuquerque, New Mexico, and they were considering another move. Rachel was excited about the possibility, but she didn't want to go unless they were married.

Julia thought about Wisconsin, eventually going back to the farm house that was part of the family estate. She believed her parents would soften if they could spend time with the baby. Maybe she should go back east, but not with Philip getting married. Maybe she should find her own place here, but would Mark really be willing to relocate? She felt like she didn't belong anywhere. She knew that she was getting on Tibor's nerves. She just wanted to be with her children.

She grieved that she wasn't there to put Rossie to bed, to hear his prayers or to sing to Alexander, to watch Thomas in the Greek play his class was performing. He had written her a funny note, saying he was "Hades" in the Persephone play, and how he had to wear her sandals. Imagine him wearing her own 8½ size sandals. But how did he feel, not having her there to hear him deliver his lines, without her there to congratulate him. She felt his need like a hardened fist inside her, and when she tried to loosen it, make it drift away, by morning it had returned, that lump in her solar plexus.

Martine wanted Julia to come over to the city for a big parade. "You've got to get your mind on other things, outside yourself." But Julia felt that she was too pregnant for such a crowd.

Martine admitted later that even she had been almost afraid, "There were so many people, at least 50,000." Tibor had played his trumpet in the marching band and Martine had tagged along beside him. She described the music as festive, the crowd, magnificent, with every affinity group you could imagine. "There was the usual stuff," she said, against intervention in Nicaragua, the pro-Salvadorean group, Free Prisoners, get out of Israel, the Gray Panthers, Brits out of Ireland, the UFW, the UFW and friends, a City of San Francisco bus in the middle of it all, plus these two school buses full of waving children. "They were so cute!" Postal union clerks, filmmakers, the Communist Party, Marin Concerned Citizens, Lesbians against everything, the Bay Area Anti-Sexist Men's League with a giant banner at the foot of it all.

"Did I miss anything?" Julia asked.

"Not really."

Tibor was off on his next project, trying to help the homeless, and attempting to advise a group of poor black families in Oakland, who were being evicted from their apartment building. He was always trudging off to this meeting or that, after being in court all morning. He was all over the place, as if the slightest breeze affected him, but in his spare moments, late at night, he was still able to focus on Martine.

Martine wrote Kate: *Some day I'll write and tell you it was all worth it, right? But right now, I wonder. I really think these adoption people get some kind of vicarious charge out of gobbling up all the private musings of our lives. I realize there's fierce competition out there for babies, but do I really have to market myself? Perfect Prospective Parent with Pleasing Partner? Too bad the histories belie the resumes. Too fucking bad I'm considered grandmother material in Brazil or we might have had our own little beauty by now. How I'd love to have a dark-haired child, with big brown eyes. Too bad there aren't more romantic teenage girls out there, willing to carry a baby like I did, just to give us a chance.*

I'm trying to get Rachel to organize a baby shower for Julia. I'm tired of being in charge of everything all the time, and Rachel never puts much energy into our friendships when there's a man around. You know how I feel about Richard. Can you believe they're thinking of moving to New Mexico? That would certainly be a full circle. It does look like he wants a child of his own, and she's offered to have yet another operation to get her tubes untied, but he's unsure about marriage until the operation's proved successful, and she doesn't want to go through with it unless they're hitched. Going nowhere fast.

As good as Tibor is to me, sometimes I'd like to go out and just screw some stranger. I'm dying to flirt, but I don't feel sexy. I have lost all sense of passion. Desire has only one object, this unknown, nameless infant. I do worry endlessly. What if it all came true? You know how I resent doing laundry, and I need my sleep!

Last night I talked with this young birth mother, and she was so obnoxious, asking the weirdest questions, mostly about religion and my eating habits. Did I believe in reincarnated relationships, and would I ever smoke dope in the presence of "her" child?

Tibor is losing his ebullience, tired of his own goofing perhaps,

200

tired of keeping up the happy face after so many variations on disappointment. Funny how I almost feel better when he's low, happier when he's a bastard.

Most women would settle for a good man and a good job, and I know I should feel lucky, but I was made to crave more. I would like to adopt a hundred children.

Rachel wrote Kate: *Lianna's birthday was simple, yet ebullient. Several children, godmother Julia holding the helium balloons, looking a bit like a balloon herself. We had this glorious birthday parade, with musical instruments down Divisadero, Lianna leading on her red bicycle with training wheels, which Richard bought for her. It's so nice to be with a generous man for a change. She rides it around the dining room table, to our chagrin. But she's an amazingly centered being, who gives me strength and courage. Vergil had stomach flu yesterday — threw up and flushed his retainer down the toilet. $300. YIKES! It couldn't be helped, poor darling.*

Anyway, Richard does want a child of his own, and Kate, you know, it makes me so sad to have to think — is this really appropriate? Sometimes I think SURE — I love this guy, and I'd risk it even if the operation weren't successful. But if it wasn't, then would he want to find someone else? I know it would have been better for me to have met someone who already had kids, but I'm crazy about this man and think we're terrific together. He makes me laugh hard, is extremely kind, thoughtful, loves bed and board, has a wonderful lucid mind, a mensch instead of a dredle.

He does make me move forward in a more realistic way, but even that goes against the grain, for I'm used to the leap of the dance in romance, and I think he is sometimes shocked at how crazy life can be with children running around. This does bewilder me, you know, for either he's with us, or he's not. Sometimes I'm terrified that this is just another rehearsal for pain. Why can't it all be more simple? I know my life has been messy and complicated, while he likes to have things exact, in control. All I've ever really wanted was to have a solid family, and now I feel like I've sabotaged the boat. Kate, do you see how complicated this path has become?

Julia wrote Kate: *My own state of mind still takes me by surprise, as fierce as these Braxton Hicks contractions. I know you always warned me, and it's clear that I was blinded, but I am still so obsessed by this man, it makes me despise myself. I just wish I had your strength of will, and could do as you would — forget him! I know that silence and absence are the only things that can help, and I'm hoping the labor will release me. Light a candle for me, o.k., when it begins. We'll let you know. I miss you so damn much. You are my lifeline connection to those boys, and you have been an angel. You don't know how wild I am to see them. Meanwhile, I've been doing a huge series of these tiny watercolors — odd painting in miniature, and I finished working on the design for Rachel's book. I hope you will forgive me for flogging the above subject matter ad nauseam. I know I'll get over him, and what a relief that will be. Could you lend me the baby sweater with the ducks on it?*

Three days before the boys were due to arrive, Julia woke up at 3:33 a.m. She lay there in the darkness wondering — what brings labor on? She wasn't sure if these cramps were "true labor" or just the intense Braxton Hicks contractions she'd been feeling for weeks. She decided to go downstairs.

"What's going on?" Martine looked half-asleep. She had heard Julia moaning.

"I think it's started," Julia said.

Martine didn't seem to comprehend, "But this isn't even the right month." Martine grew more awake as Julia walked slowly down the uncovered wooden steps. She had an over-whelming urge to water the house plants.

Martine followed her down, helped her light several candles, and it was rather nice, prolonging that wavery, flickering world of semi-darkness, stopping when a contraction came to lean against a wall, moaning softly like a foghorn, round, open, low, expelling the abdominal tension, going under the wave, rather than trying to ride it out on top.

"Can you time me?" Julia leaned on her friend. Ten minutes between contractions, obviously no progression, but Julia assured her that she wasn't hurting too bad, and the hot water bottle pressed against her back gave her some relief.

A deep hot tub helped even more. She could barely feel the contractions, submerged in the total warmth of that wet relax, and she thought about the baby in utero, enjoying its last perfect hours, how the baby was suspended in fluids just as she was in the bath, glad to be taking the beginning of this labor nice and slow. And so she rested there with the steam and candlelight, letting her fingers float, letting her mind swim out, as Martine began preparing a basket of food, some goodies they could take to the hospital.

But the labor didn't really get moving that night. Julia was able to go back to bed, catching winks of sleep between those spaced out contractions. When daylight finally did appear, she made her promised phone calls, first to Rachel, then to Kate and her boys. Mark answered. She almost felt the impulse to call him, "Honey," like she had, for she couldn't help thinking of the three other times when she had been like this, in early labor, how he had stood by her, so attentive, helping her through it all. He seemed to remember that too, and his voice betrayed him.

"The boys will be disappointed," he said.

"I know, I hate to postpone them. But at least they'll get

to see the baby now when they come. Tell them that I'll call as soon as I know."

"Are you going to be o.k.?" he asked. But she couldn't tell him how afraid she was, bringing this baby into the world without a man beside her, how she needed someone big and strong to lean against. She made him wait a minute when a contraction came.

"All right," she breathed out. "That was a long one."

"Maybe the boys can come for Thanksgiving. I was hoping to be in Boston."

This admission cut into her, but she only said, "Perfect, fine."

"We'll all be thinking of you," he seemed so affable now.

"Thanks," she answered. "I'm sorry."

"I know," he said, "but it's o.k."

Even this generosity saddened her. He was happier now without her. Then another contraction hit.

Most pain is persistent, while contractions simply appear and disappear. When one comes, you are thrown completely into the present tense, riding out that minute on a twisting, internal bronco, and when the contraction ends, it's as if some fairy godmother had just tapped you on the head—*ping*. Feeling fine, just walking around, talking on the phone, when—*ping,* the spell is cast for another moaning minute—the world stops and the underworld starts to spin—to grind, to halt, to groan—*ping,* but then the morning sun shines through and all the sparrows are singing—*ping.*

The morning passed, and Martine hovered close by, brought Julia a cup of beef bouillon. Nothing ever tasted so good. Reminiscent of childhood sickroom scenes, its very aroma meant sustenance.

Dr. Chou wanted her to be examined that morning, but the check-up indicated that nothing was wrong. She was coming early, but the baby was in a good position, and a healthy size. He told her not to call back until the contractions were five minutes apart.

Martine suggested that they take a walk up at the Rose Garden and pick one special flower, which they could take to the hospital. "Remember," Martine reminded, "it's good to try and visualize an opening rose, turning gradually open," but then another contraction came, and flowers were the last thing on Julia's mind.

"Funny," Julia said, "how it feels like it's tightening, when it's actually opening you up."

It was lovely early evening, the city foggy clean, the Golden Gate a sober grey, and the clouds above appeared to be building. Because of the hour and atmosphere, the colors were intense.

They looked out across the water toward the Golden Gate, the gap beneath it like an open cervix, leaving them in utero, on the inside of the bay, and looking toward that gate, Julia wondered out loud, "I just wonder who we are waiting to meet." She caressed that little being, who was getting a strong muscle stroke from its mama's heavyweight bag.

"I heard that the uterus is the strongest muscle in the human body," Martine announced. She always had these facts. "And that includes the biggest bicep of the strongest man on earth."

Julia smiled. She liked the idea, but she remained quiet, internal. They walked the amphitheater of roses, from one level to the next, focusing on those flowers. When the gardener asked when she was due, Martine responded, "Any minute." He leaned over and picked her a beautiful, almost blue flower, lavender blue, one of her favorite colors.

Back home, Martine made herself a hamburger, while Julia ate a slice of cantaloupe, more bouillon and a bite of burger. She was getting pretty hungry, and doubted if her stomach had shut off as it was supposed to do. Would nothing make these contractions get serious? But as she went upstairs for bed, she knew it was changing. As soon as she lay down, she began to have contractions five minutes apart, and her legs began to shake. "Martine!" she cried. "Call Dr. Chou."

It had started to rain, and a light effervescence pumped the air, cool, damp, exhilarating. Oh, but these contractions were getting intense now, very urgent. Martine dropped her at the night time emergency entrance to Alta Bates, right where Julia had brought Rachel, laboring with Lianna.

As soon as they reached the deserted lobby, Julia's stomach hit stop. She rushed toward the bathroom down the corridor, banged in and let it go, heave after heave. She probably shouldn't have eaten.

"You'll feel so much better now," Martine encouraged, but Julia only felt overwhelmed.

The nurse in charge of Labor & Delivery was phoning for the A.B.C. assistant. She arrived within minutes. Everything was clicking — Dr. Chou was on call, the rain — a good sign, the quiet evening on the floor, the availability of the room. Martine was right beside her, concerned, as present as her own body, and they were moving together in this. Julia tried not to think of Philip, how he should have been there too. She jerked herself back from that thought with the start of the next contraction. She needed the Lamaze breathing now. Martine held up 2, 3, or 4 fingers, for a rhythm of pant-pant-blow. The labor was getting so strong, and Julia felt that she might get weepy. Thank God Martine was with her.

The nurse said that she was already six centimeters dilated, and Julia was beginning to shift into that other world of intense concentration, the rugged, strained part of the climb, no switchbacks now, transition.

Dr. Chou appeared and the room buzzed with extra activity. They got the lighting right, and now her moans were getting higher, harder to keep down in the low zone. Between contractions, Julia stripped off her clothes. She didn't want anything on. It was all so fast. With every extreme contraction, she began to throw her head about, almost frantic.

"Look at the rose," Martine reminded, "look into the opening rose." She turned the flower on the bedside table, and Julia tried to focus, but she only wanted to look out, far far away, absenting herself from her body. She looked to Dr. Chou, and felt like her eyes were pleading, helplessly pleading with him to help. It hurt *it hurt* It Hurt IT HURT, beyond bearable, beyond a sane amount of pain, and when Dr. Chou examined her, it felt like human torture.

"If you feel like pushing now, you can push," Dr. Chou said calmly, but that seemed next to impossible. They had just arrived. How could it happen so fast. It never had before.

"Pretty soon you're going to have your baby," the nurse whispered, wiping her forehead with a cool washcloth. Julia took it in her hands. She wanted cool! clean! hands! But she didn't feel the urge to push. Why not?

"I feel no urge," she protested.

"You're definitely ten centimeters," the doctor said, with his hand inside her, and Julia's waters burst, spraying his glasses and hospital gown. He was laughing. They were all laughing, everyone but Julia, who wanted them all to Shut Up! She was so serious, engaged, in the middle of a fierce contraction.

And so she began to push, not with the urge so much as from memory, from training. She knew how to grab the outside of her knees, and press down with a chest of breath, pushing with all her upper muscles. It did seem to help control the contractions, pushing down on their incredible intensity with her own. As soon as the contraction was over, she wanted a tiny ice chip, and Martine was there to serve her, reheating washcloths for her perineum, cold washcloths for her face and hands. She only had a minute to get ready for the next bout. Her hair seemed drenched. She was sweaty and slippery. "And I never even perspire," she laughed, weakly, but then—OH! She pushed *she pushed* She Pushed SHE PUSHED with all her might, and out came, shit. She lay her head back on the pillows, while they wiped it up and whisked it away, making nothing of it.

"Nothing's happening," she wailed.

But Martine said, "Just push that baby down and out. A little further, a little past the place where it was before." With Martine's encouragement, and the nurse's optimism, Dr. Chou's kind face, things progressed—"You're doing so well! That's great, Julia. Embrace the pain, reach out to it. *Now* you're really getting somewhere."

She had no idea of how much time was passing, adrift in another world, thrown into it, laid back from it, though sometimes she felt lost in it, rather than making the best of each contraction, not bearing down thoroughly enough, missing the rhythm. Then she began to think that they were lying. They were simply being nice, at her expense. Encouragement was a useless token. The head *wasn't* descending. She couldn't believe it when Dr. Chou said that the head was through the cervix, and the body was entering the birth canal. It didn't feel that way at all.

But what was this? They wanted her up? They wanted her up on her feet and off to the bathroom. Sitting on the toilet, they said, would give her the advantage of gravity, help get that baby down. Their hands supported her on all sides, as she walked, bending and shuffling forward, and then squatting, she pulled at the back of Martine's blue jeans, until she thought she would rip the pockets off.

"You have to push through the pain, push *through* it," Martine coached, and Julia felt it descend. The nurse was pressing on Martine to support the weight, the mightiness of it. Yes, this was helping. Back, she was maneuvered to bed, in a near weepy, out-of-it state, not sure if she could keep this up much longer.

Then they held a mirror down for Julia to see how her

perineum was changing. But she only saw a mess of blood, and wanted it wiped away. Now she could see she was flattening out, and the nurse instructed her to place her fingers inside and touch the baby's head. Two inches inside she could feel a jellied mass that was her baby's head! She realized that this little person was close, so very close. She really felt that she was in the hands of God, and God's force was moving through her, and this seemed neither bad nor good, just a fact, and even though she thought — "This is agony," the pain almost had an exquisite quality.

The nurse wanted her to keep her fingers inside with the next push to feel the progress.

"Why don't you speak to the baby," Martine said. These would be the last few moments her baby would be living inside her. But suddenly everyone seemed to be getting excited. Dr. Chou was putting on his gloves. They just had to get it down under that pubic bone, down and up and out and here. She was becoming more determined now. Down, down, come on baby, the gut crusher of will power. Every muscle in her neck, face, jaw, shoulders, arms, back and abdomen, was straining, pushing, out and under and *down.* "Just a couple more pushes and you'll have your baby," the nurse's tone brought Julia back again to the bigger reality, that this wasn't just a fight against her own body, but a process that involved another human being, who was working too and being worked. And yet it seemed to go on. Martine held up the mirror, and yes, she thought she could see the littlest part of head crowning, and then a good fifty-cent-size piece of brown wet hair, and that made her push even harder, though she was filling up past the full point, stretching now past all possible limits, burning, and she thought, cool, *Cool,* to no avail, for it felt like a raw hot split, felt like she would split up there, stretching with nowhere to go. But then after that contraction, the head slid back in a ways.

"That's good, Julia," the doctor said. "Just one more push

like that and you've got it." She believed him, and put all her strength behind it.

Martine felt like a witness on some other level, pouring heart and energy into these last few moments — the anticipation, the struggle with the strain of it, the immensity, awesome, and it was almost as if huge music were on the way and she could hear it approaching, getting closer and closer, and stronger and more powerful, mounting up to overwhelm them all, and then, as if in a movie, "I've got to do a little snip here now," the instant decision, the ready move, when he saw that she wasn't going to give, and with that one easy snip he reached in for the chin, she was howling *ugh,* and crying *Oh,* and she thought she'd be ripped apart, and Martine saw the head coming out as Julia's flesh tore like a split-open grapefruit, and the head, which had appeared to be small, became gigantic. They pushed Julia over on her side, to turn the shoulders and then suddenly gush, so primitive, this huge chubby person was between her legs, humped up in a ball and she only felt what — immediate relief.

It was squirming in the doctor's hands, and Julia asked, "What is it?"

Somebody said, "I think it's a girl. Yes, it looks like a nice big baby girl."

Julia looked to the child and cried, she just started to bawl, "A girl? A *girl!* I can't believe it. Oh my God, a baby girl." And then Martine was crying too, and hugging her hard, and then Julia lay back, all quivering and high on the gut swinging chorus of altitude awe, booming and soaring, a tangible heart clap, sweet purse of the body rising straight up the spine, and it felt like the lid of the entire room, the entire building was blown right off with this arrival, and there was such gratitude too, as Julia took that baby on her belly, touching her real live skin, her head, and leaning forward, tears fell upon the child and she smoothed that little back, as the nurse began to work on her. She had to gently massage Julia's uterus, while Julia continued to stroke the baby there on her chest, and out came the placenta easily, and then Dr. Chou began to sew, but nothing could distract Julia from this wonderful being, fresh from another world.

The nurse was rubbing the baby vigorously, trying to get her going, her little whimper cries, sweet beginning noises. They put a blanket over her, and they were hot and soft just skin to skin, so intimate, together. She encouraged the little one to nurse, but she wasn't proficient, not like her boys had been right away. Such dark brown, silky hair—that was different also. So pretty, firm and round. She already seemed such a person, yet calm, observant and calm.

When Julia passed the baby to Martine, she said, "I could never have done this without you."

Martine nodded, and felt such amazement, holding that baby, gently rocking her in her arms. She walked her carefully around the room. "She's so beautiful, Jule. She's incredible."

The nurse suggested that Julia try to get up, slowly, very slowly, and take a shower.

She let the water hit her back, and it seemed to cleanse her through and through. When she finally came back out, the bed was changed, sheets stretched tight, inviting, and Martine was still humming to the baby. Julia lay down and opened her arms, while Martine then went to spread camembert on crackers, and they drank glass after glass of apple juice.

The nurse explained that it would be best to just hold the baby through the night, skin to skin. She was six pounds, three ounces, much smaller than her boys had been, but she appeared full term in every way, even though she'd come early. The white vernix smear on her skin was an indication that she'd been a little premature, but the nurse had rubbed that in with olive oil, and now her skin was butter soft. Julia looked up and down her arms, her little shoulders, her hands, her toes. Finally, the baby buttoned on, and drank her first real deep drink, and the nurse and doctor waved goodnight, and the room seemed very silent.

"Would you like me to spend the night?" Martine offered, and Julia asked her if she would.

"I don't want to be left alone yet."

The air felt clear, the storm was over. Martine slipped off her blue jeans, and climbed under the covers. "It's 3 a.m.," she said.

"We better wait to call."

"Are you going to tell him?"

Julia shook her head, no. It felt odd, having Martine and this new baby girl in bed. It eased her mind to have her friend close by. Martine clicked off the light. "What do you think you'll name her?"

"I have no idea."

"Maybe you'll have a dream."

"Kate dreamt that the baby would be called Frimp."

"That's got a nice ring," she laughed. "I just can't believe that the boy producer conceived a girl."

"I'll tell you, it's something different. I can't wait for the boys to see her."

"I bet it will make it easier for them."

"You're probably right."

"You tired?"

"No," Julia answered, "but maybe we should get some sleep." She had both hands on her baby's back.

"Well, goodnight my dear," Martine murmured, rolling over. She was asleep within minutes, while Julia lay awake in that small, dark room, and held onto that immediate knowledge of skin, aware that she had sailed through it, that she'd reached some other shore, alluvial, and that Martine had reached it with her. She was lying there now with part of herself, part and proof of their love, but so apart—connected for a lifetime, even after the life line, after the breast is gone and divisions are made, and she knew she'd always hold this evening like a quiver, knowing that the body doesn't always give so easily, that it must lose what it holds, come floating back from the sharpest distance, washing up on the opening fan. The baby was drinking so fast, she had to stop to catch her breath, then back to the nipple and her sigh song. This first, this brand new season, they both curled in.

It was the second day of her baby's life. Julia had just finished nursing, and was lying back on a pile of hospital pillows, her hair spread out and luminous. She was holding the child against her left shoulder, rubbing her back in small circles, such a comfortable little bundle, now utterly asleep.

The floor nurse slipped in and seeing the baby, whispered, but with an urgency, "Somebody here to see you." Julia wasn't expecting anyone. "It's not visiting hours," the nurse acknowledged, while giving her this wondering expression, "but we can always bend the rules for such a handsome young man."

Julia's face contorted, as if her brain had been freeze-dried, while her entire body grew panicked, hot, and she wanted to hold out—"Wait," for who else could it be, but there wasn't time to even stop this progression of events, for the nurse was gone, and she imagined him there in the doorway, in his yellow cabled sweater.

This moment will never change, she thought, as if she were looking through a camera, and the shot of the open and empty door was sealed and shocking, caught forever. She pictured the mixed emotions on his face, the guilt and tenderness, not knowing how he'd be received, the sharpness of his features, softened now by feeling, but this extreme of thaw was happening way too fast for her.

"Hey!" he said. It was William. Her face must have registered shock and relief, happiness and disappointment. She burst into tears as William strode in. "Glad you're so happy to see me!" he kissed her hello. "A mere 3,000 miles, and what do I get? Bad weather."

It was raining again outside, and she laughed through her tears, "You silly Willy Sam."

"You didn't think I'd turn against you, did you?"

"You surprised me," she said. "What a sweetie you are."

"Well, do I get to hold my firstborn niece or what?" The baby was still sleeping, and Julia turned her, held her down in her lap, before handing the small bundle to William. He held the baby close, in against his side, but awkwardly, perhaps a little low, whereas a woman would have held the baby right up to her heart. "I had business out here, so I hopped the first flight. Mom and Dad called," he added. "I guess they're going to get over it, and they're happy you had a girl. Have you named her yet?"

"I was so certain she'd be a boy, I never considered girls' names. I don't think 'George' particularly suits her."

"She looks like, like a little wood nymph," William tried to describe her, and a spark seemed to flash melodic in Julia's brain.

"Sylvanna," she said. "What do you think of Sylvanna."

"Different," he said, "like a flash cube."

"Well, go ahead, take our picture. You were the first to know."

He unleashed his camera and took a shot, then another. "I'll make copies," he offered. "You can send them around. Have you had any word from Philip?"

"He's getting married," she said.

"I don't think so."

She had another jolt of hopefulness. "Why do you say that?"

"Winthrop saw him at The Yale Club, in New York. I guess it was pretty clear."

"What was? What was clear?"

"He was with some guy. Win was properly grossed out."

"What's *that* supposed to mean?"

"*Julia,*" William said. He didn't quite know how to speak about this with his sister. "The guy came up to Win, and was very drunk, saying stuff like — You're the most handsome man I've ever seen, and Win almost laughed in his face."

214

"Philip says that about everybody—he always exaggerates."

"Win just thought, he asked me, you know, he thought you should have your blood checked."

"Are you sure this was Philip Mercato?"

"Well he didn't have horse shit on his shirt, but—Winthrop knew who it was. They talked! And then he went off with his arm around this guy."

"That sounds like Yale to me, doesn't it?"

"I wouldn't know."

"I'll have a test, sure, if it'll put the family at ease. This is just too peculiar, my God." She looked down at the baby in her arms and wondered. What if Winthrop were right? Then—If there's anything wrong with this baby!

"Just try not to think of it now. I'm sure you'll be perfectly fine."

Suddenly everything fell into place. Why he had never really wanted her, wanted her in the deepest way. Maybe she'd been blind to the obvious. "He never really loved me," she said to her brother. "I think he wanted to. He would have liked to."

"I'm sure he did," William reassured her.

But somewhere inside, she knew she was right. She felt closed off like some infant abandoned in a wicker basket where she had been left to just cry and cry, never having received that first total love you need in order to believe you are someone worth loving. Though rationally, of course, she knew her friends, and children, her parents and brothers loved her. She remembered how Kate had responded once—Of course it's not rational! Understanding totally.

She could admit that she had really loved this man. She had loved how his seed had flown into her, how she had pulled all of him into her, gripped him with her arms, wanting to catch his soul—for that moment flying into her, and yes, she did, she caught it—she had caught his seed that day and would be returning with a daughter now.

She realized that even her hatred had been a form of holding onto him. Now she'd have to give that up too. It was as if the floor had dropped out from beneath her, and she had nowhere to go. Only her mind kept revolving, and the image of his absence, she knew, would accompany her everywhere, and she would always feel him there, inside her, but gone. There in the middle of some meaningless movie, or out on the street, seeing his green car parked, or standing stock still in the grocery store, holding a jar of quince jelly, or just trying on shoes, tears dropping onto the black patent leather, thinking over and around, thinking on forever, how every detail of her life had been truly given over, to him, her every breath, every brush stroke and item of clothing, every glance in the mirror, not for her, but for him, every time she lay down or woke up, clutching the pillow, every moment of changed weather, every evening she held their child, every star, every wish, every meal, had been made in some motion of love for him, and suddenly it was no longer the same. Something had stopped, and refused to go further. She was observing the end, the actual, the last frame melted out by the light of the camera, the snuffing of her shining countenance.

When the phone call came for Martine, it was as sudden, unexpected, as waters breaking. She said yes. "Yes," they would go. That night. She called Tibor, as if her own labor had just started. She said, "Hurry, just hurry home." He was there within an hour, and she'd already packed their bags, had called to make flight reservations. She had doused her cigarettes and crumbled them up in the trash. She called Kate, but no answer, so she phoned Western Union. Martine was in a state of animated shock. She got dressed, then undressed, and took a shower. Her hair was in wet dark ringlets when Tibor flew in the door. They stood there for a moment, then

216

hugged with all their might. She felt like she'd never let him go.

"You should call your parents," Tibor said, but she didn't want to stop and stumble over anyone's reaction. She would call her family later. She wrote Julia a note, and left Rachel a message on her machine. They had to get going. They had nothing prepared — no crib, no blankets or infancy clothes, but she thought about the Jewish tradition, how one waited for the birth before obtaining anything. She didn't know if it would be a boy or girl. The agency had been unclear. That didn't matter. The child would be a newborn. The world seemed small. They would cover half the globe to be there, to receive their child and bring that baby home.

Rachel was wearing a turquoise scarf tied under her chin, with a big straw hat, sunglasses from the fifties. "You look like you're hiding from your fans," Julia kidded her, thinking Rachel did look like some kind of movie star in disguise, casual in her offhand glamour.

"It is such a *bother, Dahling,* being bothered wherever you go," Rachel affected, sashaying a little as she went.

Renay, Rachel's mother, was with them, visiting her daughter for a week, and she took a plastic bottle of sun block from her supply bag, "Rachie, I want you to put this on your face. You have to protect your skin."

"Mother thinks I'm going to wrinkle like a California Raisinette," she whispered. It was a glorious, bright day, late November. The first rainstorms had already turned the hillsides green. Julia's boys had come for Thanksgiving vacation to see their baby sister. The children were all tumbling down the path ahead, Vergil and Thomas, old buddies, in the lead, while Lianna held onto her mother's hand, and Sylvanna, strapped in her front pack, was comforted by their rhythmic descent.

"She's such an easy baby," Rachel patted that small,

round bottom, before dutifully wiping some sun block across her cheeks. "Thanks Mama," Rachel said, her voice sounding more southern than usual, as she handed back the bottle, and winked at Julia, putting her sunglasses into her pocket.

"You can't be too careful," Renay added, walking a bit ahead.

The children seemed to almost pounce down the steep path that led from the top of Mount Tamalpais down to the ocean. The waves crested in miniature, rolling up onto the bare strip of sand. Rachel and Julia walked side by side, in silence for a while.

"I just hate to think of us going off in different directions," Rachel said finally. Julia would be flying back east with her children later that week, and Rachel was planning on moving back to Savannah, the city where she was born. Kate had called over Thanksgiving to announce that she was pregnant, and Martine was overwhelmed by her new adopted baby son.

"Sometimes it's hard to get what you want," Julia said. "But it does seem like we're all falling into place. Look at those kids. What a wild bunch we've conceived."

"I'm glad I didn't go for more. I've always liked an even number."

"Me too," said Julia. "Two's enough and four's plenty."

"Plenty," Rachel repeated. "That's a tasty word. I just feel so thankful sometimes to be alive on a day like this. To have survived it all."

"You survived Richard anyway."

"Thank God," Rachel said. "What a mistake that would have been. If there's one thing I can't stand, it's a man who's ambivalent."

"Maybe you just make up your mind faster. And once it's made, it's over."

"In this case, I was just reading the signals. It is peculiar though, isn't it? That we could be so crazy about these guys, I mean, ready to lay down our lives, and then . . ."

"And then feel next to nothing. I know, it worries me."

"Well it worries me when men treat life like a business. They think they can run their homes like a business, and their love lives, like some kind of practice."

The boys had climbed up on a big rock, and were resting, waiting for their mothers, and Alexander called out, "Can *I* have a ride?"

Thomas admonished him, "The baby is sleeping," but then Thomas slid down the rock, opening his arms to catch his little brother, taking him on his back for a good twenty feet, which seemed to satisfy Alexander. Lianna ran ahead now to join the boys, looking up to Ross and smiling.

"Remember when he used to feed her his bottle?" Rachel said. "When she was still in utero? What a champ."

Lianna stopped for a moment to pick a few wild flowers for her grandmother, who was about to tell her that she shouldn't pick anything out of nature, but Renay caught herself and said, "Lovely!" instead.

They wound down around the mountain path, back away from the view of the ocean, into a darker, ferny grove, dense with oak trees, twisting above the small stream's scatter of rock. It was cooler, moister, on this side of the hill, and they could smell the earth. "Isn't it amazing that Martine and Tibor had to go all the way to India?" Julia conjured the distance.

"The lengths we all go to are amazing."

Returning to Massachusetts was no longer frightening. She almost looked forward to the bleakness of early winter. November was one of her favorite months. Perhaps that was perverse, but there was something very pure and visible about the greyness of the forest before snow, something honest about that state of absence.

As they came around the bend, back out into the sunlight, Rachel admired how the sun shone on her friend's wavy blond hair, how she seemed to have melted from a lioness into a graceful, satisfied woman. They both noticed how the beach appeared closer now, how far they had already come.

"How's it going with Renay?" Julia asked. "From all appearances, you're doing an admirable job."

"Renay," Rachel paused, "will always be a pain in the butt. At least now I know *she* won't change, and my reactions can loosen. I mean, I don't find myself so eager to react. I just wish she'd be more of a grandmother. Sometimes I think it's hard for her to admit she's sixty-four years old."

"I wonder what we'll be like at that age."

Rachel looked pleased, yet wistful. "I just love to think of us, you and Kate, Martine and me, all of us sitting out on some mesa, our kids all grown, yakking our heads off, thinking about all this, what we went through, and how tumultuous it seemed."

"But how logical in retrospect."

"I think we should start planning right now. Just the four of us."

"Yes," Julia said, but she seemed so tender today, something just beneath the surface. "I want to look in on Paul, before I go," Julia said. "Having those blood tests unnerved me."

"We were lucky," Rachel added. The children were sitting on the side of the path, complaining of thirst now, saying that they couldn't go on, that Alexander had a stone in his shoe, and Vergil was hot, "Really hot," but Julia and Rachel just walked past their complaints. They didn't even say — *You sad sack of bones* — because they could see the complaints weren't serious.

The two of them led the way, descending, "So what do you think," Rachel asked. "Do you think you'll contact Philip when you return?"

"I doubt it," she said. They took the switchback in the path, both of them feeling the strain in their muscles. "I just want to get back to work. For the first time in my life I feel like it's all right to be alone."

"Well you're not exactly *alone*," Rachel reminded her, waving to all their children. "What I'd give sometimes for just one week to myself. Do you think you'll start riding again?"

Julia thought about that. She had always liked riding alone — it was easier to enter that other form of communication with your horse — visceral rather than verbal.

By spring she would be riding again, comfortable in the filtered light of the forest, smelling the scent of crushed pine, the cool of river on rock.

It was a perfect scintillating day, and at the crossing of the paths, she took a right, remembering how the three of them had ridden there once. She leaned forward to grip Eagle's coarse, white mane, as she trotted over the pine roots of the path, going way back into the woods. Perhaps she was just trying to retrace some light-hearted amazement of love she had felt there, but it was all right now to be riding alone, wanting to go further than they had ever gone.

She felt stoned by the clarity of the day, the light shimmering through the brightness of new oak, that tender stage of green, when suddenly, on her left, she saw the opening of the quarry down below, parting the density of the woods. The path descended to the left, and entering the quarry, she realized how funny it was that imagination rendered memory inaccurate, for what she had remembered was part of a bigger fabrication — she had imagined the floor of this place as a bit of grassy light, comforting, enfolding — but it was raw, exposed, with heaps of scattered rock shards. Still she wanted to take everything in, every detail, the chalky color of the light. The quarry lent itself to a kind of absence of sound, as if it were baking the dimensions in a sound proof box. Only toward the end did she hear the splash of water upon rock, as she urged her horse on to where the quarry narrowed. A stream of water fell from above, playing over the damp stone wall. She held out her canvas hat, and collected a drink there, getting sprayed with the water as it fell.

She could have turned around, but felt like exploring further. She didn't want to be afraid, but her horse seemed wary. The walls were steep and close. As they turned the corner, she saw a tunnel carved out through the limestone. It was dark and dripping, the floor muddy and perhaps unreliable, with pools of shallow water, and she wondered if the floor would hold. Eagle stopped, and refused to move forward, as if sensing something up ahead, something Julia could neither see nor smell, but every fiber of the horse refused. It made Julia believe that there might be something there that only the astral certainty of an animal could pick up on. Eagle had never expressed such physical hesitation before, but Julia was determined to overcome that, and urged her gently on, speaking all the while, comforting the horse with her own assured voice. She didn't want to get harsh, but still the horse refused.

So Julia got off, deciding to walk first, leading her horse through the tunnel. This seemed to reassure Eagle. The horse relaxed, lowering her head as she followed, but Julia wasn't so certain at this point. What if there was something within this dark cavern? Her horse could easily be frightened, and might even run, and she would be miles from anywhere. Still, she had the impulse to get to the end of this place before leaving, not to let fear overwhelm her.

The tunnel opened up into a cave-like room, the rounded ceiling chipped away, dark and damp, so cool with the dripping that surrounded her. The cavern made her feel chilled, but she walked to the end of the place, pushed her hand against the damp grey wall. There at the very end, she saw how the roof to this cave room opened, as if tunnelling straight upward, into the leafy light of the sky, and she wished that she too could ascend there, go right up that small shaft into the air. Like Frank. She thought of Frank cruising the heavens, way above her, and she believed that the dead must have compassion for the people they loved still on earth, who were caught in their own stone rooms. She wanted some bigger arena.

She got back on her mare and rode out, stroking the warm, smooth side of Eagle's neck, hooting as she left the echoing tunnel, returning to the welcome of daylight. And as she rode on out of the quarry, she urged her horse into a canter, and felt this unspeakable grace, that it was given, it was hers, and she took all of it in, like the first milk of human kindness.

Rachel took Julia by the elbow then, "Maybe everybody at some time feels that way, totally isolate. I know I felt that way when Daddy died. I learned something then, that you can experience the extreme of that, of separation, and at the very bottom of it you know that you'll survive, that you're a part of everybody else, and like everyone too, alone, but not alone, ever, like being born or even dying. I guess I've come to believe in The Great Out There, and I love you," Rachel added, "So cheer up, gumdrop."

The children were following now, and they could hear Renay, "You just have to walk with your own two feet. We're almost down. Can't you feel the ocean?"

"Rach?" Julia asked. "I just have to ask one question. It's been bothering me for some time." Julia looked tickled, pleased with herself. "Not bothering me exactly, but it's something I have to know."

Rachel stopped then, turning slightly, and Julia asked, "Will you marry me?"

Rachel threw back her head and the sun shone on her face, "Of course I will," she laughed.

Julia gazed out over the blue that merged with the horizon. "But I'm serious," she said, and they both could hear the waves breaking clearly now.

"Well so am I," Rachel answered, as they turned and walked—out onto the opening beach.

Printed October 1989 in Santa Barbara & Ann Arbor
for the Black Sparrow Press by Graham Mackintosh &
Edwards Brothers Inc. Design by Barbara Martin.
This edition is published in paper wrappers; there are
250 cloth trade copies; 125 hardcover copies have been
numbered & signed by the author; & 26 copies handbound
in boards by Earle Gray have been lettered & signed by
the author.

Photo: Lisa Sheble

LAURA CHESTER is the author of over ten volumes of poetry, fiction and non-fiction. Her most recent books include *Free Rein,* new writing from Burning Deck Press, *Lupus Novice,* an account of her struggle and personal breakthrough with the auto-immune disease, S.L.E., published by Station Hill, and *In the Zone: New and Selected Writing,* Black Sparrow Press. One of the founding editors of the innovative small press, The Figures, she went on to edit several important anthologies, *Rising Tides, 20th Century American Women Poets*; *Deep Down, The New Sensual Writing by Women*; and *Cradle and All, Women Writers on Pregnancy and Birth.* She is planning a final sequel anthology, *The Marriage Bed,* and working on a new collection of short fiction, *Bitches Ride Alone.*